Trivial Pursuits

Trivial Pursuits

THE LOVE GAME: BOOK SEVEN

ELIZABETH HAYLEY

WATERHOUSE PRESS

ISBN: 978-1-64263-345-0

To Rocky Flintstone for proving humor always has its place

Chapter One

VERONICA

I'd gotten up to get another drink at the bar, leaving our group of friends to hang out at the Yard, the additional outdoor space and deck attached to Rafferty's that Drew ran. Since they'd put outdoor heaters up, the place was still crowded even in the colder weather, and the bartender took a few minutes to get to me.

I ordered another margarita with extra salt and asked Reed to add it to our group's tab. Owen, who'd followed me to the bar, asked him for another IPA, and as we waited for our drinks, we turned back toward the Yard to take in the action around us.

Groups of people—mostly college age—laughed around tables or gazed at each other longingly from across intimate high-top booths. There were even a few customers who looked to be older than us, still in business attire. Had they come here for a drink after work and found themselves still here hours later, ties loosened and sleeves rolled up, holding their sixth bourbon and thinking about how they were getting home?

Reed came back a moment later with our drinks, and I started to walk back toward the gang.

"Hold up a sec," Owen said, putting a hand on my arm and then quickly taking it away.

When I turned around toward him, he was leaning against the bar, bopping his head like he could hear some sort of music I couldn't.

"What's up?" I asked.

"Nothing," he said way too casually to be believable. "Just thought we could hang here for a second."

Why is this guy so strange?

I'd never met anyone quite like Owen. I didn't know him well, but he seemed like a puzzle I'd never be able to put together because some pieces had gone missing.

He was usually super chill, but tonight I sensed an edge to him that he couldn't quite cover. I'd always been a good read of people, and most of the time my instincts were spot on. I liked to think it was sort of a sixth sense I'd been born with and honed throughout the years, but it probably had more to do with the fact that my family's connections and dealings weren't always on the up and up. I'd been aware of some shady shit and interacted with enough sketchy people to pick up on mannerisms that indicated when something wasn't quite right.

And tonight, I'd gotten that vibe from Owen more than once.

"You seem nervous or something," I told him. "What's going on?"

It was possible that Owen was simply attracted to me. I'd gotten that vibe too. But tonight he seemed distracted.

Shrugging, he pursed his lips a little before saying, "I'm fine."

"Okay," I said, not completely convinced but not wanting to force the subject. "I'm gonna head back, then." I started making my way back to our group.

"Vee, hang on."

With a sigh, I turned around to see Owen barreling like a bull in Madrid through a group of guys crowded near the bar.

I half expected one of them to shove him or at least yell at him to watch himself. Instead, when they'd caught sight of who'd caused their sea of dude-bros to part unexpectedly, their broad shoulders and puffed-out chests relaxed a bit.

Owen excused himself after he'd come out the other side, and the group immediately returned to discussing their protein intake or arguing about which brand of T-shirt had the tightest sleeves.

And that was when I realized Owen's superpower. He was basically the human version of a labradoodle—despite whatever trouble he got into, people couldn't help but like the guy.

"Okay," he said. "So, I wanted to get your opinion on something."

"No, your haircut doesn't make your ears look too big."

"What?" He looked confused but also a little self-conscious as he moved a hand to his ear. "I knew I should've stayed with my old barber."

"Kidding. Bad joke," I told him. "Sorry. What were you saying?"

"I know you have like...connections or whatever, and since you helped with the whole Brad thing, I thought you might be a good person to ask."

"Please don't tell me you have a psychotic stalker too."

He shook his head, appearing more serious than I'd expected him to.

Now I was the self-conscious one. "I'm really batting a thousand with the jokes tonight." When he still looked concerned, I added, "I was kidding again."

"Right." He pulled his phone out from his pocket and abruptly handed it to me.

There was a text on the screen.

Just heard the old lady kicked it. I'll be by around noon tomorrow to get my shit. You better be there this time.

"Am I supposed to know what this is referring to?" I asked.

His brow wrinkled into deep furrows. "I think Minnie owed them something, and now they want to collect."

"Okay," I replied, drawing out the word. I had no idea what any of what he was saying had to do with me.

"Sorry." He ran his hands through the waves of his dirty-blond hair and then rested them on his head like he didn't know exactly what to do with them. "Let me backtrack a little." Owen began walking farther away from the bar, and I followed him over to a high-top table, where it would be a little easier to talk. "The woman I lived with died," he said after sitting.

"Oh my God, that's terrible!"

"Thanks. It's okay though. I mean, it's really sad and I've been pretty bummed out, but it's not like I didn't know it was coming sooner rather than later."

I was struck by how easily Owen seemed to accept her death. I wondered how long they'd been together, but it was none of my business, and I didn't want to ask him about their relationship.

Still, I couldn't help but ask, "Was she sick?"

Owen leaned against the table and narrowed his eyebrows. "No, not that I know of?" It was almost a question he was just considering a possibility now. "Not any more than anyone else her age, I guess. I mean, getting older definitely doesn't sound like a ride I'd wait in line to buy a ticket for. Unless you practice regular strength training, your muscle mass decreases by about ten to fifteen percent after about age thirty. Even then, diminishing testosterone levels have a negative effect on muscle fibers. And when you consider the decline in the functionality of the eyes and ears after about age forty or fifty, I'm sure she had difficulties I wasn't even aware of."

Did Owen always spit out random statistics when he was stressed? It sure seemed that way.

"The majority of the geriatric population have medical problems that go undiagnosed," he continued. "So who knows?"

What the fuck?

"Geriatric?"

"It means elderly."

"I know what it means. But..." *How do I ask this?* "So your girlfriend was ... of an advanced age, then?"

Owen jerked his head back before giving it a quick shake. "No. Oh my God. No! Minnie wasn't my girlfriend. I just rented a room from her. If anything, she was more like my grandmother. Though if you ever meet my grandma Jimi, don't tell her I said that."

"Your secret's safe with me. That makes...so much more sense." I was surprisingly comforted by the fact that Owen had only been sharing a home and not a bed with this Minnie person. I liked to think that age was only a number, but when that number made someone old enough to be your grandparent, I had to draw the line.

"Now I can stop wondering if you gave Minnie sponge baths."

Owen stared blankly at me.

"Sorry, I really need to stop talking. That was insensitive."

"And also mentally disturbing."

"That too," I added. Then I gestured to his phone, which I was still holding. "So this text . . . do you know who sent it?"

"No idea. And I don't know how they got my number. But she must owe this guy money or something." Owen shook his head and sighed. "This is way too deep for me. I don't make a habit of associating with questionable individuals."

I nodded toward the table across the deck where our group was laughing boisterously.

"Brody left college and hired Drew to impersonate him for a whole semester, and then he pretended to be married to me and let his parents plan a wedding so the rest of his family could celebrate. Taylor and Ransom fled the state after they thought they accidentally murdered her ex, and Hudson owed so much money to bookies that the rest of the group decided to execute an elaborately planned heist at the home of the previously mentioned ex's father," I said almost in one breath. "Then they kidnapped him and called me for help," I added.

"Well, when you put it like that . . ."

I leaned down to take a drink and brought my gaze up to look at Owen as I sipped on the straw. "So," I said, "what's my role in all this . . . whatever *this*—"

"Threat. I think it's a threat."

"It's not a threat."

"Mmm," he said, cocking his head to the side. "It kind of is."

"What was the threat?"

Owen looked back at the text. "I mean, it's more of an implied threat than a direct one."

"So it's ... *not* a threat."

"No," he conceded. "I guess not exactly. But he probably didn't want to threaten me in writing. But when he comes over tomorrow and I don't have his 'shit,'" he said, using air quotes, "there's no telling what he'll try to do to us."

"*Us?*"

"Yeah. Well, I kinda thought it'd be a good idea if you were there with me. Maybe you can bring your uncle or ... brothers or dad or ... some other scary male relative who'll keep this dude away."

"How do you even know it's a guy? And you don't know what this so-called *shit* is. It could be Minnie's sister asking for her loom back or something."

"Minnie said her sister died a few years ago, and I don't think they were close. Besides," he said, "no one uses a loom anymore. She wasn't *that* old."

OWEN

After about ten minutes of heavy persuasion, Vee managed to convince me to text back and at least ask what the *shit* was that they were referring to. Now we just had to wait for the answer.

"I need another drink," I said, downing the rest of my beer and standing abruptly with what could probably be described as the least amount of chill I'd ever had. I'd probably been calmer as a toddler.

"Try not to freak out yet. You don't know that it's bad."

She'd told me that numerous times since I'd shown her the text, but the words held no real meaning.

"But I *feel* like it's bad. And my feelings are usually correct."

"Well, I feel like you're panicking before you need to, and my feelings are usually correct too. One of us has to be wrong."

"That person is you," I told her. "I'll grab us some more drinks."

When I returned a few minutes later, Vee had picked up my phone from the table and was typing away. I should've been angry that she'd looked at it and was *using* it without asking, but all I felt was curious. And maybe a little thankful that she'd chosen to involve herself. She definitely had a better shot of making this dude back off than I did.

"What? What is it? Did he text back?"

"Yeah." She looked up at me, her thumbs still hovering over the screen of my phone but not moving. "It's fine. It's someone named Mickey. He just asked about brownies she used to make. It must be for a bake sale or something, because he said they promised them to people and he needs them."

"Seriously? You're buying that shit?"

Vee's bullshit detector should've been sensitive enough to pick up on something so stupid.

"Yeah. Why is that so hard to believe? I mean, I didn't know her, but how hard is it to imagine that Minnie would have agreed to contribute to a bake sale?"

"So, *Minnie*," I said slowly, "promised some dude named *Mickey*," I said even slower, "that she would donate brownies to a bake sale?"

Vee sucked in a quick breath as she let the observation

sink in fully. "I hadn't thought about the names."

"Yeah. Fake name, fake story. Simple as that. This guy's probably some con artist or identity thief or something."

The phone buzzed in her hand, causing her to look down at it. At first I assumed it was another text, but when it didn't stop, I realized I was wrong. She thrust the phone at me.

"He's calling." I could hear the panic in my voice as I stated the obvious. By the time I answered the phone, I sounded positively traumatized. "Hello?"

"Put it on speaker," Vee whispered as she moved closer to me.

"Hi. Um, my name's Owen."

I figured honesty was the best policy. Plus, I always heard that offenders are less likely to commit murder if the victim tells them their name. I also figured that chances were if they had my number, they also had my name, so giving them a fake one would only piss them off.

"So," I said, doing my best to sound casual, "how did you know Minnie? Did you go to church with her? Or maybe from that consignment sale she was always asking to go to?"

"Does it matter how I knew her?"

My eyes darted to Vee, who gave me an uncertain shrug with widened eyes that did little to comfort me.

"Uh...I guess not. I was just curious about the connection."

"The connection is that she's my dealer. Or *was* my dealer. But now you'll have to be that person until I can find someone better."

"Honestly, anyone's better than me, so maybe just go over to the local high school and find some dude with long hair and an unruly beard, and he can probably—"

"Listen. I promised six of my best customers I'd have a batch of brownies for each of them by tomorrow, and I already paid her, so do whatever you need to do to make that happen, because I'll be over tomorrow to pick them up."

"So by brownies, you mean ..."

"Yeah, dumbass, I mean with Minnie's marijuana in them. I don't know where she gets it or how she makes the brownies so perfect, but I can't replicate it. You lived with her, so you better hope you picked up some of her skills."

"How do you even know that?" I asked, but he hung up without responding, leaving me looking at the screen and wondering what the hell I'd gotten myself into without actually *getting* myself into anything at all.

For some reason, I found myself staring at my phone as if that would make "Mickey" come back on the line. I had a million questions and no way to get any answers.

"So ... the sweet, old woman who was kind enough to rent you a room was also a drug dealer?"

I finally looked up from the phone and slid it into my pocket. "It appears that way, yes. I mean, I knew she made pot brownies because I've eaten them, but I assumed it was medical marijuana and she was just being hospitable by sharing." I shrugged. "I didn't know she had a legit business going."

"Well, I'm not sure you can call that business *legit.*"

"Which is why I need *your* help. Who knows what these people are capable of?"

Vee was quiet for a moment as she stared back at me with her deep, dark eyes that I found myself getting lost in. "She never showed you how to make them?"

"Nope. Which is really a shame because Mickey's right. Hers are the best. The ones I used to get off a guy in my old dorm tasted like chalk."

"We could just give back the money," she suggested. "Might be easier than making brownies that we don't know how to make with drugs I'm assuming you don't have."

I sighed. "I don't. Or at least, if I do, I don't know where. God, this is such a mess." I scrubbed my hands over my face. "And who knows how much he gave her. Considering my bank balance is near zero, I kinda doubt I have enough to cover it."

Vee's lips twisted a little as she seemed to process our options. Then she sighed heavily. "If I help you, what's in it for me?" She raised her eyebrows as she waited for me to respond to a question I hadn't anticipated.

Anything you fucking want. I can't have these guys after me.

But I had no idea what I possibly had to offer her. "Uh ... maybe just like the intrinsic satisfaction that comes with helping someone in need? You know, like altruism and shit."

Her face told me I should try again.

"A hug?" It was more than wishful thinking, but I did hope it would make her smile.

Thankfully, I was right. Though if I had to guess, I'd say her smile was more due to amusement than actual happiness.

"What did you have in mind?" I finally asked.

"Well, since I've somehow become the Scooby Gang's get-out-of-jail-free card, I'll need to give this a little thought."

Jail. I hadn't even thought about that.

"Literally anything," I said. "You can have anything you want if you help me get rid of these guys. I can't go to jail, Vee! Dudes in jail don't like guys like me!"

She smirked a little, as if she found my admission entertaining. I was fucking freaking out over here, and she was practically laughing.

"Oh, I don't know. I think there would be plenty of guys who'd take a liking to you."

Oh God! "Damn it, Vee. I can't share a cell with some long-bearded psycho whose idea of a good time is tattooing people with rusty paper clips." I knew how panicked I sounded, and the fact that I was now clutching Vee's shoulders didn't help.

"Okay, okay," she said calmly. "How long are you able to live at Minnie's house before her family takes it or sells it or whatever?"

"Forever," I said with a shrug. "Minnie left it to me. Why?"

Vee looked taken aback at that. "She left you her *house*?"

"Yeah. Why? Is that weird?" Which was a stupid thing to say because I knew it was weird. It was also kind of sad. The only people Minnie seemed to have had in her life were me and a drug dealer named Mickey.

She gave me a look that screamed *Duh!*, but she didn't say it. Instead, her look turned thoughtful. "So," she finally said, "if I help you, you'll do *anything* for me?"

"Uh, I mean, I guess within limits. I'll have to draw the line *some*where." I just wasn't sure where that line would begin and end until Vee tossed out whatever crazy request she had dancing around in her head. "I'm not gonna give you the house, if that's what you're thinking." Minnie had left it to me for a reason—though I wasn't clear on that reason—and I wasn't about to just give it away.

"I don't want the whole house," she said simply. "Just a room for the fall semester."

Well, shit. I didn't exactly feel like cohabitating with a beautiful woman was much of a compromise on my part, but I tried to temper my excitement.

"Sure. Yeah," I said as casually as I could manage. "The house is pretty big, so that shouldn't be a problem. I'll just need to clear out some stuff from one of the spare rooms, but I've been meaning to get rid of it anyway."

Vee smiled broadly. "Great! Now I can save some money on rent."

"Okay, so are you gonna call your uncles or brothers so they can meet us at the house tomorrow?"

"Nah. I got a machete in my trunk. Thought I'd handle this one myself."

I felt the blood disappear from my face, no doubt leaving me ghost white.

"I'm kidding, Owen."

She smiled, but it took me a moment to recover.

"Oh. Okay, so what's the plan, then?"

Maybe her family would just threaten these guys from a distance. Call them and tell them they better stay the fuck away from Vee and anyone she was friends with. Or maybe they'd dig up some dirt on these fuckers and blackmail them. Really anything was possible.

Except . . .

"We're just gonna make the brownies."

Chapter Two

VERONICA

"So that's what you got for me?" Owen stared back at me. "We're just gonna make the brownies? Why didn't I think of that?"

"I don't know," I tried to joke. "I wondered that too, since doing what they asked seemed like the most obvious solution."

"Well, it would be if I had any clue what the recipe was or where the hell she stashed her famous marijuana. She didn't tell me where she kept it."

"Come on," Vee said. "How hard can it be to find? She probably has it in a coffee can in her cabinet or something. I'm thinking these guys'll be willing to overlook the fact that we used mix from the box as long as we remember to put the pot in. Let's just go check the place out and see what we can find. We have"—I looked at my watch—"almost twelve hours to make it all come together. That's more than enough time to make a few batches of brownies."

"Again. We don't have *any* of the ingredients," Owen said. But he was already walking toward the parking lot. "Not to mention, there are probably no stores open to get what we need. And you have to infuse the butter, and I think that part alone takes a few hours."

"I thought you said you didn't know how to make them?"

"I don't, but it seemed unsafe to eat something like that without knowing the process involved, so I Googled it once."

I wanted to tell him it was probably unsafe to eat drugs made by strangers no matter what process was used, but we didn't need a D.A.R.E. moment right now.

Suddenly, he stopped walking and turned toward me. "Wait, do we even *want* to make them right? If we do a good job, they'll want us to do it again. And again. And then we'll end up like Walter White and Jesse, cooking meth out of a trailer in a desert somewhere."

"Only if I get to be Walter," I told him.

We started walking again, and the sea of parked cars suddenly made me more alert. "We've both been drinking. You don't plan on driving there, do you?"

Did he even have a car?

I followed Owen as he rounded the corner of Rafferty's and headed toward the back alley. It was then I saw Owen's mode of transportation leaning against a rickety fence near the dumpster.

"Does riding a bike count as drunk driving?" he asked.

"Yeah. It does, actually."

"Huh." He seemed to ponder my response as he grabbed on to the handlebars and hopped onto the seat. "I totally wasn't expecting that."

"I feel like that statement might be true for a lot of the things you find yourself involved in."

"Probably," he said. "We'll be fine, though. Would you

rather ride on the pegs or handlebars?"

"Um..." I looked at the blue bicycle. The tires seemed to deflate a little when he sat down, and the whole thing seemed too small for him. Did he steal it from a rack in front of a middle school? "I'd rather not ride at all."

Owen rolled his eyes. "We could walk or call an Uber, but both of those will take more time. Time that we don't really have if we're going to find Minnie's stash and make six batches of brownies."

I didn't move.

"What if I promise to stay on the sidewalk?" he asked.

"Where pedestrians and dogs are?"

He stared at me like he was trying to come up with some other way to convince me I might be making the biggest mistake of my life if I didn't jump onto a kid's bicycle in the freezing cold and let a buzzed twenty-three-year-old ride me to a house he inherited from a low-key drug-dealing grandmother.

But since at least part of that scenario was my fault, I let out a sigh and grabbed on to Owen's shoulders.

"Pegs," I said.

OWEN

"Can you get out the eggs?" Vee asked as she grabbed the oil. Thankfully, we'd found a store open not far from the bar, and it had what we needed. "Other than that, we just need water."

"And the marijuana, which we still have no idea where to find."

"Well, yeah. But we'll find it. I feel like it's gotta be in the kitchen somewhere. When we find it, we'll just mix it in with the butter and roll with it."

"That's not at all how it's done," I informed her, probably sounding too smug for a man whose knowledge came from the internet.

I cracked an egg into the gigantic bowl before grabbing another. "And what makes you think it's in the kitchen? It could be under a floorboard in a bedroom. Or maybe behind a wall or something."

"I doubt it. I just don't think a woman in her nineties would want to pry up part of the floor every time she had to make a batch of these brownies. Which, by the looks of how many boxes of brownie mix she has stored in her cabinet, was probably pretty frequently." Vee pulled down six boxes from the cabinet Minnie used as a pantry, leaving about four up there. "At least we don't have to make them from scratch."

She moved quickly around the kitchen, measuring the correct amount of water and oil. It was impressive to watch, actually. It also made my mania a little less obvious. I hoped anyway. Vee was as focused as she was calm, and it helped to keep me from freaking out more than I already was.

"Are you counting them?" Vee asked as I cracked another egg and dropped it into the bowl.

I hadn't been, but I could easily count the yolks now. "Of course I am."

She looked at me, raising her right eyebrow a little higher than her left before turning back to the bowl. "Okay, you finish with the eggs, and I'll look for a whisk or something to stir this with."

While Vee was opening and closing cabinets and drawers, I finished putting in the last couple of eggs.

"Do you think they'll want brownies that are more cakey or fudgy?" I asked. "Because if they want them more like cake, it says we should add an extra egg per box."

When Vee didn't answer, I turned toward her. She was riffling through a cabinet and had already pulled out some baking pans and set them on the floor behind her.

"Thoughts?" I added.

"I think they're more concerned with what's *in* the brownies than their consistency."

"Well, right now we don't have anything to put in them, so I want to make sure they at least taste good. So I need your opinion. More moist or less?"

"Don't say that word. It's so gross."

"What word?"

"Moist." She shivered as she spoke it.

"But it's on the box. And how come you can say it and I can't?"

"I can't say it either." She pulled out another pan.

"But you did say it."

"Just so you knew what you weren't allowed to say it anymore."

"Are you always this bossy?"

"Are you always this annoying?"

Her comment might've been insulting to anyone else, but I couldn't help but laugh. Then I picked up some of the pans off the floor and set them around on the counters. It was already after one in the morning, and we still needed to mix, bake, and cool all six batches and, in addition to that, probably cut all of them and put them in Ziploc bags or Tupperware or something. Even though Minnie was gone, it didn't feel right to give her cookware away, especially to a drug dealer.

Vee returned to the bowl holding an electric hand-mixer, but she paused when she caught sight of the bowl.

"What?"

"You put *all* of the mix in?"

"Yeah, why wouldn't I? We need all of it." The bowl was certainly big enough to accommodate all the ingredients at once, so I wasn't sure what the big deal was.

"We have to stir it by hand first, then."

Did Vee understand what the point of an electric mixer was?

She must've read the confusion on my face because she said, "Otherwise all of the mix will fly out of the bowl and get all over us and the kitchen."

I wanted to point out that that particular problem wasn't our biggest concern and that we just needed to get this shit done as quickly as possible, but Vee had already grabbed a wooden spoon and placed it in my hand. "You get to work on that, and I'll look for the secret ingredient."

I stirred the batter slowly until most of the dry mix had been incorporated into the eggs, oil, and water mixture, rather than sitting on top like a volcano of chocolate powder ready to explode when the mixer touched it. I hated to admit it, but Vee was probably right about not using the electric mixer right away.

"Okay," I called to her. She was standing on the small stool Minnie kept in her kitchen and opening the cabinets over the fridge. "I think I'm done. Any luck?"

"Nah," she said it with the same amount of emotion that would've been warranted had someone asked her if she liked eggplant. "Not with the coffee like I thought." Vee stepped down off the stool and came over to me. "Why don't you give it a shot while I mix?"

"Okay, but only if I get to lick the batter off the beaters afterward."

I spent the next five minutes or so looking around the rest of the kitchen before heading into the dining room where no one ever actually dined. Minnie had decorated it with floral wallpaper back in the sixties, and it had stayed that way ever since. Other than some of the paper peeling and the bright pink fading from the sun to a paler version of itself, the room had been unchanged. She even had the same large china closet that I hadn't ever seen her open.

But that didn't mean she didn't. I reached to grab both knobs of the glass doors and pulled hard, but they didn't budge. When they didn't open, I went to the drawers below. If I couldn't open those doors, Minnie wouldn't have been able to.

Vee stopped the mixer. "I'm going to let Gimli out," she said.

I'd put him in the basement when we got back to the house because I knew he'd be overly excited to meet Vee, which would involve lots of jumping and licking. And since we had a mission to attend to, I'd thought it best to keep the beast contained until we'd at least finished making the brownies. With food in the equation, there was no way Gimli would leave us alone.

He'd settled down a few minutes after we'd gotten home, but the electric mixer seemed to have provided him with a second wind, because now I could hear him yelping.

Vee walked over toward me, licking one of the beaters. She handed me the other, which I took gladly, and then walked over to the basement door.

"Wait, let me—" I called as her hand touched the knob.

But it was too late. As soon as Vee had pulled open the

door a crack, Gimli's brown and white face had pushed it the rest of the way open. And though he wasn't very big, his adrenaline made up for his size.

Vee stumbled back a little off balance, and once Gimli propelled his wiggly body at her, she was on the ground in no time.

It all happened so fast, it was hard for me to tell if he'd knocked her over by force or if she'd realized resisting him would be futile and had given in. Either way, the end result was Gimli alternating licks between Vee's face and the brownie batter.

I know, buddy. I want both too.

"Gimli!" I yelled as sternly as I could. But even the dog knew I was all bark and no bite, so to speak, and the worst I'd ever do is pull him away. I definitely wasn't the alpha in our relationship, and Gimli and I both knew it. Thankfully, the little furball was relatively well-behaved *most* of the time, because I certainly didn't have a future as a dog trainer.

Gims tried his best to maintain his place in Vee's lap, but I managed to grab him off and hold him, despite his wiggling and thrashing in my arms. By the time everyone had calmed down, all three of us had brownie batter smeared across our bodies, and both of the beaters had fallen to the floor.

"I'm so sorry," I said to Vee. And then to Gimli: "That's like the complete opposite of how to get a girl to like you."

Vee patted Gimli's head and spoke in a baby voice to him. "He doesn't know what he's talking about. I already love you. You're just excitable, that's all. But you'll get used to me, and soon we'll be best friends, won't we?"

I was pretty sure Gimli thought anyone who gave him food or attention was his best friend, and since Vee had done both within a few seconds of meeting him, she was a goner.

Gimli followed us into the living room as we lifted couch cushions and opened drawers in end tables, and I was sure he'd never leave our side for the rest of the night, no matter how tired he might be.

"I think if we don't find the weed," Vee said, "we make the brownies without it and hopefully that'll buy us a little time."

"You think they won't realize?"

"I don't know. If the brownies are all supposed to go to other people, I doubt they'll eat one right there. It's not like cocaine, where they can rub a little on their gums or something. We'll just wait until they call us out on it and then apologize profusely for the mix-up. If we both blame the other for not adding it and argue a little bit about whose fault it was, maybe they'll take sympathy on us."

Gimli jumped up onto the couch—a luxury he wasn't afforded when Minnie was still living. For some reason he knew Minnie's rules without her ever having to explicitly teach them.

"Mickey didn't sound like sympathy was an emotion he often familiarized himself with," I said, removing a picture from the wall, hoping to find a safe hidden behind it. No luck.

Gimli climbed up to the top of the sofa back and planted himself right below the picture I'd just taken down.

"Come on, Gims, could you be any more in the way, dude?"

Vee laughed and headed out to the porch that connected to the living room.

"Stop, Gimli," I said. "Come on."

"What's he doing?" Vee called.

"He's like . . . biting the plastic on the cushions and digging at the back of the couch. Minnie's probably rolling over in her grave right now. I can't even take care of her furniture, let alone an entire house."

Vee came back into the living room. "Wait, maybe he smells something. Maybe she hid it in the couch cushions or something. The plastic would contain the smell well enough that anyone visiting wouldn't smell it, but a dog would be able to, I'm sure."

We both looked at each other for a moment before making a silent pact to search Minnie's couch. In seconds, the plastic covers were off, the fabric of the cushions unzipped.

"Have at it, boy. What'da ya think, huh? You think there are drugs hidden in here?"

Gimli was sniffing every pillow and cushion as well as every inch of the frame, but he didn't seem to be focused on any one spot.

I groaned, completely frustrated. "It could be anywhere. This is pointless."

"Which is why I suggested we start making them anyway. We can only bake a batch or two at a time anyway, so we should put in the first few since they take like forty-five minutes each. We'll keep looking while they cook, and if we find it, we'll just mix the plain brownies with the special ones when we cut them up. If whoever is getting these happens to eat one without any weed in it while others in the same batch definitely *do* have weed in them, hopefully they'll think they just got a dud. And if we don't find her weed, at the very least, we can still buy ourselves some time."

"I don't know ..."

"Do you have a better plan?" Her question sounded more hopeful than condescending or sarcastic.

Time was of the essence, and we needed to come up

with a contingency as soon as possible. Other than Minnie's brownies, I'd given up weed, so I didn't have any contacts anymore. And while I could maybe find someone willing to sell, I didn't have the spare money to buy what we'd need. Not to mention that Mickey had said Minnie had some kind of magic weed or whatever.

"Unfortunately, no." I sighed. "We'll go with your plan if it comes to that, and if we get caught, we'll promise to give them extra in another batch."

Both of us knew the idea wasn't a great one, but it was the only one we had.

Chapter Three

VERONICA

I took out the first two batches of brownies and placed a fork in the center of each to see if they were done. Setting them down on the stovetop to cool, I called up to Owen, "Find anything?"

I had to ask before putting in the next two batches, but I already knew the answer. If Owen had found any marijuana, I would've known about it immediately.

If Owen responded, I didn't hear him. Though the house was pretty big, so who knew if he even heard me in the first place?

We needed to wait until the brownies cooled so we could cut them out and reuse the pans. For a drug-dealing baker, Minnie didn't have as many nine-by-thirteen pans as I thought she would've. This must've been a larger order than she'd been used to. Lucky us.

I wanted to go help Owen, but Gimli had his eye on the brownies, and the last thing we needed was for him to eat one. Or an entire batch. I didn't know much about dogs, but I knew enough to stand guard so Gimli didn't eat his weight in chocolate.

"Give it up, Gim."

The dog cocked his head to the side like he was trying to translate what I'd said.

I patted him on the head, feeling strangely bad for him, before hopping up to sit on the counter. If I needed to protect them, I wanted to do it sitting at least. It was going on three in the morning, and the night was quickly catching up to me. Maybe a snack would perk me up.

I hopped down and went to the fridge to poke around. There wasn't a ton in there, but I saw some deli meat in one of the clear drawers. Owen could probably use a sandwich too. I opened the drawer and pulled out the meat and cheese. As I reached down to close it, a Tupperware container caught my attention. Practically throwing the food onto the counter, I reached in and removed the container.

On the lid, written in neat script on a piece of tape, read *Cannibutter*.

She couldn't possibly have made it this simple.

"Owen!" I yelled. "Get down here!"

I heard feet pounding overhead, and seconds later, he was running into the kitchen.

"What's wrong?"

I turned the container so he could read the lid.

"You've got to be kidding me," he muttered. "Where'd you find it?"

"Under the lunchmeat. You never noticed it in there?"

"You didn't eat any of it, did you?" he asked, his voice alarmed.

"No. Why?"

He sighed. "Because I haven't been able to bring myself to throw anything of hers away yet. Some of the food may be expired."

That was sad but also kind of gross.

"Owen, this is your house now. You can let yourself... live in it."

"No, I know. You're right. Once all this is behind us, I'll start getting things in order."

"Okay, so this is good. Minnie did most of the legwork for us."

"Yeah. Let me just look at the recipe to doublecheck we're doing this right."

I waited while he read his phone.

Finally, he said, "We just need to wait for it to get to room temperature. The site says not to microwave it because that can ruin the marijuana."

I set the butter down on the counter and bent down to pet Gimli. When I looked back up, Owen was smiling at me.

"What?"

"We make a pretty good team."

"Guess we do," I said, smiling back.

Gimli jumped up between us, and Owen scooped him up into his arms so he could give him a big kiss. Gimli returned it with one of his own that left trails of slobber across Owen's cheek. At least I was in good company.

"Don't worry, Gims. You're part of the team too."

OWEN

Once we'd found Minnie's butter, the process was smooth sailing.

"Want one?" I asked Vee, who was icing them with chocolate frosting we'd found in the cabinet in an attempt to make them look—and possibly taste—slightly more appetizing.

She turned toward me, slowly licking a knife covered in chocolate.

Until now, I'd never thought about what it would be like to be a piece of silverware, but I decided right then that if I could come back in my next life as the knife Vee was holding, I'd wish for my current life to be over stat.

"I don't know," she said skeptically. "I've only ever taken one hit of a joint one time, and it was when I was in high school. I'm not sure it's a good idea to be high when Mickey gets here."

I understood that. And even if I hadn't, I never would've pressured her into anything she wasn't comfortable with.

"Cool. More for me, then." I smiled widely.

"Don't eat all our product." She grabbed the spatula that lay on the counter and swatted me with it. Thankfully she'd chosen that instead of the knife that was in her other hand.

"Okay, okay. You're right. Don't wanna give Mickey a reason to be pissed off. We have . . . what?" I looked around the kitchen at the brownies that were cooling on various plates. "Two more batches to do?"

"Yeah, but I say we do four and scrap the first two we made. Minnie has more boxes in the cabinet, and I'd rather not chance giving them any of the ones that don't have the pot in them."

"Good call. But by 'scrap,' you mean *eat all of*, right?"

Vee grabbed one of the ones from the first batch and brought it to her lips. "Of course I do," she said before taking a big bite.

Chapter Four

VERONICA

It was ten in the morning when I woke up at the kitchen table without realizing I'd even fallen asleep. The last thing I remembered was sitting down to relax for a moment while the last two batches of brownies were baking, which was probably around four in the morning. I'd set the timer, just like I'd done for the others, but I hadn't even heard it go off. And at some point, Owen must've covered me, because I had a soft cream blanket wrapped around my shoulders and a throw pillow that had been placed under my head.

"Owen," I called when I looked around the kitchen and didn't see him. There was no sign that anything had gone horribly wrong, because the house hadn't burned to the ground with me inside. "Owen," I yelled again, this time louder.

"You're up," he said, his voice holding an excitement I hadn't heard all night. And a moment later he appeared in the kitchen doorway looking and smelling freshly showered.

I was suddenly very aware that I was neither of those two things. I was also fairly certain I had an imprint on my cheek from where I'd fallen asleep on my phone.

"We're good to go," he said. "I got the last two batches out, cut them all up after they cooled, and separated everything into six containers. Mickey better leave us alone after this."

"Either that or he'll ask for more since we did such a good job."

"Shit." Owen ran a hand through his wet hair as he seemed to contemplate the possible outcomes once Mickey arrived.

"I'm kidding. Kinda. I think once you explain that you have no idea where Minnie got the weed she puts in them and you used the last of what we found to bake these, he'll find someone who's easier to deal with."

"Hopefully." Owen went over to the coffeemaker and began preparing a pot.

"Did you get any sleep at all?"

"Nah. Once I finished with the brownies, I tried to relax, but that wasn't happening. So I cleaned up the kitchen and then took a shower. I can sleep later."

"You didn't have to do all that yourself. You could've woken me."

"I'm not that much of an asshole."

I laughed. "You're seriously like the least asshole-y person ever."

Owen grabbed two mugs from the cabinet and pulled out the pot of coffee to pour one for me before pouring one for himself.

"I actually got that superlative senior year. Least Asshole-y Person Ever."

"Congratulations," I said, taking the cream out of the refrigerator. "I'm sure your parents were proud."

"Yup. My mom put it in her Christmas letter that year. My

grandma bragged to everyone at her church about it, and then I was in the local newspaper . . . It was a whole thing."

"Mm-hmm." I smiled. "Sounds like it."

Over the next half hour or so, we sat in the heated sunroom on the side of the house drinking our coffee and talking about the previous night's adventures. Gimli seemed happy to join us as he chewed his bone on the floor next to me.

"I hate the suspense of this," Owen said. He'd looked toward the front of the house a few times since we'd sat down—it wasn't too difficult to pick up on because he had to look over his shoulder to do so. "It reminds me of when I used to forge my dad's name on bad report cards. I'd be relieved he didn't see the report card, but then I'd be worried the teacher would realize it and I'd get in trouble anyway. You know?"

"Not really," I answered honestly. "I probably would've had to find a new place to live if I'd done something like that. My parents were always pretty strict."

It had more so been my mom who'd been the disciplinarian, but when she'd died when I was younger, my dad had picked up her mantle.

Owen nodded slowly as he seemed to think about my response. "What was the worst thing you did as a kid?"

"I never really did anything bad when I was little." I hadn't thought about it much until now, but maybe following the rules was my own twisted way of rebelling. Or maybe I just liked to please people. "I'm trying to make up for it now, though, by cooking baked goods with drugs in them and rooming with a guy I barely know."

Owen laughed at that, but the sound was interrupted by a loud knock at the front door. He whipped his head around toward the front lawn, but all we saw was the grass, Minnie's flower garden, and the road—which did not have any cars parked on it. At least that we could see.

"You think that's him?" he asked with a whisper, still craning his neck until his face pressed against the screen like an indoor cat trying to get a taste of the outside.

"I don't know. He's a little early if it is."

"Are drug dealers usually early?" he fired back after turning to face me.

"Maybe some are?" It was a question since I had no idea. "Let me get it. Guys like this usually go easier on a woman." I headed into the living room and toward the small foyer.

"No way! I'm not letting *you* answer the door. What if this guy has a gun?" Owen sprinted ahead of me, but when his hand reached the doorknob, he didn't turn it. "Oh my God," he said, his voice low but panicked. "What *if* this guy has a gun?"

"I don't think he even has a car," I pointed out after peeking past Minnie's lace curtains. The only vehicles in sight were in neighbors' driveways.

"What if he had his buddies park around the corner so if this goes south and he has to kill us, no one will be able to identify the getaway car?"

That scenario was more plausible than I would ever admit to Owen. "Stop with all the what-ifs. Let's just give him what he came for." I put my hand over Owen's, and both of us turned the knob at once. Then we gave it a pull. When it didn't budge, we gave it another, harder pull. Still nothing.

"Hold on," Owen yelled. "This thing's a real bitch sometimes." He looked over at me. "Why don't you let go for a second, and I'll see if I can get a better grip while I use my foot for leverage."

I let go and watched Owen struggle with the door for a

few more seconds before finally pulling it loose. He nearly fell over when the door opened, but he found his footing quickly and straightened himself. I'd been so focused on the door and Owen that I hadn't even looked outside yet, but Owen's expression told me I should.

Standing on the porch, wearing khakis and a blue polo shirt with the logo of a nearby Catholic school, was a girl who looked to be no more than—

"What are you, like nine?" Owen asked, looking down at the girl.

"Ten, actually," she said, standing a little taller like the double digits made her proud.

I leaned in toward Owen, still keeping my eyes fixed on the girl with straight black hair, sharp bangs, and an odd smile.

"Did you have any idea Mickey was a little girl?"

"What do you think?" he whispered back.

"Hi, I'm Laila—"

"I knew it! So your name *isn't* Mickey!" Owen stuck his head out the door before walking out onto the porch, causing Laila—or whatever her real name was—to take a step back.

"Is your dad here?" he asked. "Or your older brothers or something?"

"Um, yeah, my dad's parked at the end of the block."

Looking down the street toward the end that led to a larger road, Owen yelled, "This is really messed up, you know… making a little girl do your dirty work while you wait somewhere hiding." Then he disappeared into the kitchen.

Laila stared blankly, and I probably looked very much the same. Though I'd never actually been *part* of my family's illicit activities, especially as a young child, I definitely wasn't as shocked by the little girl's involvement in them as Owen had been. I'd grown up surrounded by questionable people and decisions. Guess I wasn't the only one.

Owen returned a few seconds later holding a brown paper bag with sturdy handles, which he practically thrust in Laila's direction.

"Here. Give this to your dad, and please tell him we're done after this." His voice was stern, certain in a way I didn't think it would've been if Mickey had come here himself.

Laila looked a little uneasy, and I wondered how many times she'd had to be her father's suburban drug mule. Once she took the bag, we watched her walk down the porch steps and head down the street.

"We did it," Owen said with a long sigh that mirrored exactly how I was feeling.

"Yeah. Thank God that's over." I held my fist out to bump his, but he pulled me into a tight hug.

I felt so small wrapped in Owen's arms, like I could get lost in them, and it occurred to me how much of his size was probably masked by his baggy clothing and unassuming demeanor. He didn't feel *big*, necessarily—just taller than I'd noticed and strong in a way that made me wonder if his body looked as solid as it felt.

But my thoughts were interrupted by a hard knock at the door that made both of us jump.

The door opened much more easily this time, and standing on the porch steps were Laila and who I guessed was her father, Mickey.

Shit.

He was shorter than Owen, but he had the presence of someone who could handle himself in a fight.

How could we have fucked this up? Owen had eaten one

of the brownies we'd given them, and he'd thought it tasted fine. Mickey would just have to accept that this was the best we could do and go somewhere else next time.

"What do you think you're doing, giving these to my daughter?" He held up one of the Ziploc bags to make his point.

Owen looked unable to speak at first, so I answered. "Sorry. We didn't see you and figured you sent Laila—"

"You figured I sent my ten-year-old daughter to pick up brownies from strangers?"

"Yes?" Owen answered almost as a question. "Do you *not* want them?"

"No, I don't want them!"

Shit.

"Did you taste them?" Owen asked. "They're pretty good. I don't know if we put the same amount of pot as Minnie usually uses, but we put in whatever she had left. I looked up a recipe on Google and everything."

"They were baked with love," I chimed in with a sweet smile.

With that, he thrust the bags toward us and then put an arm around his daughter. "Take your brownies back before I call the police."

That was a threat I hadn't anticipated. "So is this you asking us to make more? Because we don't have—"

"No, I'm not asking you to make more! I'm asking you—I'm *telling* you—to take these and don't come near any of my kids again."

I wanted to tell him that his daughter was the one who'd come to *us*, but I had a feeling that observation would be ill-received.

So instead I went with, "I'm confused."

"*You're* confused?" he yelled. "I'm still trying to figure out why you gave drugs to a fourth-grader."

"Me too," Owen said, putting a finger to his lips thoughtfully. "It's definitely a conundrum."

This was not the way I saw any of this going.

"I'm sorry" was all I could come up with.

Though his complexion was darker than mine, he was turning redder as we spoke.

Then another man, much larger than him, emerged from a black car that had parked in front of Minnie's house. Another guy followed close behind him.

"You Owen?" he yelled as he headed across the grass.

What the hell?

"Yes?" Owen said, sounding like his answer was a question.

"What? You don't know your own fuckin' name?" said the guy behind him.

"Watch it," said the first guy. "There's a kid right there." As he approached us, he added, "Sorry to interrupt. This'll just take a minute. I'm just here to pick up ... some brownies. For my daughter. She's got a real sweet tooth." He smiled, but it faded quickly.

What the hell? Did Minnie have regulars that we didn't know about? Was she running some sort of marijuana Subscribe and Save out of her home?

"Wait, I'm sorry," I said. "Who are you?"

The man jerked his head back, looking almost insulted. "I'm Mickey. I talked to Owen last night."

"*You're* Mickey?" Owen and I said at the same time. Then Owen turned to Laila's father. "So that means you're *not* Mickey."

"Nope," he said, shaking his head slowly in anger.

I wished I had a shell I could retreat into, like a hermit crab trying to play dead. Were hermit crabs smart enough to play dead? Leaning toward Owen, I whispered, though I knew everyone else could hear me.

"I think that also means we gave drugs to a little girl."

"I know what it means," Owen said through clenched teeth.

"Wait, seriously?" Mickey almost laughed, but he looked slightly more appalled than he did amused.

Owen nodded, clearly ashamed.

"That's disgraceful," Mickey said. "Jesus. She could've eaten them. Or handed them out to her friends. You could've gotten a bunch of kids high."

Please stop.

"Why would you do that, Owen?"

"Because I thought she was you." Owen sounded exasperated, and for good reason. We were so *not* cut out to be drug dealers. Or bakers. Whatever. "Or I thought her dad was you, even though he wasn't with her. God, I don't know. Does it even matter? Just take the brownies."

"Well, obviously I'll take the brownies. I don't need you to tell me to take the brownies." Mickey reached out toward Laila's father, and the man handed Mickey the brown bag. "I apologize for the mix-up."

"It's fine," Laila's father muttered.

"So, hold on." Owen pointed between Laila and her dad. "If you weren't here for the brownies, why *were* you here?"

It was a good question. Minnie's house was on a dead-end street, and clearly Owen had no idea who Laila was. Maybe Minnie had known her? But her dad was parked down the street, which meant she didn't live on the block. And it also meant Laila hadn't come to visit Minnie, or her dad would've most likely been with her.

Laila looked to her dad, and he gave her a nod like she had his permission to speak to us.

"Um," Laila said quietly, "I'm doing a fundraiser for soccer, so my dad dropped me off at the end of the street so I could see if anyone wanted anything."

"You know," Mickey said, "it's probably not a great idea to let your child roam the neighborhood unsupervised. Never know what kind of weirdos are out there." He eyed Owen and me as he said the last part.

Laila's dad eyed Owen too.

"What are you selling?" Owen asked, his voice full of hesitation.

"Yankee Candles," the little girl answered, sounding more excited than she had a moment ago.

"Great." It looked like Owen was doing his best to try to smile. "I'll take ten."

Laila's father laughed a little and then revealed a satisfied smile. "You're goddamn right you will."

Chapter Five

OWEN

"Only a couple more days until your future wife moves in, huh?"

I looked over at Carter, who'd asked the question with a smug grin. "*Vee* will be moving in soon, yes." Though I'd love to be able to call her my future wife. Hell, I'd settle for girlfriend. But she'd seemed to friend-zone me pretty quickly. And pretty permanently. Sadly, baking pot brownies together was evidently not the way to her heart.

"Don't try to tell me there's not something there," Carter chided. "You two sneak off like, uh, like, um…" He glanced around until his eyes fell on Toby, who was chatting with Aniyah and Xander.

We'd all gathered at the Yard to celebrate the recent graduation of many members of the group I'd become friends with over the past year.

"Tobes," Carter said. "What're the names of those two people who fell in love when they weren't supposed to?"

When Toby gave him a blank look, Carter continued.

"Their family blew up a gas station."

"Oh! Romeo and Juliet?" Toby supplied.

Carter snapped his fingers. "Romeo and Juliet. That's it. You're like them. Except hopefully without the dying."

Taylor, who was sitting near us with Sophia and Ransom, looked over. "Gas station? Pretty sure that play predates cars."

Toby came closer and sat with us. "He's talking about the movie with Leonardo DiCaprio. We watched it a few weeks ago."

"It's awesome," Carter enthused. "People were shooting each other, and the soundtrack was a banger. There was a lot of crying, though, which was kind of a bummer."

"And Vee and I are like that how?" I asked, knowing I shouldn't bother but being unable to resist hearing Carter's logic.

"Because you made a love connection and none of us even realized it. Like when Romeo fell for Juliet through a fish tank." He looked around thoughtfully. "Was there a fish tank involved that night?"

"Why would there have been a fish tank?" Sophia asked.

Carter shrugged. "Just would've made for a cooler story. The ultimate meet-cute."

"I'd like to go the rest of my life without hearing you say 'meet-cute' again," Taylor said.

"You're just jealous."

"Of what?" she asked.

Carter stared at her for a second and, seemingly unable to come up with a reply, fixed his attention back on me. "Anyway, so the two of you spend a night together, and then she's moving in, just like Romeo and Juliet got married right after meeting."

I eyed him skeptically. "I feel like moving in together and

marriage have quite a few steps between them."

"Do they, Owen?" he asked in the most patronizing voice I'd ever heard from him. "Do they really?"

"Yes?" I drew out the word, uncertain of how to respond to the lunacy that encapsulated the very essence of Carter.

I knew I could end all of this by just telling everyone what had really happened the night Vee and I had disappeared from that party a few months back. The gang had questioned and teased me about it mercilessly since, all of them assuming I'd hooked up with Vee. And while I didn't want them to have that impression, I wanted them to know Vee had helped me carry out a drug deal even less. Surely everyone thinking she'd slept with me was better than people thinking she was involved in the marijuana trade.

Or maybe that was wishful thinking on my part. For all I knew, Vee would prefer to be likened to Pablo Escobar than be rumored to have had sex with me.

In my defense, I'd never *told* anyone I'd slept with Vee. I'd even denied it, though I'd been so unconvincing no one had believed me.

It was just that I was such a shitty liar, it had been easier to keep quiet than to make up a reason for why Vee and I had snuck away.

"And Romeo and Juliet would've moved in together if they hadn't died, so it's like almost totally the same."

Jesus, he's still on this?

"She's moving in because she needed a place to stay and I have the space," I argued. "Not because we're star-crossed lovers or whatever."

"Did you know it's actually bad to be star-crossed lovers? It means you've crossed the stars, like pissed off fate," Ransom explained. When we all stared at him, he picked up his beer bottle, looking self-conscious. "What? I can know stuff."

Taylor patted his hand. "We know you know stuff. That was just...super random."

His eyes narrowed. "You guys must've had shitty English teachers if that's random knowledge."

"I never even read it," Carter said.

"Really?" Sophia asked. "I thought everyone read that in high school."

"Oh, I'm not saying everyone else in my class didn't read it. But I definitely didn't. Come to think of it, I don't think I read anything in high school. Maybe that's why I was always so much busier in college."

He suddenly looked contemplative, so I left him to it and looked at everyone else.

"You guys excited about being done with school?"

Pretty much everyone in this group had just finished up their time at Lazarus University. Carter had graduated after finishing his fifth year due to redshirting a year while he played football, and Sophia, Toby, and Aniyah were all finished as well.

Ransom had completed his master's program in sports medicine at a different local school, and Xander had earned enough credit hours to graduate but had randomly decided to change his major. He and I weren't close, so I wasn't quite sure what was up with that. Maybe he really liked school?

Taylor had graduated a semester earlier and would coincidentally be headed to the same law school Vee had chosen. Everyone planned to stay in the area except for Aniyah, and even she was only moving an hour outside the city.

With a year left until my own graduation, thanks to the

year I'd taken after high school to explore the US in my dad's fifteen-year-old minivan, I was thankful I'd still have my friends around.

Granted, I had other friends at school. A lot of them. But those relationships all felt more casual. This group had been through some shit together, and it showed in the regard they had for each other. There were no better people to have your back than the people currently gathered at the Yard with me.

They all seemed to share the same feelings—that they were excited to have graduated but nervous to start the next chapter.

I could relate since I shared those feelings about what was in store for me.

Most of me was thrilled I'd have Vee living with me. I'd been enamored with her since the second I'd seen her. Who could blame me? With her olive complexion, sleek dark hair, and shrewd but kind eyes, she was absolutely gorgeous. But my feelings were also unrequited, and I wasn't sure how well I'd be able to play off how into her I was.

If I could avoid following her around like a lovesick puppy, I'd consider it a win.

Speaking of puppies...

I drained my glass and stood. "I gotta head out. Gimli probably thinks I've forgotten about him."

"Say hi to him for me," Carter said.

"Will do."

I said my goodbyes to the rest of the group and then hurried down to where my beat-up truck was parked. I hadn't had a vehicle up here until I'd inherited Minnie's house. I hadn't really needed one, and I also didn't want to put out money to buy one when I was already struggling to pay for school. But when I'd inherited Minnie's house, which needed a lot of fixing up, it had made sense to get something I could haul materials with.

Thankfully, my dad was able to talk my grandpop into getting a new truck, leaving me to inherit his old one. Old Clarence was a little clunky and cantankerous, but he usually started when I needed him to and got me from A to B with minimal fuss.

The drive back to Minnie's was quick, and I pulled into her tiny driveway and made my way to the front door. It still surprised me that she'd left me her house. We'd gotten on well and had definitely been close, but it had still been completely unexpected.

It made me a little sad to think that Minnie hadn't had anyone in her life more important than some college kid renting out her basement.

Pushing open the front door, I was immediately assaulted by my bestest friend. I bent down as he licked my face. Gimli was always an exuberant greeter.

I rubbed behind his ears as he gave me a contented snort before I stood and made my way to the kitchen, Gimli hot on my heels. There were tarps and materials scattered around the house, but I did my best to keep the floor as clear as possible. The last thing I wanted was my favorite guy taking a nail to the paw or something. I'd never forgive myself.

Grabbing a treat for Gimster and a bottle of water for myself, I surveyed my kitchen. It was coming together slowly but surely. Having to do the work myself in between classes, homework, and my job at a hardware store made it a slow process.

Which reminded me, I had an early shift the next morning.

I hadn't even applied to work at Mark's Hardware. After Minnie left me the house, I'd started going in there almost daily to pick up things I needed for various projects. Minnie's house had never *looked* rundown, but once I'd started poking around, it was easy to see how years of neglect had worn on the place. Once I got one thing fixed, another popped up.

One day, I was wandering the aisles of Mark's when a woman came up to me and asked me questions about a leaky sink she had. After helping her, I noticed Mark, the store's owner, watching me. He nodded once before disappearing into the back. He returned a moment later with a Mark's Hardware shirt and welcomed me to the team.

My parents had been wary of me working while in school. I tended to do well in classes when they were my sole focus, but my brain had a tendency to wander when I had a lot going on. I'd been called flighty more than once, and while I didn't think that was an entirely apt description, I understood why people got that impression.

But the job had come in handy—especially with its employee discount—more than once, and I truly enjoyed working there. It would also allow me to stay up here for the summer instead of returning to Virginia like I had every other summer.

I'd managed to keep my family in the dark about Minnie leaving her house to me. My family was great and they'd always been incredibly supportive of me, but they also didn't give me a whole lot of credit. And I got it. I did. I had a total *come what may* attitude wrapped in a surfer-vibe personality. I hadn't ever had to deal with many real-life issues. Part of me worried that they'd insist I sell the house, but I didn't want to do that.

Minnie had *chosen* to give her house to me. Granted, she

may not have had many other options, but she could've just not left it to anyone. Or she could've donated it to charity or done whatever the fuck people do with houses when they die. But she didn't. At some point, she must've taken whatever steps were needed to add me to her will. She left it to me, and I was going to take care of it.

I wasn't naïve enough to think I'd live there forever. Maybe I would, maybe I wouldn't. But I was going to love it first. I was going to rebuild it to its initial glory before I made any decisions.

I owed Minnie at least that much.

VERONICA

I taped another box closed while doing my best to ignore the looming presence in my doorway. Or *presences*.

"Who taught you how to tape a box?" one of the loomers asked.

I turned to glare at my brother Manny. "What's wrong with how I'm taping them?"

He scoffed. "Nothing, if you don't mind them popping open as soon as we lift them."

"I don't remember asking you to lift anything."

His eyebrows shot to his hairline. "Oh yeah? You gonna lift all these yourself, *princesa*?"

"Maybe the random dude she's moving in with will help," my other brother Franco said. "Though the *last* random dude she moved in with was pretty useless, so I doubt this one will be better."

I gritted my teeth, mostly in annoyance that his barb

hit its mark. My dad had been less than thrilled when I'd told him I was moving in with *another* man he'd never met and who I'd never even mentioned before announcing my plans to cohabitate with him.

Manny looked contemplative for a moment, which didn't bode well for me.

"Is it that men who actually know you don't want to spend much time with you? Because *that* I get."

Ugh. Older brothers are the worst.

I flipped them off and continued taping up boxes. I only got one more closed before they were beside me, Manny ripping the tape out of my hands.

"Are you using Scotch tape?"

"It's all I could find," I defended, though it came out as more of a whine. These two jerks always reduced me to the bratty little sister, even when I was actively trying to shed the role.

"How have you even survived this long?" Franco said with as much derision as he could probably muster.

My hands met my hips in an indignant stance that was well-practiced when it came to tangoing with these two. "Please, you can't even boil water. If we're comparing survival skills, I'm pretty sure cooking trumps closing boxes."

Franco traded a look with Manny before turning back to me with a smirk. "Oh, you can cook, huh? So that wasn't you who gave us all food poisoning that time you made us shrimp scampi?"

"That was five years ago, you jerk. And how was I supposed to know you couldn't leave shrimp out for more than two hours? It didn't say that anywhere in the recipe."

Both of their eyes widened.

"Because it's common fucking sense!" Manny yelled.

"You're the person they put directions on shampoo for, you know that?" Franco added.

"Says the guy who couldn't pass freshman year Spanish, even though he's been speaking the language since he was born," I countered.

"How many times do I have to tell you? That teacher had it out for me."

"I'd have it out for you too if you proposed to me with a ring pop on the first day of class."

Franco pointed a finger in my face, which I quickly slapped away. "She and I would've made beautiful children. Instead she married some bald, white dude who looks like he irons his khakis. No way do they have the chemistry we had."

"How do you even know who she married?"

He suddenly looked uncomfortable. "I found her online."

"Oh my God! You're the creepiest stalker to ever stalk!"

"Shut up. It's not like I peeked in her windows or anything. It's not my fault she has a public Facebook page. I mean, isn't it like Teaching 101 to lock down your social media?"

"I'm sure if she knew she had Ted Bundy on her trail, she would." I couldn't help the laughter that erupted from me. This whole thing was hysterical.

"Whatever. I hope she's happy with her three children who probably all have a thing for collared shirts and loafers."

I put a hand on Franco's shoulder. "Your stereotyping is second to none."

He sniffed. "Thank you."

For fuck's sake.

"Can you guys leave now so I can finish this?"

Manny dropped onto my bed with a bounce. "Nah. I

wanna talk about the guy you're moving in with. What was his name again?"

"Owen," Franco supplied.

"Oh yeah. *Owen.* I guess it's better than that other dude's name. Brody. What the hell kind of name is that, anyway? His parents must've hated him from birth."

I wanted to argue that his parents actually loved him more than he sometimes deserved, but there was no need to invite more conversation.

"You're breaking Dad's heart, you know?" Manny, always the king of transitions, said.

"Yes, I can totally see how my acceptance to a premier law school would be devastating for him."

"There are good law schools in New York. You don't have to keep fleeing the state at every opportunity." Manny could teach a master class on inflicting guilt.

"I'm not fleeing. I'm pursuing opportunities."

"With *Owen*," Franco added.

"Owen is just a friend who has a spare room. Stop acting like I'm starring in a remake of *Pretty Woman*." The image of sweet, clueless Owen as Richard Gere was laughable. Though I had to admit, there was something endearing about Owen. Quite a few somethings, actually.

"Please," Franco muttered. "Like you'd be cast in that."

"Are you calling me ugly, Frannie?"

"Yes. And don't call me Frannie."

"What are you gonna do about it?" I inched into his space, my eyes narrowed into a glower as I stared up at him.

Both of my brothers were as big as tanks. Franco was taller at nearly six foot three, and Manny was one of the shortest men in the family at six foot even. Only my Uncle Ricky was shorter at just under six feet. I was tiny by comparison at five foot four.

Before I could even grasp what was happening, Franco had me in a headlock and was rubbing his knuckles against my scalp.

"Stop, you animal. Dad! I swear, if you don't stop, they'll never find your body. Dad!"

The clomping of boots on hard wood approached as I attempted to wrench myself away from my brother.

"If you don't get off of me, I'm going to make your life miserable."

Franco laughed. "Too late."

A heavy sigh interrupted my next, more colorful threat.

"Doesn't it ever get old?" my father asked, sounding weary. How the three of them worked together always amazed me. But they all seemed born for keeping Diaz Construction—one of the few legit businesses Uncle Ricky funded—up and running smoothly. Ricky always joked it helped his image to have a few honest businesses in his name, but we knew the real reason was that my mom told my dad she wouldn't marry him if he wasn't on the straight and narrow. And since everyone had loved my mom, Uncle Ricky was happy to help.

I hoped practicing law fit me as well as my dad and brothers' occupation fit them. I'd loved my internship last year and had worked in a local Legal Aid office during the past year to make sure it was what I wanted before I spent a gazillion dollars on law school.

I'd always loved learning about the law, but I was still worried I was making a costly mistake.

I squirmed to push my head back so I could see my dad, even though he appeared upside down and the position probably made me look like something out of *The Exorcist*.

"Let her go," my dad ordered. He'd always seemed a giant amongst men to me, tall and broad from years of heavy lifting.

Franco did with a muttered, "She started it."

"You're twenty-six, Frankie. It's time for new material," my dad said as he stepped into my room and surveyed the boxes. "Almost all packed?"

The question sounded innocent, and anyone who didn't know my dad well would've missed the tension in his jaw and the stiffening in his shoulders. But I knew he was worried. He'd always worried about all of us, and it had only intensified when our mom died when I was fourteen. But he'd tried to not let that worry stifle us. And even though I was sure he didn't like it, at twenty-four, I was a little past him being able to determine what I did and who I lived with.

"Yeah, just a couple more boxes to fill, and then I'll be all set."

He turned to my brothers. "You good to drive her down there tomorrow?"

Manny crossed his arms over his chest. "She hasn't even *asked* us yet."

"She didn't ask because I already told you to do it. Asking if you were good was just a formality."

I stuck my tongue out at them behind my dad's back, just to be a brat. They acted like we hadn't worked all of this out weeks ago over a family dinner. Hell, they'd *offered* to drive me. There was no way they were going to miss an opportunity to intimidate Owen into treating me right. Not that Owen would ever treat me *wrong*, but they didn't know that, and I respected that their overprotectiveness came from a good place.

"Guess we'll just do the princess's bidding, as usual," Franco griped.

"Jesus, you two with the drama. I'll be out of your hair for the foreseeable future. You'd think you'd be happy to dump me at my new place."

Franco took a step closer and put his finger in my face again, but I didn't knock it away this time. "You'll always be in our hair, Ronnie. You're like a hideous knot that's easier to leave alone than try to comb out. So don't act like you moving away means you won't be seeing us."

It was as close to a declaration of undying love and affection Franco would ever deliver, and I took it for what it was.

Tears pricked my eyes, and I leaned forward and wrapped my arms around his thick chest. "Love you too, Frannie."

"Stop with the Frannie shit already," he said as he flicked my head before dropping a quick kiss there. Then he pulled away from me and left the room, my dad giving him a hearty slap on the back as he went.

Manny came over to me then and said, "You know we're gonna scare the shit out of this Owen kid before we leave you there, right?"

I smiled. "I wouldn't expect anything less." But I'd have to text Owen and tell him to expect a less than warm greeting from my brothers.

Once they were both gone, my dad fidgeted his hands as he looked around my room. "I'm sorry I can't drive down with you guys. But Frankie and Manny will be more help to you, and with them gone, I need someone to watch over the crews."

"I know, Dad. It's no big deal."

He nodded absently. "We'll take a trip down when things slow down and we can all get away. You can show us around your new city."

"New York will always be my city."

That made him smile. "That's what I like to hear."

My mom had always been the nurturer, the caregiver. My dad was those things too, but he was less demonstrative with them. My brothers and I felt his love every day, but he sometimes struggled to take the first step in showing it.

So I did what my mom would've done. I put the poor guy out of his misery.

I stepped close and hugged him tightly. "I love you, Daddy."

He sank into the embrace, the tension leaking from his limbs as his body molded around mine. "Love you too, baby."

Maybe I was crazy to leave a family who loved and supported me so thoroughly. But I couldn't shake the feeling that there was still more for me out there. And I was determined to find it.

Chapter Six

OWEN

My day had begun with an ominous text from Vee.

My brothers are probably going to try to scare you. Stay strong! See you soon :)

What exactly did *try to scare* me constitute? How did they know what I found scary? Would they try a variety of things until one worked?

I imagined her brothers popping out from behind doors in an attempt to startle me, and the image made me laugh. Obviously I knew they'd likely try to physically intimidate me. And who would really blame them? They were dropping off their gorgeous sister with a guy they'd never met. I couldn't begrudge them a little macho posturing.

The problem was, I wasn't afraid of things like that. I doubted they'd beat the shit out of me or anything, and at the end of the day, what else was there to be afraid of?

But I didn't want them to think I didn't understand *why*

they were trying to intimidate me. *Do I pretend to be scared of them? How scared should I pretend to be? Do I lower my eyes like a submissive dog whenever they glare at me, or do I call them sir or something?*

"What do you think?" I asked Gimli, who was lying at my feet.

His response was to groan loudly and roll onto his back.

"I think showing my stomach sends the wrong message." I stared at Gimli, waiting for further suggestions, but when he didn't move, I bent down and rubbed his belly.

He wagged his tail, and I wished everyone was as easily pleased as the Gimster.

I stood, withdrew my phone from my pocket, and typed out a quick message to Carter.

How do I keep Vee's brothers from wanting to beat me up?

My phone rang almost immediately.

"I thought people in our generation preferred texts," I said.

"Are they there?" Carter asked, his voice sounding slightly panicked. "Why do they want to beat you up already?"

"What do you mean *already*?"

"Owen!"

"No, they're not here yet. Jeez."

"Then how do you know they want to hurt you?"

"Vee texted that they were going to try to scare me."

"Oh," he replied, as if their wanting to do that made perfect sense. "Then why did you think they were going to beat you up?"

"I said they *wanted* to. Not that they would. But I'd prefer for them to have a good impression that makes them *not* want to resort to assault and battery."

"They're her big brothers. I think it's pretty much their job to make sure you know they'll kill you if you hurt their sister."

"How do I show them I have no intention of hurting her, though?"

"Maybe just be super welcoming and helpful. And be as nonthreatening as possible."

"How do I do that?" I didn't think anyone had ever been threatened by me in my life. Not that I was small or a pushover or anything, but I was pretty sure I emanated chill. "Should I, like, make everyone brownies or something?"

Sans the pot this time.

"Yes. Yes, you should definitely do that. And when you're done baking them, you should text me, and I'll come over and . . . sample them."

"Why would I need you to sample them?"

"Dude, it won't help your case to feed them shitty baked goods."

"*Dude*, I have perfectly functional taste buds."

"But then I can also hang around and provide backup in case you need it," he added.

That was . . . tempting. But did I want to seem like the kind of guy who needed backup? Did I want to *be* the kind of guy who needed it?

My family had raised me to face my problems head-on. Not that Vee's family was a problem necessarily. Ugh. Why was I such a mess over this? I rarely got all stressed out about . . . well, anything really. I was a *come what may* kind of person. I didn't worry about what *might* happen.

Until a beautiful Colombian goddess helped me bake pot brownies so I wouldn't be indebted to a bunch of low-level dudebro drug dealers. When it came to Vee, it seemed I worried about *everything*.

Hopefully as we got to know each other—and my heart got the memo that she was my roommate and nothing more—I'd settle down. But as I stood in my house and spiraled, I wasn't too sure that would be the case.

"Owen? You still there?"

"Yeah, sorry. I was contemplating your offer. But I think I'm okay. I don't want them to think I can't handle myself."

"But what about my brownies?" Carter whined, and I tried not to be offended that he'd clearly only offered to come over so I'd feed him snacks.

"I'm not going to make brownies. That seems like overkill."

He gasped. "Brownies are never overkill."

"I think getting some bagels makes more sense. I'll buy you a brownie next time we go out somewhere."

"What if where we are doesn't have brownies?" he asked, a pout still clear in his voice.

"Then you can get something else."

He didn't reply for a second, probably thinking it over, before saying, "Fine."

"Okay, well, I guess I'll talk to you later, then."

"Yeah. But Owen?"

"Hmm?"

"If they end up being giant dickheads, call me. I'll be around all day. No desserts required."

His offer warmed me from my toes to my forehead. "Thanks, Carter."

"Anytime."

After hanging up and putting the phone back in my pocket, I looked down at Gimli, who was still at my feet. "You'd protect me, wouldn't ya buddy?"

He stared at me for a second before closing his eyes.

Maybe I should make some brownies after all.

VERONICA

If there was anything worse than sitting in a cramped truck with two men who sang along to R.E.M. songs at the top of their lungs, I'd yet to experience it.

"Seriously, who under the age of forty even knows the words to R.E.M.?" I yelled over their off-key rendition of "Everybody Hurts."

Does everyone hurt, Michael Stipe?

Because, right then, it felt like the only one hurting was me. And goddammit, how did I even know the name of the lead singer? I'd been infected!

Both my brothers slowly turned their heads to glare at me—even Manny, who was driving.

"Watch the road," I chastised.

"R.E.M. is one of the greatest bands of all time," Franco said, his voice low and menacing.

"You're part of a Colombian mob family fanboying over one of the whitest bands in history. You should be ashamed."

"Well I'm not. And your prejudice has no home here."

"I'm not prejudiced. I just want it to stop."

"Want what to stop?" Manny asked.

"You two singing. If it can even be called that."

"How dare you," Manny said. "Franco has the voice of an

angel."

"And Manny sings like a cherub," Franco added.

"That's just another name for an angel."

"Exactly," Franco replied, as if it made sense.

"Can we please listen to something else?" I begged.

Manny lowered the volume of the music and said, "Sure. We can listen to you tell us more about Oliver."

"Owen," I corrected. "What do you want to know?"

"I dunno," Manny said. "His social security number, medical history, whether he has a criminal record. Stuff like that."

"Is he an organ donor?" Franco asked.

"Why do you need to know that?"

He shrugged. "Just for planning purposes."

"You two are seriously impossible."

"Fine," Manny said. "If you don't know anything useful, you can tell us when you first knew that you *lurved* him."

"Ew. Who says *lurved*? And I don't. We're just friends."

"Hear that, Frankie? They're *friends*," he said. I could see his eyebrows bouncing in the rearview mirror.

God, I hated him.

"Oh, I bet. I have lots of friends who'd let me move in with them rent free."

"How do you even know that?" I asked.

Franco turned in his seat to smile at me. "I heard you telling one of your friends. Like an actual friend, not whatever this Orson guy is to you."

"He *is* just a friend. And his name is Owen."

"*Tsk*. It's not good to lie to your family, Ronnie," Manny said.

"Yeah, Ronnie," Franco added. "Think of how good it'll

feel to tell us all about your feelings for Oscar."

"Owen," I growled.

Manny looked over at Franco. "She seems to be in denial."

"Or maybe she just lacks the self-awareness to express herself freely," Franco suggested.

Manny shot me a quick, serious look. "I think it's time."

"Time for what?" I asked.

"I agree," Franco said, ignoring my question. Then he turned in his seat again so he could face me. "You see, Veronica, when boys and girls reach a certain age, they start to feel things for each other that goes beyond friendship."

"For fuck's sake," I groaned.

"It's called attraction," Manny said, picking up where Franco left off.

I wondered if they'd rehearsed this or if being asswipes just came naturally to them.

"And when a boy named Oz—"

"Owen," I interrupted Franco to correct him *again*, even though I knew they were doing it on purpose.

"And a girl named Ronnie—"

"Veronica," I cut in on principle.

Franco whipped around. "Not everything is about you, ya know? I can name my hypothetical couple anything I want."

An eye roll was all I could muster in reply.

"Anyway, when Omar and Ronnie figure out they're attracted to each other, they begin to explore what I like to call the Base System. First base is—"

I'd never unbuckled a seat belt faster in my life. I had the thing off and was leaning into the front so I could reach the console before Franco was able to utter another word.

"Let's see what's next for good ole R.E.M., huh?"

Turns out it was "Losing My Religion," which was

incredibly fitting considering the car ride with my brothers had nearly cost me my will to live.

Chapter Seven

VERONICA

"Honey, I'm home!" I yelled as I swung open the door. Maybe I should've knocked, but since I was moving in, I figured what the hell. May as well barrel on in.

The sound of Gimli barking startled me. I'd somehow forgotten about him, so I bent down to give him some love. He was a mangy thing, but his tongue lolled out as I scratched behind his ears, and since that was one of the best receptions I'd ever gotten from a man, I decided to be flattered.

"Aw, he still likes me," I said when I saw Owen coming down the stairs.

"I'd question his sanity if he didn't," Owen replied.

It wasn't the first time Owen had complimented me, but I was thrown by the ease with which he did it every time. Even when we'd texted back and forth, he was so free with his flattery, it flustered me. And turned me on a bit, to be honest, but this was Owen, and we were friends and roommates, and for once in my life I would *not* make a situation more complicated than it needed to be.

He stopped beside me, and I took a second to drink him in as I stood. He was in a tank top and shorts that stopped a couple inches above the knee, both of which revealed a surprisingly muscular body.

Owen had a certain stoned surfer boy quality about him that made it seem like he'd be vegged out on a couch for the bulk of his life. But the way thin veins popped out of the tight skin stretched over lithe muscles, it was clear Owen took care of himself. He wasn't bulky or shredded, but rather functionally fit. The kind of guy who wasn't intimidating to look at but was probably fluent in some kind of martial art.

"Do you know Krav Maga?" I asked him, my voice flying out of my mouth before I even realized I was speaking. *Krav Maga?* What the hell was I even talking about?

Owen looked just as perplexed. "Uh, no. Why? Did you wanna learn?"

The way he said it sounded like he'd be willing to learn it just so he could teach it to me, and I found myself charmed by him again.

I shrugged. "I dunno. Never thought about it."

"Oh. Okay. Well, if you do, I'm sure we could find somewhere."

"Are you offering to take classes with me?" I asked, suddenly hoping the answer was yes because there wasn't much that sounded more fun than learning something like that with him.

"Sure."

I smiled at him, unsure of what to say to that. Thankfully I was saved from having to say anything by my rude-as-hell brothers pushing the front door open so wide it banged into me, jolting me forward into Owen.

He wrapped his arms around me as I fell against his chest. I couldn't help but notice how firm it was, because I'd evidently become a total perv.

"Well, well, well. Ronnie, you could've just told me you knew all about the Base System already," Franco said with a shit-eating grin on his face.

I looked up at Owen, who still had his arms around me, and saw his confused expression.

"Base system? Like . . . in baseball?"

Manny snorted. "Yeah, man. Just like baseball." He set down the box he was carrying and extended his hand toward Owen. "I'm Manuel, Vee's brother."

"Owen," he said as he shook Manny's hand before introducing himself to Franco, who offered his hand and name in response.

"Where are we taking this stuff?" Manny asked, hoisting the box back into his arms.

"Oh, uh, follow me." Owen spun around and started up the stairs. "I fixed up a room for you. If you don't like that one, I can start working on the one you want. I probably should've FaceTimed and shown them to you so you could pick."

"I'm sure whichever one you worked on will be fine," I assured him.

I'd known when I agreed to move in that the house was a work in progress. I was fully prepared to live with some holes in the walls and dust everywhere. Since I wasn't paying rent, as long as it was livable, I'd be happy.

He stopped outside a door and ushered Gimli inside, closing it quickly behind the dog. "He'll be fine in there until we're done." Then he moved to a second door and looked back at me. "Okay, well, don't be afraid to tell me the truth. I don't mind changing things so that you're comfortable."

I nodded once to show I understood, and then he opened the door and stepped inside. I followed, my eyes wide.

The room was beautiful. The walls were light blue, but color streaked across them as sunlight filtered in through a beautiful stained-glass window.

Damn, people really knew how to build houses back in the day.

There was a four-poster bed made up with a white down comforter and a large dresser in the same dark wood as the bed.

"I'm sanding a desk to put in here. I can stain it so it matches everything else," Owen said.

Manny whistled as he came in and set the box down at the base of the bed on the wooden bench that looked to have a top that lifted for extra storage.

"Owen, I'm . . . I'm speechless. You've done an incredible job in here."

Owen shrugged, his face reddening slightly. He didn't strike me as someone who blushed often. It was adorable.

"I thought you'd enjoy the window. But if not, you can keep the curtains closed. I got the ones that block out sunlight, just in case."

"This is a nice-ass room, *princesa*," Franco said.

I wanted to call him out on the patronizing nickname, but right now I did kind of feel like a princess.

And damned if Owen didn't make the unlikeliest of princes.

OWEN

I took my first full breath that morning when I saw how much Vee liked her room. Truth be told, I'd spent more money in there than my budget allowed, but I hadn't been able to help it. I wanted her to *want* to be here, not just stay because it was a free place to crash.

She stared around in wonder as I stared at her. She was dressed casually in tight black shorts and a burgundy workout top. Her hair was piled on top of her head, and her face seemed to be free of makeup.

She was the most beautiful woman I'd ever seen.

"Okay," Franco said with a clap. "Let's get moving. The quicker we get her shit out of the truck, the quicker we can abandon her here and never look back."

Vee cocked her hip and set a hand on it. "Please. You two will probably cry all the way back to New York."

"Tears of joy, dear sister," Manny said as he threw an arm around her. "Tears of joy."

She shrugged him off and rolled her eyes. "Whatever you say. Lead the way."

They bantered that way for the rest of the day. I was mostly quiet, taking in the casual ease with which they teased each other. Being an only child, I'd always wished I had someone I could mercilessly make fun of while still knowing they had my back.

I mean, my grandma and I were kinda like that, but it was still different. And I basked in the experience, hoping to soak up some of the sibling bond by osmosis or something.

"Man, I'm starving," Manny said, shooting puppy eyes at Vee.

"Oh shoot," I said. "I meant to order pizza or something, but it slipped my mind when we got so busy." What I'd really been *so busy* doing was casting subtle but nonetheless longing looks at Vee while she shuffled boxes and unpacked items as we dropped them in her room.

They'd fit a surprising amount of stuff in the truck, and it made me feel happy that Vee had seemed to bring everything she owned with her. She'd clearly intended to stay for the long haul.

"You're letting me stay in your house rent free and helped me move my stuff all day," Vee said with a smile. "The least I can do is feed everyone."

"The very least," Franco agreed.

"You could do the most and pay us for our time," Manny added.

"Mmm, yes, I suppose I *could.*" She let the words hang there a moment . . . and then turned to me. "Is there somewhere nearby that you like?"

"Uh, yeah, there are a few. College town and all," I said with a chuckle that came out way too awkwardly. "I have a few menus in the drawer next to the fridge."

She smiled at me, making my heart thump harder. She was going to send me into cardiac arrest if she didn't stop shining the full megawattage of that smile on me. Though I had a similar reaction when she spoke to me too. Or looked at me. Or came within five feet of me.

Jesus, this was never going to work. I was going to expire before we'd even cohabitated for a week. Then she'd be left alone in this huge house that was in complete disarray because every time I started one project, another more pressing one popped up.

A throat clearing brought me out of my downward spiral, and I looked around to see Vee gone and her two brothers glaring at me. They really were big men.

"So...Owen...tell us about yourself," Manny said in a way that was meant to sound like a threat hidden in casual conversation.

"Oh, um, well, I'm from Virginia. I'm going into my senior year, even though I'm already twenty-three. I took a gap year. Let's see, what else? I, uh, oh! I'm friends with Vee's friends. The ones she lived with before. So that's...good. Right?"

They didn't look like that was good.

"I think I'm gonna go make sure Vee found the menus," I said as I gestured toward the door and moved in its direction.

Franco slid into my path, and I nearly bumped into him. "As fascinating as all of that was, we'd like to know a few things that are a bit more specific."

"Like what?"

"Like if you have a criminal record," Manny said.

Oh God, do they know about the pot brownies? Did Vee tell them?

Still, I hadn't gotten caught doing anything wrong, so I could still be truthful.

"No."

"Involved in any illegal activities?"

My brow furrowed as the irony of the situation hit me. "Isn't your uncle a mob boss?"

They shared a look I felt conveyed horrible things for my well-being before they both widened their stances and crossed their arms over their chests. It made for an intimidating dance I had no interest partnering in.

"We weren't talking about us," Manny gritted out. "We

were talking about you."

My brow furrowed. "But ... why?"

"Why what?" Manny asked.

"Why aren't we talking about you? I mean, I get what this is," I said, waving my hands in front of them as I spoke. "Your sister is moving in with some guy you don't know, so you wanna interrogate me or whatever. But the truth is, it's I who should be the worried one. Your family could do way more to me than I could ever do to you. And while I get leaving her here will probably be hard for you, what do you really expect me to reveal in the next few minutes that will set your minds at ease? I could say anything, and you'd have no way of knowing if it was the truth or a lie."

"So you're saying we'll, what? Just have to trust you?" Franco asked.

"No. I'm saying you'll have to trust Vee. We both will. You'll have to trust that she knows what she's doing and that she'll let you know if she needs help. And I have to trust that she won't call you to beat me up the first time I leave the toilet seat up." I shrugged. "She seems like a good person and, honestly, a lot tougher than me. So I'm willing to put my faith in her that everything will work out."

Her brothers looked a little shocked by my words but still unsure.

"So if she wants to move out?" Manny asked.

Then I'd probably assume the fetal position and cry for days.

"Then she moves. You know I'm not charging her rent, so the only thing I get out of her being here is company. Which I'm thankful for," I rushed to add so it didn't seem like I didn't want her here. "It's definitely been lonely being in this big house on my own."

"Why didn't you put out an ad for more roommates?" Franco questioned, his tone suspicious again. "You have the room, and I'd suspect you could use the money."

I shrugged again. "I wasn't sure that Vee would be comfortable living with anyone else. I'm open to roommates, but the house needs more renovations first. Which is why I'm not charging Vee anything. She offered to help me fix the place up, and I figured that was a fair trade."

That wasn't explicitly true, but I figured she *would* help me if I asked, so the words fell off my tongue easily.

Franco snorted. "Our sister? She's going to help you fix up a house?"

"Yes, she is," a decidedly feminine and assertive voice said from the doorway, where Vee stood giving her brothers a withering look. "And if you're quite done trying to scare my roommate, the food will be here soon."

"We weren't trying to scare him," Franco mumbled.

"We just needed to feel him out a bit," Manny explained.

Her lips quirked. "And how did he feel?"

I expected the two men to balk at her phrasing, but they each regarded me for a moment before turning back to their sister.

"Eh, he'll do," Manny said.

"Yeah," Franco added. "But we'll still make him disappear if he treats you wrong."

Alarmingly, Vee smiled widely. "I'd expect nothing less."

Chapter Eight

OWEN

"Well, *I'm* excited about this!" I plopped down onto Vee's orange swivel chair and used the edge of the small desk to push myself into a fast spin. I was glad that she'd happily agreed to put it in a common space instead of her room. While I'd done a decent job making her room look about a million times better than the rest of the place, none of the bedrooms were as large as they were in newer houses.

I guess people a hundred years ago had a lot less shit.

When I came to a stop, Vee was sitting at the kitchen table looking weary but relieved.

After Manny and Franco had left, we'd spent most of the afternoon settling Vee into her room. I'd hooked up her TV and gotten her connected to the Wi-Fi while she organized her clothes in her dresser and small closet and put brand-new sheets on her bed because she had some sort of superstition about old sheets and a new house or something. Apparently it didn't matter that the house was a century old. It was new to her, and when you slept somewhere new, it needed to be on new sheets.

"Excited about spinning?"

"No. Well, yes, spinning too." I gave myself another push. "But I meant about living together. It'll be fun to have a roommate who doesn't make me repeat myself every time I try to talk to her."

"What?"

Vee held a hand to her ear, and I tossed a pencil at her because it was the only thing within reach.

"Better watch it or I'll give you lead poisoning." Pencils were made of graphite now, but the threat sounded better when it included a deadly toxin.

"I think I might get lead poisoning anyway," she said, letting her eyes scan the walls. "Seriously, though, did Minnie ever have this checked for lead or asbestos or anything? This could be bad."

"As bad as selling drugs to young children?" I tried to laugh, but I still felt like an idiot. An idiot who could've gone to jail for a very long time. In addition to whatever drug charges I would've faced, had Laila's dad decided to press any, they'd probably tack on a few child-endangerment charges as well.

"Maybe not quite as bad as that. And we technically *gifted* the drugs, and it was only *one* child, so that's not as bad." Vee was grasping at straws, and they were the ones given out by environmentally friendly restaurants—the paper kind that disintegrated in your mouth the second they got wet.

I'd almost made a joke about how she'd make one hell of a lawyer with a defense like that one, but I didn't know how she'd take that.

"Totally," I said instead. "That gesture could be considered charity. We should write it off on our taxes."

We both laughed at that, and Vee's smile lingered in a way that made me think it might be from more than just amusement. But I didn't have time to overthink it any more than I already had because we were interrupted by the doorbell.

"I'll get it," we both said at the same time, followed by, "Jinx," which caused us to laugh again.

"It's our first visitor," Vee said excitedly. "The pizza doesn't count."

Not sure who it might be, we both headed to the door together, and when we pulled it open, we saw Drew, Sophia, Toby, Ransom, and Carter, who was holding several bags of something that smelled fucking amazing. The pizza had been more of a late lunch than an early dinner, so there was still room in my belly for whatever these guys had brought with them.

"Congratulations," he said, practically thrusting the bags toward me. "We brought food."

When I took them from him, I noticed he was holding... *is that a spring roll?*... with a few bites taken out of it.

"Nothing says housewarming like Thai food and beer," said Toby, giving a nod toward the six-packs Drew was holding.

"Um, thanks, man. You guys didn't have to do that." I meant it. I hadn't been expecting anyone to come by with food and drinks.

Carter took another bite of his spring roll and gave me a look of complete confusion. "Yeah, I know. That's what makes it a random act of kindness."

Toby put his hands on Carter's shoulders and squeezed them like he was tightening the collar on a dog before he lost all control of him. "You'll have to excuse him. He forgot to take his meds today."

"No I didn't. You saw me take them." Carter shook his head like Toby was the crazy one and plopped himself down on the couch. The plastic squeaked beneath him. "This is..." He rubbed his hand over it and narrowed his eyes like he was trying to make sense of the design choice. "Oh shit, did you guys put this on so you can have sex on here and not get any"—he leaned in and whispered—"fluids on it?"

The comment had been directed at me, but his hushed tone did nothing to stop everyone else from hearing.

This was like some sort of bad dream I wouldn't ever wake up from. I swore I could feel the heat from Vee's stare pierce my skin.

Or am I blushing?

"What? No!"

"I mean, I know you'll still get some on there, but it won't go through the plastic and ruin the couch, which is the point, right?"

The couch was ruined the second you mentioned fluids.

Unfortunately he continued. "It's like a couch condom." Carter looked pleased with the term he'd just coined.

"Come on, buddy," Toby said. "Let's go bring the beer into the kitchen and put it in the fridge."

"Drew can do it. He's already holding it."

"Jesus Christ," Toby whispered through his teeth.

"I think I have some chocolate chip cookies in there," I told him. It was a lie, but it would probably take Carter a while to figure that out, and it would momentarily rid me of any more comments about bodily fluids, so that was a win.

At the promise of cookies, Carter practically leaped off the couch and bounded into the kitchen. Drew and Toby followed, leaving Vee, Sophia, Ransom, and me in the living room.

"Where's Taylor?" I asked. Xander, Brody, and Aamee weren't here either, but it felt weird to have Ransom here without his decidedly better half, especially when he was already a little down since his sister Hudson had gone back to Georgia to live with their mom again. "You two are like peanut butter and jelly, or Bert and Ernie, or—"

"We're nothing like Bert and Ernie," Ransom interrupted.

"Yeah," Sophia agreed. "If anyone is Bert and Ernie, it's Toby and Carter."

There was an awkward silence between all of us before Ransom thankfully spoke again. "Taylor's got a shift at the Treehouse tonight, but she gets done around ten thirty. So if we're still here around then, I'm sure she'll come by."

"Stay as long as you'd like," Vee said. "It's great to have so many people I already know here. It'll make adjusting to the move and law school so much easier."

Vee smiled at me after she said it.

Did she feel especially grateful to be here with *me*?

I couldn't help but warm at the compliment, even though I knew I'd read too much into it. The last guy she'd lived with was Brody, so I was sure anyone was a step up from that experience.

VERONICA

I'd been tired after moving all morning and getting settled in the afternoon, but once our motley crew had shown up, I'd gotten a second wind. They were always so full of life. At Minnie's large oak table, we'd spread out the containers of

Thai food and passed them around like we were sitting down to some sort of Friendsgiving.

I was used to having a lot of people around the table since we frequently had extended family over for big dinners. Between all the yelling over each other and Franco and Manny snatching rolls out of each other's hands, I wasn't a stranger to big, loud gatherings.

Which was good because about halfway through dinner, Aamee and Brody arrived with more beer and a bottle of something Brody said a buddy of his made in his backyard. I wasn't about to touch whatever was in that bottle, but Owen seemed pretty excited about it.

"Did you fuckers save any food for us?" Brody asked, leaning over the table to peer into what was left of the containers.

"Sorry," Drew said. "We didn't know you were coming."

"Coming." Carter shook his head and snickered. "That reminds me. Before you guys head out, make sure you check out the condom couch."

"Ignore him," Owen said. "He has the sense of humor of a second grader."

"Really?" Carter replied. "You know a lot of second graders who make jokes about ejaculating on furniture?" His question sounded more genuine than sarcastic, which would've been at least moderately concerning for anyone who didn't know Carter.

"Ejaculating is an impressive word for you," Aamee said. "Did Toby teach you that? And here I thought trisyllabic was your limit."

I watched as Carter scratched his blond head for a moment before shooting her a bright smile that looked like a light switch had been flipped inside him.

"Thanks! Now where do you keep those cookies you promised me, O, because I looked through all your cabinets and didn't find shit."

Toby patted him on the shoulder. "I'll get you a cookie on the ride home."

"Can you get me two?" He sounded almost sad. "From the place below Brody's apartment?"

Toby nodded. "Sure. I'll get you two."

Those two were so cute it was practically sickening.

Eventually, Xander and Taylor made it over, and after giving the whole group a tour of Minnie's Palace, as Owen called it, we went out to the large picnic table out back to play cards.

"So, Owen," Aamee began, sitting back in her white plastic chair. "You said you don't believe in ghosts, right?"

We'd had this conversation a few months ago at the bar, and it had surprised all of us to know that Owen was more than skeptical of the supernatural. The opinion seemed in such sharp contrast to his very nature. He always seemed so open-minded, so accepting of anything and everything, it was hard to believe he would dismiss anything as a possibility, no matter how remote.

"I don't," Owen replied. "Why?"

Aamee was sitting facing the house, and she pointed to a window on the top floor. It must've been the attic, or a third floor that Minnie had used for storage or something, because Owen had never shown it to me or to the rest of the group during the tour.

"A few minutes ago, a light went on in that room, and then the curtains moved a little," she said. "I thought I saw a woman standing there."

"Nice try," Owen said.

"I'm not kidding. What's up there? That wasn't part of the tour."

Owen shrugged. "Probably old photo albums and antique furniture or something."

"Wait." Brody leaned forward, looking excited. "You've never even been up there?"

I thought Owen seemed a little uneasy at Brody's question, but he quickly went back to his casual self before answering.

"Nah. I'm not into hanging out in dusty attics."

"Maybe we should all go up," I suggested.

"I'm not going up there," Aamee said. "No way. Even without a ghost, that place is probably crawling with bugs or bats or something."

"My point exactly," Owen agreed.

"I'll go," Drew said, looking at Sophia, who let out a heavy sigh but then agreed to come along.

"We're not going up there." Owen sounded almost stern—serious in a way that made me hope everyone dropped it. Maybe he'd tell me why eventually, or maybe he wouldn't, but clearly Owen didn't want to talk about that attic.

"So you *do* believe in ghosts." The comment came from Aamee, who was practically singing with enthusiasm. "What's your deal? Did one sexually harass you or something?"

"No. I was not sexually harassed by a ghost."

"It's cool, man," Xander said. "Everyone's got their own shit." He tossed down a card and picked up another.

"Yeah, but in my case, my shit is not that some spirit was throwing unwanted sexual advances my way."

"Oooh, so you liked it." Brody gave a nod of approval. "Was she hot?"

Owen took a sip of his beer and then glanced around the

table at us. "How did I become friends with so many weirdos?"

Brody opened his mouth to speak, but Owen beat him to it.

"The question was rhetorical. And so we can finally put this to rest, the reason I don't go up there is because Minnie told me not to."

I could feel the pulse of the group change with his admission. A second ago we'd been joking about ghosts molesting him, and now it seemed *some*thing was up there that Minnie didn't want anyone to know about. Even Owen, the person she cared about enough to leave an entire house to.

"What do you think's up there?" I asked.

Minnie definitely had her secrets—like baking pot brownies—but the fact that she'd directly told Owen to stay away from there gave me goosebumps despite the warm temperature.

"Dunno," Owen said. "But if she wanted me to stay out of there, then it's none of my business, and I'm going to respect that."

"But what if it's a treasure chest filled with gold coins?" Carter beamed.

"Oh, or one of those…" Drew snapped his fingers as he seemed to be trying to recall whatever it was he couldn't remember. He turned to Sophia. "What's that thing you said you found in your mom's drawer when you were ten?"

She shivered. "Ew, I really hope an elderly woman isn't storing unique sex toys in her attic."

Brody looked absolutely horrified and, for once, unable to speak.

"Nice," Taylor said. "Didn't know Kate Mason had it in her."

"I think I drank too much," Brody said, already getting up. "I'm gonna be sick."

Taylor laughed a little as Brody headed to a part of the yard where he couldn't hear about his mother's sex life. He leaned into some bushes and began dry heaving.

"Sorry," Taylor said, though her lingering smile told me she wasn't. "Maybe not the best choice of words."

"Not the toys," Drew said. "That pin thing that was worth a lot of money."

"Oh, the broach?" Sophia said.

"You can come back," Aamee yelled to where Brody was near the tree line. "He meant a broach."

Brody returned to the group reluctantly and begged us to change the subject to basically anything else. When Owen seconded that, the rest of the bunch decided to acquiesce. Something told me it had more to do with Owen's request than Brody's, but I was just happy they'd all moved on.

The night continued much as it had begun—everyone swapping ridiculous stories, poking fun at each other, and drinking more beer.

Owen had his own in the fridge in the basement and had stocked it only with IPAs and raw cookie dough, which Carter pointed out could have been used to make the cookies he wanted so badly earlier.

It felt so comfortable, so natural. Like this was a group I'd always been a part of. Or maybe it was more that I felt I always *would* be.

Chapter Nine

OWEN

Mark's Hardware had been unusually slammed since I'd walked in. We usually got fairly steady traffic, but it had been insane all morning. It seemed everyone was doing home renovations in preparation for summer.

I could relate.

Usually I had time during my shifts to wander around and think about what materials I could use for my place. A lot of my ideas were pipe dreams. Things I'd do if money weren't an issue.

But it was an issue—hence why I was at work—so I was forced to be more practical in my actual spending.

Vee had turned out to be a surprising role model in that regard. I supposed even a male feminist like myself could succumb to gender stereotypes from time to time. I'd expected Vee to be more... reckless with her spending. Though, when I analyzed it, I perhaps could attribute that less to her being female and more to the fact that it seemed like she had a family who doted on her.

That made it sound like I thought she'd be a spoiled brat, which I hadn't. But I definitely hadn't expected her to be so thrifty and hands-on. Like with refurbishing and selling the furniture. She'd done an amazing job so far with all of it and had even managed to sell a few pieces already. Some of it had been long, tedious work, but she'd never once complained.

Living with her in general had been a surprise, but maybe not for the reasons I'd expected. I'd anticipated her either staying completely to herself or to leave her stuff everywhere. But she'd managed to achieve a middle ground that made me like her even more. Though, if I were being honest, *everything* she did made me like her more.

Vee had wholeheartedly, no holds barred, moved in. There was no awkward grace period where we tiptoed around each other and were overly accommodating. From the moment she'd moved in, she'd simply begun ... living.

Whether it was a pair of shoes left neatly beside the door or her mug in the sink or a bag casually draped on the back of a chair, Vee didn't try to erase herself from the house, but she didn't take it over either. She pitched in when something needed to be done, and she offered to share her meals and her time with me.

And I was more than happy to share mine with her in return.

My mind continued to drift to her as I wondered how her day was going. She was training with Drew so she could start her new job as a server at the Yard. She'd been anxious about it because she'd never worked in a restaurant before, but I was sure she'd do fine. To me, there was nothing Vee couldn't do.

"Excuse me," a soft voice said from behind me.

I whirled around to see an elderly woman clutching a hammer.

"Yes, ma'am, how can I help you?"

She held the hammer out in front of her. "Can I knock a wall down with this?"

I furrowed my brow. "Like a wall in your house?"

When she nodded, I reached out and took the hammer from her. "I think a sledgehammer would be more appropriate. I can show you where they are."

She followed behind me as I led the way toward the back of the store.

"Are you knocking the wall down yourself?" I asked.

She couldn't have been a day under seventy. And while I wouldn't have wanted to tell my grandma she couldn't do something, I also knew the odds of this tiny woman being able to take down a wall—or tell if it was load bearing or anything like that—were slim.

"Oh, I'm not knocking down a wall."

I stopped suddenly and turned to face her. "I thought you said that's what you needed the hammer for."

"I want one that *can* do it. But that's not what I'm using it for."

"Okay. Can I ask what you *are* using it for? So I can make sure I get you the right tool?"

"I want it to break all the windows out of my husband's car. But I also may want to leave a few dents in it too. It depends on how I feel after the windows."

I widened my eyes. "Oh, I, um . . . I'm not sure I can sell you something you're going to commit a crime with."

She scoffed. "What's a crime is that he thinks he can get away with spending time with that hillbilly harlot Miranda Jacobs. Giving her a ride home, my ass. That hickey on his neck came from somewhere, and I damn well know it wasn't from me."

Wow. That was … wow. "A hickey?" I asked, because that was obviously the most interesting bit. "What, is he in high school?"

She nodded emphatically. "That's what I told him. What eighty-year-old man walks around with a hickey on his neck?"

"Could it not be anything else? Like a bruise or something?" Didn't older people bruise more easily? Maybe the old guy deserved the benefit of the doubt.

"No. He admitted it was a hickey. But he said he gave it to himself with our Roomba."

"No," I gasped, scandalized. "He thought it was better to tell you he was having his way with the Roomba instead of Ms. Jacobs?" I slid my arm onto a shelf so I could lean in as we spoke. This poor woman.

"Yes, the idiot. And then she had the nerve to show up at my house with a peach cobbler the next day. She says it's a family recipe, but we all know it's from the Betty Crocker cookbook. Anyway, she only makes that for special occasions." She put her hands on her hips. "Now you tell me. How is someone being neighborly and giving her a ride home all of the sudden worth a peach cobbler she only makes once a year?"

"It does sound very suspect," I agreed.

"So I figured I'd start busting out windows on his '55 Bel Air until he told me the truth. But he hid all his tools when I threatened that, which is why I'm here."

I let out a low whistle to show I understood the gravity of her situation, while my mind reeled with my own predicament. Did I try to reason with this woman so she didn't vandalize her husband's prized possession, or did I help her avenge her honor with a sledgehammer? Decisions, decisions. "Well, Mrs. …."

"Hannity," she supplied. "Though I may be the ex-Mrs.

Hannity in a few hours."

I smiled at her conviction. "Mrs. Hannity, are you sure breaking his windows is the way to go?"

"Do you have another suggestion?"

I shrugged. "Maybe you could beat him at his own game. Go home with a hickey of your own and say the Roomba really gets around. See what he says then."

Her face scrunched up in doubt. "But where would I get a hickey? Unless..."—she moved closer to me and smiled— "you're offering."

I made a loud choking sound, causing her to slap me on the back.

"Um, I don't...I mean, I can't... It would be unprofessional."

She looked crestfallen. "Then what do I do?"

"Makeup?" I suggested.

"Hmm, that's less fun than getting it the old-fashioned way, if you know what I mean."

Unfortunately, I did.

As the conversation continued, I'd realized how off-track it had gotten. I would've been better off just giving her the hammer and letting her destroy some property.

"Or maybe you could just talk to him again?" I suggested. "Be honest with him about your feelings and see if you all can work it out."

She thought for a moment before saying, "Maybe you're right. After all, I should really be angry at Miranda. Hal hasn't been able to get it up for close to a decade, so anything that happened was surely her idea."

"Oh, yeah, okay, I didn't need to know any of that, but yeah, that seems like sound logic."

"Thank you, young man," she said. "I'll pass on the hammer today, but I may be back for some duct tape, depending on what I find out about dear old Miranda."

With that, she walked away, and I tried to forget that she'd basically just confessed to a possible future kidnapping.

Thankfully, the next few hours passed without any more threats of crime. Sadly, it also passed with excruciating slowness. The rush had ended by noon with only a few customers coming in to mostly browse. I'd nearly fallen asleep at the register, when the bell on the door chimed midafternoon.

"Welcome to Mark's Har—" I started but stopped abruptly when I saw Vee walking toward me.

Walking probably wasn't the right word. Dragging her limbs like a zombie would've been more appropriate.

"What's wrong?" I asked as she reached the counter and curled over it, with her arms stretched out and her head resting on top of them.

"I'm a shitty waitress," she said, her words muffled.

"Why? I'm sure you're fine." I couldn't imagine Vee being shitty at anything, but I also recognized I was likely biased.

"Drew had to practice deep-breathing exercises while he was training me. Drew! The calm, patient guy who manages to not get annoyed by Sophia's schemes and drama. It was like pushing Mother Teresa over the edge." She lifted up enough to rest an elbow on the counter and support her head with her hand. "He was too nice to fire me before I even started, but I could tell he wanted to."

"Are you sure you're not being too hard on yourself?"

I didn't want to make assumptions that Vee was overreacting or being a drama queen, but her description did sound pretty un-Drew-like.

"He told me we mostly used plastic cups outside so I should be able to avoid touching glassware. Then a few minutes later, he made it a rule that I wasn't *allowed* to touch anything made of glass. And when he realized that didn't include plates or bowls, he amended his rule to include anything at all that's breakable. He said he'll have someone else run food until I get the hang of it."

"Well, that's good that he thinks you just need some practice," I said in an attempt to infuse some optimism into the moment.

Vee gave me a skeptical look. "He told me he'd start me out as a hostess so I could ease into it. I also need to help clear off tables, as long as there's no real glassware on them, and help the servers where they need it. I feel like a little kid whose mom won't let her help make dinner."

"But he's letting you set the table," I offered and received a glare in return.

"Yeah, but just with silverware and napkins," she said dryly.

"When do you start?" I asked.

"Tonight. I'll probably spill stuff everywhere and make a fool of myself."

I tried to think of ways I could make this situation better but came up empty. The only thing I could offer was support.

"I don't have plans tonight if you want me to come hang out."

"So you can have a front-row seat to my demise?"

I laughed a bit at that. I'd never seen this pouty, whiny side of Vee. It was oddly endearing.

"I was thinking more so you'd have someone to talk to if you needed a break."

She perked up a bit at that, a small smile even making an appearance.

"Yeah? That'd be great."

"Great."

"I have to go in at four to help set up."

"I work until four thirty, so I'll go home, shower, and then meet you there."

She sighed heavily, but it sounded like one of relief. "Sounds good. I'll see you later, then."

"Later."

She gave me one more smile before turning and leaving the store.

I watched her go with a smile of my own.

VERONICA

"Wow, you're really bad at this."

I tried to muster a glare at Aamee and her blunt critique, but I couldn't fault her. I *did* suck at this. But I managed to find some sarcasm deep down inside.

"Why do you even still work here? Don't you have a big-girl job?"

She smiled, but it looked almost predatory.

"Following that logic, does that mean you're not a big girl? Since you're working here?"

"You know what I meant," I grumbled as I dumped the tray of overturned plastic cups I was holding onto a counter in the kitchen. "I can't believe all of these fell over as soon as I got to the table. At least nothing spilled on anyone."

"Yeah. This time," she said, unhelpfully reminding me

of the two times I *had* spilled things on customers. "And to answer your question, everyone hangs out here anyway, so I figured if I was going to be here, I may as well get paid."

"Makes sense," I grudgingly admitted as I threw the cups into the trash and wiped down the tray. "I don't know why I'm so bad at this. I'm not typically such a klutz. Or so scatterbrained. Hell, I did amazingly on my LSATs. It doesn't make sense."

Aamee shrugged. "We can't all be good at everything."

I rolled my eyes at her and made my way back to the floor.

Aamee had been tasked with babysitting me. My main responsibility for the night was hosting, but since it was an outdoor bar, that really meant bussing tables and running drinks when the servers were busy. I'd started off on my own, but it must have become clear fairly quickly that I needed a shadow to keep me from chasing away all the customers, so Drew had told Aamee to help me out.

I understood why he'd done it and couldn't blame him, but Aamee's watching my every move only made things worse. My errors had gone from cleaning up drinks that customers weren't finished with to directing people the wrong way when they asked where the bathrooms were to spilling pretty much everything I came into contact with. I'd even knocked over a fake candle that had somehow made a paper napkin smolder.

How do those even get hot enough for that to be possible?

That was me. A miracle worker who specialized in disasters.

As I fumbled with a retort, Aamee's gaze shifted over my shoulder.

"Your boyfriend's here."

I whirled around to see Owen reach the top of the stairs that led up from the parking lot. He looked good in black jeans and a plain, light-blue T-shirt that framed his lithe torso and hugged his defined biceps. Manual labor had definitely done that body good.

He gave me a stilted wave that would've looked awkward or childish from anyone else, but it was just so...Owen. He owned everything he did with a confidence that I could tell came from deep within himself. I'd never met someone more comfortable in his skin than Owen.

When his brow furrowed, I realized I'd been staring and gave myself a mental shake. Had I just been checking out Owen?

What the hell?

"He's not my boyfriend" was all I could think to reply to Aamee, and it may have been the lamest thing to ever come out of my mouth.

"Yeah, the way you were just drooling over him really hammered that point home."

Before I could give it any thought, I reached up and wiped at my mouth. Aamee's obnoxious laugh told me she hadn't meant her words literally. No wonder people were always talking about murdering her.

Owen made his way over to me, his hands pushed into his pockets, his posture relaxed.

"Hey. How's it going?"

I opened my mouth to reply, but Aamee took it upon herself to respond.

"Like she belongs on *America's Funniest Home Videos*. Is that show still on? Because you could definitely win."

I turned to glare at her. "Thanks for that."

"You're welcome," she replied in a chipper tone that made me fantasize about what it would be like to strangle her. "I'm going to go check in with my tables. Why don't you stay here? Like, right here. Please don't touch anything until I get back."

I wished evil intent on her retreating form before turning back to Owen.

"That bad, huh?" he asked with a wince.

"It's actually probably been even worse than you're imagining."

His eyes widened comically as he mouthed a *Wow*.

"Yeah."

"You know this isn't the only job in town, right? You can just find another one if this isn't for you."

I sighed. "I know. I'm just not used to being bad at stuff."

"I've been bad at pretty much everything I've ever tried for at least some amount of time. I'm a quick learner, but I'm not usually good at things right off the bat. I need practice."

"You're good at the hardware store," I argued.

"That's because I spent years being yelled at by my dad for handing him the wrong tools when he was working on cars and fixing things around the house." He smiled as if being yelled at was a good memory for him, which made me laugh.

"You're good at cheering me up," I said. I meant the words to come across as lighthearted, but they were breathier and more sincere than I intended.

A small smile spread across his lips, and he looked down at his toes, seeming almost bashful.

When he looked back up, he said, "I guess that's one thing I'm naturally gifted at."

We shared a long look that seemed to say a lot, but it was as if I didn't speak the language. My thoughts and feelings were muddled where Owen was concerned, and I wondered if that was because he was constantly surprising me. He wasn't at all who I'd thought he was when we baked pot brownies in his kitchen.

"What kinds of jobs have you had in the past?" he asked.

"Huh?" I replied, eloquent as ever.

"Maybe we can find you a job doing something similar to what you've done before. That way you'll know you'll be good at it."

"Oh, uh, well, actually . . . I've never had a job before."

"You've never had a job?" he asked, not in the mocking way people usually reply when they hear I've never worked, but rather one of genuine disbelief.

"Not like what you're talking about. I helped out with some of the office stuff at my dad's company in the summers, but I mostly worked on my own. I never dealt with customers or anything. And I didn't work many hours because my dad always wanted me to focus on school. And I guess I'm maybe a little bit spoiled," I added timidly, not wanting to come across as the princess my brothers always claimed I was.

I'd never seen myself that way, though. I was expected to work hard, earn good grades, participate in activities, and basically set myself up for success every way I could. And in exchange for those things, my dad met all of my basic needs and gave me spending money to boot. It also hadn't hurt that my uncle had thrown money at us kids whenever he saw us.

Owen's eyes narrowed. "I don't think you're spoiled. You had other things to focus on." He smiled. "Though I guess those other things aren't super helpful to you now."

I looked around the Yard. "No, definitely not."

Owen cleared his throat and looked like there was something he wanted to say but was too uncomfortable to say it.

"What?" I asked.

"I'm worried what I have to say will come out the wrong way."

"Say it anyway."

"It's just . . . I feel like you're missing out on some helpful character building."

"In what way?"

He sighed. "Having shitty jobs as a teenager isn't only a rite of passage. It's kinda necessary."

"How would having a shitty job be necessary?"

"Lots of ways. To learn how to deal with difficult people and how to work in a tough environment. It helped me learn how to persevere and be responsible and do stuff I didn't really want to do. I know that even a dream job can be a nightmare on certain days."

"And you think I don't know those things?" Honestly, I was a little hurt he thought I was so naïve. I didn't expect life to be sunshine and rainbows every day—especially in my future profession. There were future days and weeks that were going to be a grind from sunup to sundown.

"I think knowing them in theory is different from having experienced them in reality."

"But I have experienced them. My undergraduate program was incredibly competitive. And I've had internships in law offices. I know what I'm getting into." My irritation must've bled into my tone, because he thrust his hands out in front of him in a placating gesture.

"This is coming out wrong. I'm not implying you're unprepared to be successful in your chosen field or that you won't put in the effort necessary. I know you've worked hard. I'm sorry if it seemed like I was selling you short."

"So what are you trying to say?"

He looked around helplessly for a moment before his eyes seemed to light up.

"Take Aamee."

"Take her where? To a mental hospital?"

"Take her as an example. Granted, I don't know her well, but from the stories I've heard, she used to be quite, umm... How should I say this?"

"A bitch?" I supplied.

His face scrunched up. "I don't like calling women that word."

"You didn't. I did."

"Okay, well, I guess I'll accept the loophole in this case. So yes, she used to be fairly unpleasant."

"She still kinda is."

"Is she? Or is that just the role she plays within this quirky little friend group?"

I thought for a second before replying. "I'm pretty sure she is."

He shrugged. "It doesn't really matter in terms of my point. Pretty much everyone was surprised she came back to work at the Yard this summer. Except Sophia."

I raised my eyebrow in surprise. "Aamee's archnemesis wasn't shocked Aamee would work a job she didn't really need?" Honestly, I found it surprising as hell.

"No. Sophia said this job reminded Aamee what it's like to be human. And in a sense, that's what I was trying to say to you. I think it's easy to become absorbed with your job and think it's the most important thing in the world. But I think it's good to be reminded that there are other things and people that exist outside of that."

"So basically having a bunch of crappy jobs as a teenager would've allowed me to, what, relate to people better?"

"No. I think they would've allowed you to relate to *yourself* better."

"You've lost me, Obi Wan."

He huffed in what sounded like frustration. "How are you ever going to know what it's like to be asked to remake an Italian hoagie seven times because you're supposedly layering the meat incorrectly? Or be asked to refund a customer because they didn't like the movie they just spent two hours watching. Not losing your shit on those types of people isn't a skill we're born with. It needs to be honed over time. And while I know you've worked with difficult people, you probably haven't encountered a lot of stupid ones. And I mean deep down, *would you please fill this milk jug with gasoline* type of stupid. And it's jarring when you encounter it for the first time. Don't you want to be prepared?"

"But I've met stupid people, Owen. I don't live under a rock."

"It's not just stupid people. It's also arrogant people, judgmental people, prejudiced people, entitled people. Now picture all of them gathered in one place, such as this"—he gestured around the bar—"and all of them asking for things or blaming you for what doesn't even make any sense. How do you handle that?"

I opened my mouth to reply but shut it when I realized I wasn't sure. His point seemed preposterous and circuitous and quite frankly didn't even make a whole lot of sense in some parts, so I hated to even entertain the notion that he might be right. But . . . maybe he was?

Because, truth be told, a lot of what was messing me

up was that I was worried about how people would react when I made a mistake. And because of that, I was making nothing *but* mistakes. Maybe I would've cared less if I had a bigger frame of reference for dealing with people who were disappointed in me.

I'd always been a sort of golden child. Until I'd walked into the Yard. Here, I was a walking disaster. Maybe it was fear that was making that happen. Or anxiety. Or a lot of different things I needed to get over fast, because I could not spill water all over my first client or accidentally forget to print out the correct briefs for a case.

I looked at Owen, likely a little maniacally.

"What do I do?"

He looked unsure for a second before a smile overtook his face. "I'm not sure. But I'm confident we can figure it out."

Chapter Ten

OWEN

As the night wore on, Drew found less and less for Vee to do.

It was almost painful to witness her make mistake after mistake. If I hadn't known better, I'd have thought she was screwing up on purpose. I mean, seriously, who gave a woman seltzer instead of a Sprite? The woman had been so jarred when the reality hadn't coincided with her expectations that she'd sprayed liquid all over the man across from her.

At least it had been clear. Judging by the horrified expression on the woman's face, she hadn't known the man well—perhaps a first date, even. I sincerely hoped the guy stuck it out for a second date.

Jesus, what if Vee had cost this woman her soulmate by serving her the wrong carbonated beverage? Would Vee ever be able to balance out that kind of karma violation?

Thankfully, that had been the worst of it, at least cosmically speaking. Though I wouldn't have been surprised if Drew had comped more food and drinks than he'd sold.

Once Drew convinced Vee that she could take the rest

of the night off, she settled in beside me at the bar and had a drink, which she drained in one go. She waved her empty glass at Xander, who'd shown up to work the closing shift.

He made her another drink and brought it over, smirking as she grabbed it from him and took a large gulp.

"I was tempted to put seltzer in there, but I figured you'd suffered enough."

"Thanks," she said dryly.

"Anytime," he replied happily before moving away to help another customer.

Vee took another sip and then turned to me. "So what are we going to do about me and the great job conundrum?"

I sighed. I'd been thinking about it as she "worked" but hadn't come up with any clear plan to make what I was envisioning happen. "I was trying to think of a way to get you experience at a bunch of different types of jobs in as short of a time span as possible. But other than having you volunteer—"

"Which I can't do," she interrupted. "I need something that brings in a paycheck. And I don't think this"—she gestured around—"is it. I know Drew won't fire me, but he should. I'm a liability here."

I didn't want to hurt her feelings by agreeing, so I focused on the crisis at hand. "Do temp agencies hire people for just a day or two at a time for customer service jobs?"

"I don't think so."

"Well they should. Think of how convenient that would be."

"How convenient what would be?" Xander asked as he stopped in front of us.

"A temp agency that hired people to cover shifts at restaurants, stores, and stuff like that," I explained.

"You mean like Temp Me?" he asked.

I scrunched up my brow in confusion. "What's that?"

"Pretty much exactly what you just said. It's an app where businesses can post short-term job opportunities to find workers."

"How does that work?" Vee asked. "People have to fill out like eight thousand forms when they work somewhere. Seems time prohibitive to have different people working every other day."

Xander shook his head. "The app works as a legit temp agency. The workers are technically employed by Temp Me, so they only have to file paperwork with them."

"People think of everything," I muttered before turning to Vee. "We should download it."

She nodded as she pulled her phone out of the back pocket of her jeans and dropped it on the bar top. When she reached for it, I laid a hand over hers.

"Maybe we should do it tomorrow."

She laughed softly as she left her phone on the bar and reached for her drink instead. "Good plan."

We sat for a second and talked about things around the house she thought she could sell and what I was going to focus on fixing up next. We were interrupted by Drew sliding onto a chair on the other side of Vee.

"Hey, so, uh … I wanted to talk about your next shift. I think maybe—"

Vee held a hand toward him. "I get it. I'm a mess."

Drew, being the nice guy he was, immediately scowled. "No. You just need more training. I can come in tomorrow—"

Vee shook her head. "I really appreciate your willingness to help me, but my conscience won't allow me to keep working here."

"Your conscience?" he asked.

"I know I cost you a good bit of money tonight. I'd feel too guilty to keep taking advantage of your friendship when I'm clearly not a good fit for this kind of work."

"You just need more training," Drew insisted.

Vee smiled kindly at Drew. "You're so nice. Naïve, but nice."

Drew huffed a laugh of his own. "So what are you going to do?"

"We have a lead on that," I chipped in.

Vee turned to me. "I still want something more consistent, though. I don't want to wait around for jobs that may never appear."

Drew looked confused, so we told him about Temp Me.

"You know, I think Ransom said Safe Haven was looking for people to work their summer camp program. I think he and Taylor still fill in if the director's in a jam, but for the most part they've moved on, and I think a few other counselors have too. I could text him about it if you want."

While it was kind of Drew to offer, the idea made me a little wary. If her experience at the Yard was anything to judge by, foisting her on unsuspecting children was perhaps not our best move.

But before I could think of how to subtly steer her in a different direction, she was already answering Drew.

"That would be great. Thanks!" When she looked at me, her smile was radiating happiness. "Isn't that great? I love kids."

I hoped my face didn't give away my reticence.

"Yeah. Great."

May whoever the patron saint of children was forgive us.

VERONICA

The Safe Haven director had brought me in for an interview almost immediately after Ransom reached out to him about job openings at his program. Turned out they were a little desperate, which probably worked out in my favor because I had no experience working with kids.

The day camp didn't start for another two weeks, but Harry said I could start in the after-school program and then transition once summer break began—a prospect that made me happy because it would allow me to start off slow and adapt to the new experience.

When I'd told Owen I loved kids, that had maybe been a bit of a stretch. I liked them in theory—the way someone might say they liked koalas but had enough sense to know they didn't ever want to touch one.

I wasn't sure if it was the lack of exposure that ratcheted up my alarm or if it was foreshadowing for how this job was going to go, but when I walked into the Safe Haven office, I was terrified. It didn't help that I was immediately confronted by a stern-looking older woman who introduced herself as Edith and thrust paperwork at me to fill out. While I didn't know it for a fact, I suspected I'd have received a warmer welcome from a ravenous alligator.

"Harry will be with you when he's ready," she added in what I thought had to be the most unnecessary statement ever uttered. It's not like I expected him to see me when he *wasn't* ready.

I gave her a warm smile anyway in an attempt to show that I'd come here in peace, but she'd already turned her attention to something on her computer.

Thankfully, Harry didn't keep me waiting long, and after a cursory look at the paperwork I'd filled out, he leaned back and smiled—a gesture that seemed to come more naturally to him than it did his assistant.

Harry Gillette exuded warmth and compassion, and I felt immediately at ease with him. His desk was littered with photos of who I assumed was his family—his partner, three kids, and a couple dogs. He gave me a good feeling about Safe Haven.

"I spoke to Ransom," Harry said. "He gave you a glowing reference."

That wasn't surprising since I'd helped Ransom and Taylor resolve a stalker issue a few months prior. While I'd been happy to help get a scumbag like Brad off the streets, they'd been incredibly appreciative. And I was thankful Ransom had left out my mob ties when he'd told Harry about me.

Harry continued, "I also looked at all of the transcripts and other references you sent over, and everything looks great. How about I take you on a quick tour, and then we can come back here and chat for a few minutes and see how we both feel about things?"

"Sounds perfect."

He tapped his hands on his desk before standing and leading the way out of the office. "You've already met Edith," he said as we walked past the troll guarding the bridge to his office.

I nodded in answer, and Harry then led me through a door into a large, open area that had various activity centers spread around the room, leaving the center open for the kids to play. There were also some smaller rooms off the main one that had a variety of things in them, from a TV with gaming consoles to another room that looked like a mini library. I didn't study each room, figuring I'd have time to scope them all out if I was hired, but I got the impression that Safe Haven made every effort to keep the kids occupied in constructive ways.

Speaking of kids... "Where is everyone?"

"Outside. We try to spend as much time as possible out there when the weather cooperates. In the summers, we try to be outside most of the morning and then come in when it gets too hot."

"That makes sense."

"I was going to have you shadow one of our counselors for half an hour if you've got the time," Harry said. "Try to give you a realistic look at what we do here."

"That would be great."

As soon as Harry opened the door, I heard the cacophony of kids playing. My eyes took a second to adjust as I followed him out into the bright sunshine, but when they did... I was immediately overwhelmed.

Kids. Were. Everywhere.

There were kids on the basketball court, on the swings, chasing each other around the slide, playing dodgeball, and a few were sitting around with arts and crafts supplies. And while, at first glance, it appeared to be chaos, it quickly became apparent that it was, at the very least, organized chaos.

I counted six counselors who were either standing around the play area watching over the kids or actively playing with them. Harry made his way to a beautiful woman who I'd say was about my age. Her light-brown afro glinted in the sun as she stood by the basketball court wearing dark aviators and holding a clipboard. She looked like she should be walking a runway in Milan instead of watching a bunch of kids play something roughly resembling basketball.

"Veronica, I'd like you to meet one of our lead counselors, Inez. Inez, this is Veronica. We're seeing if she'd be a good fit for the team."

I didn't want to think of myself as a narcissist, but I'd always been fairly confident in my attractiveness. I'd always gotten attention—both wanted and not. But standing in front of Inez as she smiled a welcome made me feel a tad intimidated. She was almost . . . otherworldly.

"Nice to meet you, Veronica," she said as she extended a hand toward me.

"You can call me Vee," I replied as I shook her hand.

"I was going to leave Vee with you for a bit so she can get a sample of what we do here," Harry said to Inez.

"Works for me."

"Wonderful. Vee, head back in in about a half hour or so?"

"Sounds good," I replied. I watched Harry walk away before letting my eyes wander over the kids. "There're a lot of kids here."

"Yeah, almost everyone is here today. Our capacity is fifty." She was quiet for a moment before she asked, "So how did you hear about Safe Haven?"

"Oh, a couple of my friends worked here. Taylor and Ransom."

Inez looked genuinely excited when I mentioned their names. "I love them! Ransom is so fun, and Taylor was always super sweet. I was sad when they cut back to just volunteering a few hours here and there."

"Yeah, I know Ransom especially enjoys his time here."

"Has he had any luck finding a job in the area?" Inez asked.

"I think I heard he had an interview this week sometime."

"Well, I hope he gets it, but I also hope he has enough spare time to still hang out here with us a few hours a week."

I smiled. "I'm sure he appreciates knowing he's wanted."

After that, she reviewed their various practices and procedures with me in between interacting with kids as the need arose. At one point, I found myself judging a limbo contest followed by a few girls showing me a dance they'd been working on. Before I knew it, forty-five minutes had passed and I was hurrying back to Harry's office.

He waved off my apology for being late, saying he was glad I'd gotten wrapped up in playing with the kids. He answered a few questions for me, and I answered a few of his. When the discussion was done, he looked at me happily.

"So what do you think? Do you want to join us at Safe Haven this summer?"

Even though I was still more than a little terrified at the prospect of being responsible for a bunch of kids all day, every day, I wasn't exaggerating when I replied, "I'd love to."

Chapter Eleven

OWEN

I hadn't anticipated what I'd be walking into at home after my shift at the hardware store, but I should've known better.

When I'd mentioned to Vee that I should go through Minnie's things to either give to charity or sell, Vee had volunteered to take the lead on what turned out to be a project that had now somehow taken up several rooms of the house. And sprucing up some old furniture had quickly turned into an undertaking that became a slope so slippery, it may as well have been covered in banana peels and dish soap.

As I entered through the back door into the kitchen, I saw several industrial-size trash bags throughout the room, along with pots and pans piled high on the kitchen table. Vee must have heard me come in, because her voice carried from some other room.

"Oh, good. I'm glad you're home. I have a lot of the kitchen and dining room organized, but I need your input on a few things before I decide what to do with them."

I resisted telling her that she seemed to have the

organizational strategy of someone on *Hoarders* but without the crew that came in to clean the place up. Almost every inch of the floor was covered with something—from food storage containers to baskets filled with silverware to artificial plants. And they weren't sorted into piles either. Plates were in laundry baskets with light bulbs, and I swore there were about six pairs of reading glasses on a bench that held *drinking* glasses, a few pairs of scissors, books, and some cloth napkins.

I was sure Vee must have some method to her madness, but as far as I could tell, it was more madness than method at the moment. Carefully, I stepped over some of the china I recognized from the cabinet in the dining room. It reminded me of when I'd searched for the marijuana.

"Where are you?" I called back.

"In here."

"Thanks. That narrows it down," I said as I walked down the hall that led to the front door, listening for Vee's voice like I was playing a game of Marco Polo. When I heard the sound of papers rustling, I thought she may be in Minnie's study. Why someone who never studied anything—at least as far as I knew—needed a room with that name always seemed odd to me. But I guess with a house this big, Minnie had more than enough space to accommodate rooms that were hardly ever used.

As I rounded the corner toward the stairs, I saw Vee sitting cross-legged beside the built-in cabinets that wrapped almost the entire perimeter of the room. In an oversized Mets T-shirt, black bike shorts that stopped midthigh, and her hair pulled up into a messy ponytail, she couldn't have looked cuter. Surrounding her were piles of books I assumed she planned to get rid of.

"Looks like you've been busy," I said.

"So busy. I meant to start in one room and finish it, but then something would make me want to go somewhere else, and it got a little out of control." She spoke quickly, all of the words coming out in one breath. Once she inhaled enough oxygen to speak again, she gave me a small smile and closed whatever book she'd been looking at. "Sorry."

"No, don't be. Now I know what to expect when we get married, that's all."

Vee looked at me curiously, her eyebrows saying everything she didn't vocalize—my joke had missed its mark, and it wasn't funny.

"I mean, you know…" *Stop talking.* "Not that I want to marry you. Or that you would want to marry me. Or that I've thought about such things. We barely know each other, and I'm only twenty-three and you're about to start law school—" Goddamn Carter and his *Romeo and Juliet* reference. Apparently it'd resulted in a slip that would've amused Freud himself.

I thought Vee looked more and more amused with every new comment I made, but I couldn't seem to stop. I was like a leaky pipe that would keep spewing water until someone came and plugged the hole.

"It actually sounds like you've thought about us getting married a lot."

Well, that was one way to plug it.

"No. No, definitely not. It was a dumb joke that I blame Carter for, and then I felt bad so I was trying to talk my way out of it, but I've had a long day, so I was rambling—"

"Kind of like you're doing now?"

She gave me a smile that looked like she could empathize

with my embarrassment, and I wasn't sure whether that made me feel better or worse.

"Yes, exactly like that, so I'll stop now. What else have you been up to?" I asked, desperately wanting to change the subject.

She stood up and immediately began walking out of the room. "Well, I went over to Safe Haven, which went well. The director, Harry, was really nice, and I met another girl, Inez, who was sweet and, oh my God, soooo gorgeous. There were a lot of kids, which was terrifying but expected, I guess, but I think things there will go okay." She laughed awkwardly. "I mean, at least the kids are too old to pick up, so I don't have to worry about dropping any of them."

"Well, that's a plus, because if you break a kid, I'm sure you'll have to answer to someone more official than Drew."

"Shit," she said, staring off into the distance. "Oh well. We'll see how I do. I mean, I already filled out the paperwork, so I'll do my best to keep everyone alive."

"That sounds like a good place to start. I'm sure it'll be fine. And you signed up for the Temp Me app too, so if you don't love Safe Haven, maybe you'll find something else you like."

"I'll definitely try some of the temp jobs for some extra cash since I won't get that many hours at Safe Haven right away, but I plan to stick it out there even if it's not exactly what I feel like doing. Ransom and Taylor went out of their way to help me get the job, and everyone there seems really nice. And like you said, the challenge will probably be good for me."

"That's great," I agreed, happy she'd realized what I'd been trying to say even though I'd been shit at saying it. "You look like you got a pretty good start on going through some of the stuff in the house too." I looked at the piles that surrounded us.

"Yeah," she said excitedly. "Since the first few things I posted sold so fast, I figured I'd try to get a lot of the other little things out of the house first, and then we could then move on to the furniture, which is currently holding a lot of the small stuff. A lot of these are probably antiques, and they're in such good condition. I'm sure you can get a decent amount of money for them, and you can use it to fix up the house."

"You think?"

At first I hadn't been interested in getting any money. I felt bad enough giving Minnie's things away, let alone profiting from them, but Vee had a point when she'd suggested trying to sell them on Facebook Marketplace. Not only had it already brought in some cash to keep the house running, but if people paid for the items, it meant they really wanted them and would most likely take care of them.

"I don't know much about the price of furniture," I said.

"Me neither." She headed back to the kitchen. "But… Google. And I also searched for similar items on Marketplace to see what they were going for."

"So is all of this getting sold?" I motioned with my hands to the piles of items around us.

"Oh, no way. I have a system going. The ones in the garbage bags will be thrown away or recycled. It's just old paperwork or personal items like brushes, used makeup, stuff like that that no one would want. But there's a lot of stuff that people could use that won't make money or it's just easier to give away, so I found a Buy Nothing group in the area and posted some things there. Some of them have already been picked up."

"That's great," I said, but Vee continued like she hadn't heard me.

I could tell by the speed she was speaking that she was happy to help. With every sentence, her excitement seemed to grow. She told me about one woman she spoke to at a local antique shop who was interested in some of Minnie's jewelry, but Vee was reluctant to sell it.

"You sure there isn't anyone in her family who would want it?" she asked. "Some of the pieces are beautiful."

"I'm sure they are."

I knew Minnie had inherited a lot of it herself, and others had been purchased while traveling or given to her as gifts. I felt guilty getting rid of it, but if Minnie left an entire house to *me*, I doubted she had anyone in mind she wanted to leave any of its contents to. If she had, she never named anyone in her will or verbally to me at any point.

"And to answer your question, no, I don't think there's anyone Minnie would want to have it. The more I think about it, the more I think she would've liked the idea of using the money from some of her things to make her house the best it can be."

"Okay, as long as you're sure. I can call back tomorrow and bring it over. The rest of it I plan to post on Marketplace for sale or maybe eBay so we can auction it. There's also a great little consignment shop nearby where we can take some of her clothing. But then there's stuff I'm not sure about. Like her cookware, for example."

"Um, I figured we'd keep it so we had something to cook with?" I let my statement sound like a question, because really, it was. There were some things that would have to stay.

"It's nonstick," Vee said.

"I'm confused."

"Teflon, especially the kind on cookware made earlier

than the past five years or so, is a known carcinogen and hormone disruptor. When heated at high temperatures, the chemical compound is extremely toxic."

"Uh, Minnie was almost ninety when she died. It can't be that bad for you. And also, how do you know all that?"

Vee stared at me for a moment before saying, "My brain is filled with random facts that I barely ever get to use, so I'm actually pretty excited right now."

I tried not to laugh, but Vee was adorable. Her voice, her movements, her enthusiasm for something that anyone else would see as a massive burden that wasn't her responsibility. It made her even more attractive to me, and I almost hated her for it because chances were I'd never get to act on any of those feelings.

"And ninety is impressive. I'll give you that. But who knows? Maybe if she'd gone with ceramic or stainless steel, she'd still be here."

My eyes rolled at that. "Okay, so I guess give that away, then. I'm sure someone can use it." I didn't bring up the fact that we'd have to replace it all, because I was sure Vee knew that. I also knew this was a battle I'd lost before it began.

"So someone *else* can have reproductive problems?" She practically scoffed at my suggestion.

"So recycle it?"

"Can't recycle Teflon," she said. "It has to go in the trash."

"Okay, so it sounds like we're throwing it out, then?"

"Good," she said, sounding almost relieved. "I'm glad we agree."

Railroaded was maybe a better term than agreed, but whatever.

"Yeah, sure. Glad I could be of service. And speaking of,

why don't we order some dinner, and I'll help you go through some of this other stuff."

She smiled in a way that made me think she was a little embarrassed. "Is that your way of saying I got a little carried away?"

"Nah," I said, turning to the drawer that held the menus. "I mean, our house does resemble HomeGoods after a tornado, but I wouldn't say you got carried away."

Thankfully, Vee laughed at that and seemed to relax a bit.

Then I fanned out the menus like a magician doing a card trick. "What are you in the mood for?"

VERONICA

Somehow time had gotten away from us. We'd sat down to eat the wraps we'd ordered from the sandwich shop nearby and then gotten lost in all of Minnie's things. Like literally lost. At one point, I didn't even know where Owen was until he emerged from a pile of sheets with one draped over his body like a blue-and-white-striped ghost.

He made some sort of a noise that sounded like a cross between a boo and a roar and raised both his arms inside the fabric.

"Did I scare you?" he asked, pulling the sheet down and running his fingers through his sandy hair as he tried to get it back in place.

"The only thing that scares me is that you thought that was a good costume."

"It wasn't?" he asked, looking offended. "I was thinking of wearing it to our Halloween party this year."

"What Halloween party?"

"The one we're hosting. It'll be fun. We can do a theme like . . . reality TV stars."

"Those definitely sound scarier than your striped ghost." I did my best to look at Owen like he'd lost his mind, but I was already excited for the party, and Halloween wasn't for almost five months. Owen seemed like he was going to be a blast to live with.

"I'll take that as a yes to the party," he said with one of his signature smiles before walking over to a bunch of throw pillows we'd collected from the various bedrooms and collapsing into them like a kid would with a pile of leaves.

Gimli, who'd been following us from room to room as I attempted to reorganize what I'd managed to *dis*organize over the course of the day, jumped onto Owen's stomach and began licking his face with a vigor I thought he reserved only for table scraps.

"What do you think we should do with all this stuff, Gim? Huh?" He rubbed the dog's head for a minute before grabbing a pair of Minnie's sunglasses and sliding them onto the dog's brown snout.

"Stop it. That's terrible," I said, though I was trying to stop myself from laughing.

"He likes it."

I couldn't disagree exactly. The shades seemed to have had some sort of calming effect on the little guy. Instead of bouncing around like a kid who'd chased an entire pillowcase full of Halloween candy with a Red Bull, Gimli looked at ease.

"Hey, maybe we can get him to model some of the accessories."

"Right," I said with a laugh.

"No, I'm serious. I bet it'll get a lot of views. Maybe even some tags or shares."

"You're probably right about *that*, but I don't know if that'll help sell them. Would you buy a scarf that had been draped around a dog's neck for a photo shoot?" I shot Owen a look I hoped would help drive home my point, but I should've known better. "Don't answer that."

I got up to get the bin I'd stored a bunch of Minnie's photo albums in and brought it over to the pile of picture frames I'd taken down. Owen had said she didn't have any family who would want them, but I figured I'd store all of them in a big Rubbermaid bin and leave it in one of the spare bedrooms just in case.

"Some of these frames are probably worth a good bit of money." I wondered if the one I was holding was real silver. It was too heavy to be made from something cheap and synthetic.

"Yeah, maybe. We can go to that antique shop and see what they'd give us for them once we remove all the pictures." He was already taking off the back of one that held a black-and-white picture of who must've been a younger Minnie standing on a mountain. "She was beautiful," he said, sounding almost surprised. "I mean, I know looks aren't the only thing that matters, but when you only know someone when they're in their eighties, a picture like this stands out. Where'd you find this one?"

"I think that one came from her bedroom."

"That explains why I've never noticed it." When he saw me trying to look closer, he handed it to me.

Minnie had long hair and smooth skin with a smattering of freckles that covered her nose and her cheekbones. I wondered who'd taken the photo and where it had been taken.

When I flipped it over, written in neat black, cursive writing was the date *June 1962.*

I thought for a moment, trying to do the math in my head. "Minnie probably wasn't much older than us in this picture." The realization somehow made me feel closer to this woman I'd never met but suddenly wanted to know more about.

"Yeah, I guess not. I never noticed how many places she'd been. She has so many different photos of different locations. I wonder if she took them herself or . . ."

His sentence drifted off as he seemed to ponder his own question. Minnie didn't have many pictures of herself, and she had even fewer of other people. Even her photo albums were filled mostly with pictures of places she'd visited. She'd obviously traveled extensively, but I wondered if she traveled alone. And if she had, was it by choice or necessity?

"I don't know if we'll ever know for sure, but I can't help but feel sorry for her either way."

Owen looked at me curiously. "What do you mean?"

"I guess I'm thinking if she traveled with someone—a friend or lover, even—"

"Please don't use that word again in reference to a deceased elderly woman who was like a grandmother to me." He shivered as he said it, like someone had suddenly opened a window behind him on a cold night.

"I'm so sorry," I said quickly before continuing to theorize.

Owen had said that she didn't really have much family, but it still struck me as odd. Most of the photos were portraits of landscapes—beaches, meadows, mountaintops, nighttime cityscapes, even some close-ups of flowers.

"It just makes me wonder," I said. "Like, if she had a companion on these trips, that person isn't anywhere in the photos. And then I can't help but imagine the possible reasons for that. Why travel to all these places alone? Even if she chose to, that's so sad to me. Because why would someone rather experience all of this alone?"

Owen shrugged. "Maybe she just liked to travel by herself," he said simply. "Plenty of people do that. Then they don't have to worry about someone else's schedule or plans."

"It's possible, I guess."

I picked up another frame that held a small photograph of a river flanked on either side by tall trees. I couldn't tell if the picture had been taken from a boat traveling down the river or if the angle made it appear that way. Though the photograph was in color, as were most of the landscapes she'd displayed around her home, the quality indicated that they hadn't been taken in this century. Maybe the seventies or eighties, if I were to guess.

"Can you see if you can get the back off this one?" I handed the frame to Owen, who was trying to position a hat on Gimli in a way that would stay in place. "The metal tabs seem like they're stuck."

"Sure thing." Owen reached his hand out, his wide smile showing just how happy he was that I needed his help. "Need some help from someone strong, huh?"

"Yeah, but I had to ask you."

"Ouch. That's not very nice," he said, still smiling.

It wasn't nice, but I'd seen enough of Owen lately to know that it also wasn't true. I'd watched him carry twelve boxes of flooring through the house the other day without breaking a sweat, and when I'd offered to help, I found out quickly that my assistance only made the process longer, so I'd made him a sandwich instead.

Owen pushed on the small metal tabs just as I had, but they didn't budge. Finally, he found a nearby screwdriver and managed to force each one enough so he could slide out the backing and then the photo.

Or photos. There was another behind the one that had been displayed.

"What's the other one?" I asked as Owen stared longer than expected.

When he flipped it over to look at the back, I could tell that picture was pretty weathered. I thought I'd seen Minnie, but he'd turned it over too quickly to be sure.

"The Brandywine River. June 1964." His voice sounded almost empty, like he was repeating words that were devoid of any actual meaning. He handed me both pictures.

The older photo was a picture of Minnie, her hair shoulder length and curly, smiling at the front of a kayak. I held the two photographs side by side, and they looked to be in a similar location along the Brandywine, though it was tough to know for sure. Years between the two photos would've changed the surroundings, and comparing a grainy old picture to a newer color one was difficult.

"Minnie looked so happy here," I said.

When Owen spoke again, he was quieter than before, and the words held a meaning only he could fully understand. "That's not Minnie."

"Yes, it is." I grabbed the other photo out of the bin I'd put it in and held the two next to each other. "That's definitely the same person."

"You're right, it is. That person just isn't Minnie."

After a moment of studying the pictures again, I let my gaze drift up to Owen, who was facing me on the floor, now only a few inches from me.

"Look." He pointed to the woman in the picture and then to the surrounding trees. "She's in a thick coat, and there are leaves on the ground."

"I don't follow."

"So it's cold in this picture."

"Okay?" I said, still confused about what this had to do with anything. "So what?"

"So this picture was taken on a river that's like a half hour from here. Leaves don't fall in the summer. It doesn't get cold enough to wear a coat this thick in June."

As soon as he said the final word, all of it became clear to me.

"June's not the month these pictures were taken," he said.

"June's the woman *in* them," I said back.

Chapter Twelve

VERONICA

By the end of the weekend, we'd sold enough of Minnie's furniture, trinkets, eclectic holiday decorations, barely used porcelain dishes, and so many shoes that we could've competed with Amazon. Except instead of shipping, most of the stuff was picked up by random stay-at-home moms or the occasional person who'd finally found the right chair to complement their mid-century decor.

All in all, we'd gotten off to a good enough start to allow Owen to get a jump on some of the larger projects around the house. In addition to putting new flooring in the bedrooms so we could walk barefoot at night without fear of splinters, he wanted to tackle giving the entire upstairs—except my room, which he'd already done before my arrival—a fresh coat of paint after patching up the spots where the plaster had come loose over time.

"Eight hundred and forty bucks," I said proudly as Owen walked in the door from work. "I'm Venmo-ing you two hundred and five, and then I have the rest in cash." I handed over the wad I'd tied together with a rubber band because most of it consisted of ones and fives.

"No shit!" The excitement on his face made me almost as giddy. "This is incredible. Thank you! Who knew so many people wanted old end tables and plates?"

He took the rubber band off and began flipping through the stack of cash.

"It's all there," I told him.

"No, I know. I'm not counting it because I think you stole some. I want to give you your share. Twenty percent okay? I'll just make it an even one seventy." He must've counted out the remainder, because he handed me what was left.

I took it from him but held my hand in place. "Um, yeah. Thank you so much. You didn't have to do that."

"Uh, yeah I did," he replied, sounding like *my* comment had been the ridiculous one. "I never could've gotten all this stuff organized and up on Marketplace or whatever."

"I find it hard to believe you couldn't figure out how to post a few items on social media." I had a feeling Owen was stroking my ego at the expense of his own, but I'd be lying if I said I didn't like the gesture a little bit. So I figured I'd return the compliment. "You're one of the smartest people I know, and I'm not just saying that because I've been around Brody and Carter a lot."

Owen laughed at that and then walked over to the fridge and grabbed two beers. He twisted off the tops of both.

"Thanks," I said before he'd even handed me one. Opening a beer was Owen speak for *work is officially finished for the day.*

"Oh, um, did you want one?" he asked slowly, his lip twisting up a bit as I reached for one of the beers. "Because these were both for me. I'm so sorry." He held them slightly above his head, but they were high enough that I couldn't reach easily.

I watched as Owen's lips pressed together as he no doubt tried to suppress a smile as he taunted me.

"You better give me one before I have to take it from you," I threatened.

As Owen leaned against the counter holding my beer above his head, I tried to jump. But I could only make it as high as his wrist. After a few failed attempts, I gave up. I wasn't sure if I'd lost my breath from the exertion or because I'd been so close to Owen that I could smell him—a combination of soap and the hardware store.

When I caught my breath, I swallowed so hard, I wondered if he could hear the sound of my throat. But neither one of us moved. Inches from his chest, I had to force myself not to reach out and touch it. Fuck the beer. Suddenly I wanted whatever was underneath Owen's navy-blue T-shirt.

Don't even think about what's under his pants. You just thought about what was under his pants by telling yourself not to think about it. Damn it, say something.

"Can I have the beer?" I asked quietly, my lips barely moving. It was like I was worried about what my mouth might do if I opened it too wide.

A moment later, Owen lowered the beer, slowly and carefully, until it was between us. I was acutely aware of how close his hand was to my breast and how badly I wanted him to touch me.

So I did the only thing any normal, twenty-something woman who finds herself surprisingly attracted to the man she's living with would do—I grabbed my beer and the hundred and seventy bucks Owen gave me and practically ran up to my room.

In an attempt to try to forget what had just happened, I swiped my headphones from the top of my dresser, shoved them into my ears, and opened my favorite playlist on my phone. *Get out of your own head.* I squeezed my eyes shut and cranked up the volume before collapsing onto the bed like I'd just run a marathon.

Somehow my body felt weak, but my mind felt so full of energy—albeit nervous energy. I couldn't make sense of any of it. And I desperately wanted to. Did I like Owen? Of course I liked him. Did I *like* like him? Was I in sixth fucking grade? This was ridiculous.

He was a good-looking guy who I'd been living with and was therefore around frequently. It made sense that I'd feel something for him physically. It would be weird if I didn't, especially considering it'd been a while since I'd had an orgasm. I'd been so busy getting ready for the move and then getting settled in, I hadn't taken any time for . . . *myself* in a while. And right now, I knew the fire that'd been lit inside me needed to be extinguished before it raged out of control.

So after sliding over the lock that Owen had put on my door before I'd moved in, I slipped under the covers of my bed, grabbed my western romance novel, and tried like hell not to picture what Owen would look like in a cowboy hat.

OWEN

I wasn't sure if Vee had been actively avoiding me or if it had been completely accidental, but by the time late morning rolled around, I was certain her absence wasn't just a manifestation of my mind.

Like that time in high school when I'd smoked a dried banana peel and then inhaled all the nitrous out of a Reddi-wip can. My buddy Izzy had told me I'd thought one of the stones from my backyard was my pet rabbit, Snowflake. Izzy had been happy to point out that the rock was not, in fact, Snowflake, and even happier to point out that I didn't even have a pet rabbit.

No, this Vee avoiding me shit was real, and I'd had plenty of time to think about it for the hour I'd spent trying to fix whatever was wrong with the AC unit. Minnie had said she'd gotten central air installed about twenty years ago after she grew tired of "spending summers hotter than a pig on a spit in hell." She'd said it a few times, and it always conjured up an image of her skewered over a fire with Satan waiting impatiently for his meal.

Turned out I could be really fucked up sometimes.

"Damn it," I said aloud as a branch from a bush scratched my back when I stood from where I'd been crouched between the air conditioning unit and the house. Add trimming those back to the list of chores I had to take care of.

I wiped the sweat from my head with the shirt I'd tossed to the side a while ago and squinted to see the YouTube video I'd found that would hopefully help me figure out how to fix frosted coils. I definitely didn't want to have to call someone over to fix it, but we sure as hell couldn't live in ninety-plus-degree heat for the foreseeable future. Well, we *could*, but I had no intention of doing so, and I ventured a guess that Vee didn't want to either.

Vee?

I thought I heard her voice coming from somewhere but looked around to see no one.

Great, the heat already has me hallucinating.

"Owen? You out here?"

Or not. That voice was definitely real, and it was definitely Vee, which meant she couldn't be *too* mad at me for whatever I'd done last night.

"Owen?" She sounded a little closer now.

"Oh, yeah. Sorry. I'm around the side of the house." I moved toward her voice so she could see me and gave her a small wave.

She walked a bit closer but stopped when she was just close enough that we could probably talk without yelling.

"What's up?" I asked.

"Sorry to bother you. You look . . . busy," she said, her gaze moving down my body and then back up again.

It suddenly made me aware that I was wearing nothing but a pair of old camo shorts. I felt more than a little self-conscious with Vee's eyes on me. This was new. I'd never given a damn about what anyone thought of my looks. Until now.

"No, it's fine," I said. "Is everything okay?"

She looked a bit flustered. "I didn't know if you knew, but the air doesn't seem to be working." She pointed over her shoulder toward the house with her thumb.

"Yeah, I uh . . . I realized that a little while ago, which is why I'm looking at the AC unit." I tried not to sound condescending when I said it, but I was worried it came off that way anyway.

"Duh. I feel like an idiot now." She walked toward me until she was close enough to examine it with me. "Any luck figuring out what might be wrong?"

"Coils look frosted, which can't be good. I was looking up some videos to see if I can fix it myself without having to call someone, but I think the best I can do is let them defrost for a while and then turn it back on."

"That doesn't seem too hard."

"It's not, but it won't be a solution long-term. It'll only buy us a little time. It probably needs refrigerant, and a normal person wouldn't be able to replace that."

"Are you calling yourself normal?" she deadpanned.

"In this particular situation, yes." I grabbed my shirt from where I'd tossed it on the ground and brought it up to wipe my head and the back of my neck.

"I guess we can go back in while this sits since there's nothing we can do for now. It's supposed to rain later, so hopefully it'll cool off a little. I'll call my boss and ask if he knows anyone who can come take a look at it, because if I just start Googling places, it'll probably be a fortune."

Vee raised her eyebrows at me and shot me an apologetic smile that only reached one of her cheeks. "Guess it's a good thing there's a ton of stuff in the attic we can sell, then."

"The attic?"

Chapter Thirteen

VERONICA

The way to Minnie's attic was through a small walk-in closet in her bedroom. I hadn't realized it at first because the entrance had been more of a tiny opening closed up by a piece of thin wood on hinges than an actual door. I'd gone into the closet to pull out some more of her clothing I'd been planning to take over to a women's shelter this week, and when I'd taken some shirts off the bar, I'd noticed what I thought would lead to a crawl space.

So crawl I did. I'd pushed over the rest of the clothing, ducked under the bar, and crawled up onto the small platform that led to the tiny doorway. It had taken a few hard pulls to unstick the door, which I guessed hadn't been opened in a long time.

There was no way an elderly woman could've climbed through there, let alone scaled the little ramp that's only source of footing were narrow boards nailed to it. I'd had to put my feet sideways to even use them, and when I'd gotten to the top and realized that I was in the attic and not another random storage closet, I'd figured I'd put in too much effort to turn back without at least checking it out.

Even if the air conditioning were working, it would've been hot as hell up there. I had felt more than a little guilty going up there since Minnie had told Owen not to. But I also knew the house and whatever was inside it was now Owen's, and who knew if the attic was filled with gold coins or diamonds or something like that.

I didn't, however, open anything that was not already in plain view. That, I'd leave for Owen. I'd only snapped some pictures and taken some measurements of various pieces of furniture to post on Marketplace. I had no idea how some of it even got up there or, more importantly, how we'd get it down. But if someone bought it, we'd have no choice but to figure it out.

I watched Owen walk the attic floor carefully, like he was scared his footsteps might disrupt the space's perfect equilibrium.

"How long were you up here?" He passed by the large wooden chest with brass hinges and barely gave it a glance. I'd wanted to open it since I'd first set eyes on it, but I'd left it undisturbed.

"I'm not sure." *At least an hour and a half.* "Maybe like forty-five minutes or something."

He nodded thoughtfully as he moved toward a large box filled with racquetball equipment and a jumble of large-bulbed colored Christmas tree lights. He hadn't given his attention to any one thing for more than a few seconds, let alone touched any of it.

"What are you looking for?" I asked. I'd kind of hoped maybe a shirt, since seeing him without one for all this time had been more than a small distraction. How did he expect me to focus on anything except his tan, sweat-glistened skin?

"Nothing, really. Or anything," he said, reaching out to run his fingers across an old bookcase that held nothing but dust and a few stray screws. "Why do you think Minnie didn't want me to come up here?"

I wondered if his question was one that he'd directed more at the universe than at me. Like he was asking for some sort of sign or even searching deep within himself for the answer.

"It doesn't seem like there's anything strange here," he continued. "And if there is, it's pretty well hidden. It's not like I'd just stumble upon it accidentally. At least it doesn't seem that way."

I had to agree. Nothing stood out as something someone would want to hide. "Maybe she just didn't want you climbing through her closet to get up here."

"It's possible, I guess." Though he didn't sound too convinced. "Or maybe it's the ghost she's hiding up here." He turned toward me, his eyes wide at the suggestion. For emphasis, he brought up his hands and wiggled his fingers at me.

"I do believe in ghosts, but I do not believe in most of what Aamee says."

"You're not in the minority on that one." He laughed as he crouched down so he could look behind some boxes to where the ceiling sloped. "This place is kinda creepy, though, I'll give her that."

Owen didn't elaborate, but he didn't need to. The floorboards weren't all nailed down, and they squeaked as we walked. There were nails poking out of the ceiling beams that threatened to stab us if we weren't on the lookout for them, and the way the sunlight seemed to shine only through one pane of the small window at the end of the attic cast odd shadows around the room. Not to mention the only thing that it lit up was the dust floating around the air. If the space had easier access, we could have a haunted house up here for the Halloween party Owen planned to throw.

"Anything good back there?" I asked.

"Eh, not really. Some paintings, but they aren't framed, and I don't recognize the name. It's hard to even make out what it says exactly."

"What are the paintings of?" I'd learned pretty quickly there was a market for anything, so it was possible we could sell those too.

"Portraits mostly. They look like they're of Minnie, actually, the more I look at them." He pushed some boxes to the side before I saw him or the paintings he'd been looking at.

I still couldn't see them fully because the lighting was so poor and Owen's body was partly blocking them. But I could see them well enough to tell they were done by someone with some talent.

"Those are good," I said. "Really good."

"Yeah, they are," he said quietly. "I was into art in high school and was decent with charcoal sketches, but painting like this . . . oils on canvas . . . to make the human form look this realistic isn't easy by any standard."

I didn't know much about art because I'd never been good at it. "You think maybe Minnie did them? She was into photography. Maybe she painted herself from photographs."

"Nah, the signature definitely starts with a D. Oh, shit."

"Please tell me you found an original Picasso or something."

"No," he said slowly, and I could hear the weight in his voice. "I found a painting of Minnie." He hesitated before saying the last words, and when he did, I understood why he sounded so affected by the discovery. "She's pregnant."

OWEN

And there it was—the reason, or at least *one* of the reasons, Minnie had wanted me to stay away from the attic. Minnie had told me she'd never had a family, never gotten married—though maybe she *hadn't* gotten married—and I'd believed every word of it. But this painting told a different story. At some point in her life, she was pregnant, and she had a baby. What happened to that baby would probably always remain a mystery, but my curiosity about *what* she chose to keep hidden mattered so much less to me than *why* she'd chosen to keep it hidden.

There was no shame in having a baby out of wedlock or placing it for adoption. At least not in today's society. And I would've liked to believe that Minnie would've known I would never have judged her for any decision she made when she was young. I would've never judged her, period.

"Maybe she wasn't actually pregnant," Vee offered. "It's a painting, not a photograph. It could've just been artistic freedom or whatever."

"I guess."

I had a hard time latching on to that theory, though I couldn't exactly place why. Looking at the painting made me feel like some kind of voyeur peeping into a life that Minnie obviously wanted me to have no knowledge of, but I couldn't look away either.

The painting was a profile of her—her long, delicate arms covering her breasts as she gazed back over her shoulder to someone other than the artist. The painting stopped at her hips, just low enough to see her belly without revealing anything below. The artist had clearly made every effort to be sure this was tastefully done.

"What should we do with them?" Vee asked, sitting down beside me and crossing her legs like she planned to be in that position for a while.

"I feel like we should return them to the original artist. If he's even still living."

"Yeah, I guess that's probably best."

As soon as Vee finished her sentence, a rustling from the other side of the attic made both of us jump. Vee was smart enough to stay seated, but since I'd been crouching, I sprang up like a jack-in-the-box and hit my head on a ceiling beam.

"Aww, fuck!" I said, rubbing the top of my head.

"Are you okay?" Vee rose to her feet, grabbing ahold of my hand and telling me to come into the middle of the room so I could stand fully.

"Yeah, I'll be fine," I told her. I bent down so she could see the spot on my head where I'd smacked it. "I'll go put some ice on it soon."

I winced when she touched near the tender spot.

"You should wash it too. You have a cut, and there's already an egg starting. I hope you don't have a concussion."

"I doubt it. I hit my head so many times as a kid, it's a wonder I don't have permanent dents in it."

She stared at me for a moment, and I thought it looked like she was trying to suppress a smile.

"Well, that explains a lot."

"Shut up," I teased. "What even was that? Do we have a squirrel or something up here?"

"Squirrel, mouse, bird...ghost?" she offered. "What if Minnie was trying to tell us something? Like she doesn't want us giving back her paintings."

"I thought I was the one who hit my head."

"Really. Maybe she was giving us a sign. I know you don't believe in ghosts, but do you really believe that our bodies are all that makes us *us*? That we don't have a soul?"

"I definitely know some people who lack souls," I joked.

"Owen, be serious for a second. Minnie had those pictures of her and that woman June hidden behind other photos. And now we find a painting that shows her pregnant when you thought she never had any family. It's gotta mean something."

"Yeah," I agreed, already heading to the opening in the floor that led to the master bedroom closet. "It means whatever secrets Minnie had..." I tried to convey with my eyes the importance of what I was about to say. "She wanted them kept that way."

Then I headed back downstairs to get a bag of frozen peas to put on my head, hoping Vee would follow me.

Chapter Fourteen

VERONICA

It was only Wednesday, and I'd already had as many jobs as there had been days this week. Xander's friend's app turned out to be helpful in terms of finding me some work, but that work had been as random as it had been short-lived.

Monday, I was given the role of People Solution Specialist. I had to admit the title sounded important, but it was just a fancy way of saying I answered phones and listened to people complain about clothing they'd bought.

I could only pretend to give a shit about the neckline of a blouse or a stray string on the stitching of a pair of shoes for so long before I started faking a thick Irish accent just to make the time pass more quickly. It had the added bonus of most people not being able to understand me and therefore hanging up on me, which I appreciated. Turned out I did not specialize in solving people's problems.

I was thankful when Tuesday came and I had something new. Either the clothing company realized they didn't need another customer service person or I'd done such a shitty job that they'd already hired someone to replace me. I was fine with either as long as it meant I didn't need to spend another day pretending to empathize with someone who'd spent seventy dollars on a pair of socks that hurt their toes.

I was then told to help a mom named Gwen who was working from home and trying to find the right fit for her family. I could do that. I liked kids. Or at least the ones I'd met at Safe Haven. But things felt different when I was the sole person in charge of four of them under five.

About two hours into the nanny gig, I'd already second-guessed all of my life's choices that had led me to that very moment—the one where I had regurgitated formula stuck in my bra, two kids on my lap crying, another covered in paint, and one who screamed that she wanted to watch some fucking show about a whiny bald kid all day long.

I did the best I could to keep the four of them *actively engaged and intellectually stimulated*, as their parents had requested, but you can only have a fourteen-month-old finger paint her feelings for so long before one of you ends up with paint in her hair and a strong desire to sue Pinterest.

As the day went on, we transitioned from *actively engaging and intellectually stimulating* to *somewhat occupied* to *we're all really fucking tired*. By the time Gwen emerged from her office around five in the afternoon, we were all on the *barely surviving* end of the daily activity spectrum.

She looked around the family room, which was covered in pillows from the fort her son Henry had begged me to make with him and then immediately destroyed. There were no fewer than six sippy cups lying on their sides and two dirty diapers beside me.

"How did everything go?" she asked as if she didn't already know the answer.

I plastered on my best smile. Not because I wanted to come back again but because I felt bad for this woman who lived this day in and day out.

"Great," I said, infusing my voice with as much enthusiasm as I could muster. "We had fun, didn't we?" I asked the baby, mainly because he was the only one who couldn't answer with a definitive *no*.

When I'd arrived in the morning, Gwen had told me she already felt guilty enough going back to work, even if it was only to a bedroom in their own house. The last thing I wanted was for this woman to feel bad about anything else. Especially not some strange girl who'd only had to babysit for a few hours. They were nice kids, but shit were they a handful.

"Good," she replied. She knew I was lying, but neither of us acknowledged it.

After saying my goodbyes to the kids—who *were* really cute and mostly sweet—I wished Gwen good luck with everything. It was the kind of farewell you say when you know you'll probably never see the person again. And as I headed out to my car, wondering if Owen had enough alcohol back at the house to make me forget this day ever existed, I looked back at Gwen.

Her husband, Mark, had left before I'd arrived, and he wouldn't be home until after three of the four kids were in bed. He'd miss dinner and baths and tuck-ins. I wondered if he cared. And then I wondered if he was actually relieved he didn't have to deal with any of those things.

As I got in my car, I gave one last wave to Gwen and her four children, who were huddled around her like ducklings.

And as she waved back at me, an absent and exhausted gleam to her eyes, I knew I wasn't the only one contemplating my life's choices.

OWEN

"If one more thing in here breaks, I might have to sell the whole house at the yard sale too."

I'd heard Vee come in the back door, and I couldn't stop myself from bitching. Which I knew made me seem like a bitch, but right now I had to admit I kind of *was* one. I should be thankful I'd been gifted a house, even if that house wasn't in the condition I'd been prepared to take on. But a fucking leak? I'd just had to pay to have someone fix the AC last week, and now this?

"What's wrong?" Vee called. "And we're having a yard sale? When did you decide that?"

"When I realized I need to get rid of this house and everything in it."

She must've recognized the urgency in my voice, because I heard her sprint up the stairs before I saw her. Then she was beside me in no time, her eyes moving up and down from the bucket to the soggy ceiling above it and back down again. "What the hell happened?"

"Something leaked," I said dryly. I didn't mean to sound condescending when I said it, and I hoped Vee didn't interpret it like that. "Sorry. I'm not frustrated with *you*. I'm just frustrated in general." There were two things I typically stayed away from—electricity and anything involving water. The idea of setting the house on fire or possibly flooding it scared the hell out of me.

When Minnie was alive, she'd always paid for the things I couldn't—or wouldn't—fix, but now she was gone, and she'd left what little money she'd had from her estate to a charity I'd never even heard of.

When I'd first moved in, she'd spun some yarn about working the nightshift in a warehouse so I wouldn't make too much noise during the day. But in reality, the only money she had coming in was from social security. That meant that now I couldn't just call someone to come fix something just because I didn't *want* to. Plus, the house was already flooding, so to speak. How badly could I fuck this job up?

I hadn't even noticed Vce disappearing to get towels, but before I knew it, she was back with an armful of them. She put them around the bucket to absorb any stray droplets that might land on the hardwood floor.

"Did a pipe burst or something?"

"No, it's leaking in through the attic ceiling, so there must be an issue with the roof. I tried climbing out the attic window to get up there, but—"

"But it's pouring out and you're not Spider-Man, so you realized you're gonna have to wait until it's nice out and you have a ladder like a normal person?"

"Something like that," I said, sounding completely defeated.

"Well, it's supposed to stop raining soon, so hopefully the worst of the damage is done."

"I hope so. I can patch the ceiling down here once it all dries out, but the roof is a different story."

I hoped it didn't have to be completely replaced. Vee and I might have to live in a tent in the backyard while we saved up the money to deal with that. I didn't even have a ladder that would reach close to as high as the roof of this house. Why were old houses so tall when their ceilings felt so low? It was like some of the vertical feet got lost in another dimension that I couldn't figure out how to access.

"Anyway, enough about this." I gestured to the water still dripping from the ceiling, though thankfully, it seemed like it was slowing down a bit. "How was *your* day? Better than the customer service thing?"

Her face twisted, thinking of how to answer, and it made me think it might not have been.

"Well, it was...less boring than the customer service thing," she said. "But I had to play Mary Poppins to four kids while the mom worked from home. Not the easiest job when we had to stay cooped up in the house because of the weather. And the kids have a no-electronic-device rule. I understand the reason for the policy, but it made my day a little intense."

"Intense is when you total your car and then find out there was a bird's nest with four eggs under the hood that'll never get to meet their mommy."

Vee opened her mouth, but no words came out.

I cleared my throat to break the awkward silence before saying, "Not that I know from experience or anything. I'm saying *your* day makes *The Shining* seem like a bedtime story."

"I don't disagree." Vee put her back against the wall and then slid down it until she collapsed near the bucket of water like a pile of clothes that had dropped from a laundry chute.

Not that Vee had anything in common with dirty clothes. She didn't smell or have weird, mysterious spots on her or anything like that.

Thankfully I was smart enough to keep those unfortunate

thoughts in my head rather than say them aloud.

"I'm glad I did such a piss poor job that Gwen would probably let the robot vacuum keep an eye on her kids before she lets *me* back in there."

The thought of one of those little circular vacuums following four young kids around the house made me laugh. It also reminded me of my conversation with the woman at the hardware store.

"What?" she asked as I crossed my legs and lowered myself down to the ground to face her. The wood below me creaked as I settled myself onto it.

"Just you," I answered. I hoped my sincere smile might make her day a tiny bit better.

Her smile always did that for me.

In the small space of the hallway between Vee's room and the wall across from it, we sat together, our knees so close they were almost touching and our hands trying desperately to find someplace to settle. My eyes found hers—a brown so dark I was lost in them again. Like one of those roads you've driven down more times than you can count but suddenly feels unfamiliar in the darkness.

And that was always how Vee was to me—a friend who also seemed to be a stranger in so many ways. It only made me want to know her even more. Being this close to her again brought out all those fucking feelings that I'd tried to bury inside myself that night we'd shared . . . whatever that was in the kitchen and then both pretended it never happened.

"You know what would probably make us feel better?" Vee asked, and I silently prayed that we'd get to act on these feelings we both seemed to have.

"What?" I noticed how I leaned in when I said it, and I

thought she did too. Though maybe I was just being hopeful. I could feel my veins grow alive with the sudden rush of blood, as well as some other, larger parts of my anatomy.

Her teeth bit at her bottom lip for a few seconds before she let go of it and said, "I think Minnie still has some edibles left in the cabinet above the oven." Her voice was so soft, so seductive, it took me longer than it should have to realize she hadn't just invited me to lick the inside of her mouth—or any other part of her, for that matter.

"Oh. Yeah, okay. That's a good idea." *Not as good as the one I had, but it's something.* "I'll go check." I stood quickly, and when I got to the top of the stairs, I turned back. "Hey, if you don't mind, I think I'm gonna sleep up here tonight in case it starts raining again. I'd rather not have to worry about it from the basement."

"Of course. Why would I mind?"

I couldn't think of an answer that made any sense to say aloud, so I shrugged.

"Kay, thanks. I'll probably just bring some blankets and stuff into Minnie's room and sleep on the floor." The spare bedrooms both had a ton of stuff I didn't feel like moving. In addition to Minnie using them for storage before she passed and Vee using them as a place to organize all of Minnie's things she'd been going through, I'd had to bring down some boxes and the paintings from the attic so they didn't get ruined by the water.

"Why don't you sleep in her bed? I figured you'd be moving up to that room soon anyway."

"Because that's just...it feels... I'm taking baby steps here."

"Oh my God, did she die in it?" Horror swept over Vee's

face, and she brought her hands up to cover her mouth.

"No, she didn't die in it. But it's still *her* bed. Just gives me the creeps or something. I don't know. Eventually I'll get around to moving my bed up once we get hers out."

"Consider it done," Vee said, pulling out her phone. "When I posted one of the twin bed frames from the spare room, someone asked if we had anything bigger because she liked that they were solid wood and not the cheap IKEA shit. I'll message her back now and tell her we have a queen if she wants it. Should bring in at least three hundred or so."

"Perfect. I'll go see what edibles Minnie has left and be up in a jiffy."

Jiffy? Really?

I waited until I was completely down the stairs and out of sight before smacking myself in the head a few times.

Chapter Fifteen

OWEN

Vee had helped me set up camp on the floor at the end of Minnie's bed, where there was a small carpet that allowed for some extra padding in addition to the blankets and sheets I'd brought in. I wanted to be as close as possible to the bucket so I wouldn't have to walk too far in the middle of the night if I needed to dump it out.

"Not bad," I said, lying down and adjusting my pillow. I turned onto one side so I could see how it felt against my shoulder and arm since that was how I usually slept. Wouldn't be the most comfortable I'd ever been, but I could manage. "Hopefully it'll just be for tonight, and by the weekend I'll figure out what's going on with the roof. It's supposed to be nice out the rest of the week, so we have that going for us at least."

"I was thinking I could call my dad and brothers and see if they wanted to help with the roof. They deal with things like that on the reg."

"Did you just say 'on the reg'?" I smirked, trying not to laugh.

"Whatever. I've been eating these like they're Halloween candy for the last hour." She held up the box of gummies I'd found in Minnie's cabinet and smiled widely. "Should I ask them or not?"

I didn't want to admit right away that I needed help, but . . . I needed help. "Yeah, I guess so. If it's not too much trouble for them. I mean, I'm sure they're all busy, but it would definitely help save some money, which we don't have much of. Did you hear back from that woman about the bed, by the way? And only ask your dad and brothers if it seems like there's a good moment to do it." It was my house, and even though a leaky roof wasn't a minor problem, it still made me feel a little like a loser for needing their help. "I don't want them feeling like they *have* to help or anything."

"It's fine. They said they'll do it."

"What? You asked them already? When?"

"While you were rambling on about whether or not I should ask them." She held up her phone. I'd been so involved in my own thinking—and talking—I hadn't even noticed she'd been using it.

"Oh. Well, tell them thanks for me."

"I will. But they should be the ones thanking *you*. They all secretly love this whole . . . *coming to my rescue* thing."

My eyebrows went up, and I suddenly felt more alert. "Do you need rescuing?" I didn't like the idea that her family thought Vee needed some sort of help because she was living with me, even if she did. Or *we* did.

Vee looked confused by my question, which I hoped was a good sign.

"No. Rescue was a bad word choice," she explained. "But you know how big brothers and dads are, especially with daughters. They like to feel needed."

"Oh. Yeah. That makes sense."

I didn't have intimate knowledge of those kinds of relationships because I wasn't a daughter, obviously, or a dad or a big brother to anyone, but Vee's explanation seemed like a rational one—at least according to movies and TV—so I decided not to probe any further.

"I think we should make a fort, and it'll be like you're really camping," Vee suggested out of the blue.

I let my head fall to where she lay next to me. "You really are high, aren't you?" I laughed. At some point after eating an excessive amount of Minnie's gummies, we'd both lain down on the makeshift bed. I knew better than to think we'd ended up in this position for any sort of romantic reason. I was certain our proximity was one of laziness rather than anything that revealed any real intimacy.

Vee laughed but was on her feet quickly. "It'll be fun. We can drape some sheets from the bedposts to the dresser and close the other end in the drawers. It'll be like a tent." Her excitement radiated from her as she spoke. "And we could put up some of those little glow-in-the-dark star things to look at. Do you have any of those?"

"I don't."

She deflated quickly, like I'd broken the news to her that I was allergic to the baby kitten she'd just adopted and therefore had to give back.

"Oh, okay. We can get some somewhere." Then, like a cartoon character who'd thought of the perfect solution to a simple problem, a light bulb seemed to illuminate in her head. "I'll tell Brody and Carter to grab some on their way."

I had so many questions, but the most important of which

was, "Brody and Carter are coming over?"

Vee nodded enthusiastically. "They texted to see what we were doing, and I told them we were babysitting a bucket tonight, so they invited themselves over."

I nodded too but with way less enthusiasm.

Not that I didn't have fun with Carter and Brody, but they could be . . . stressful at times. And I'd had enough of a cortisol spike lately. And also, having Brody and Carter over probably meant it would end up being more than just Brody and Carter, and since we were babysitting a bucket, I wasn't in the mood to babysit everyone else too.

"Cool," I said, not even trying to infuse my voice with any sort of enthusiasm.

VERONICA

It didn't take long for Brody and Carter to arrive, and when they did, they brought in an industrial-size trash can.

"Uh, what are you bringing trash *into* the house for?" Owen asked from the top of the steps.

I'd wondered the same thing, but I'd been so shocked—though I really shouldn't have been—that I hadn't even opened my mouth to ask about it yet.

"Correction," Carter said, looking extremely pleased with himself. "It's an empty trash can. As in clean. Devoid of any trash. Sans trash," he said proudly, and Brody gave him a nod of approval, like he was just as impressed with Carter's vocabulary as Carter was.

"We stopped and got a new one so you can use it instead of whatever small bucket you guys were using," Brody added.

"No more babysitting."

The two began carrying the trash can up the stairs, Brody first with Carter holding the bottom above his head so it would be level as they ascended. I thought their strategy might be more for show than practicality, but what did I know about carrying enormous garbage cans up stairs.

When they got to the top, Carter set down his end next to Owen. He must've seen the bucket we'd been using—the kind for mopping floors—because he patted his own trash can affectionately.

"Oh yeah, this boy will last ya. The rain should be stopping at some point soon, so now you guys can go to the Yard with us. I already told the rest of the gang we'd bring you."

From the bottom of the stairs, I could see Owen looking from the trash can to the household bucket and back again.

"I'm into it," he said. "The trash can shall set you free." He raised his arms up toward the sky. "Give me like six minutes, and I'll be ready to go. I just gotta jump in the shower."

I had already started to jog up the stairs to get changed, excited that we'd be going out with our group of friends. No matter how crazy life became, I could count on them to distract me for a little while.

"You'll be ready in six minutes, and that includes a shower?" Carter looked even more confused than usual.

"Yeah," Owen said. "My showers don't take more than three minutes because I take cold ones to get my adrenaline flowing. That leaves three minutes to get dressed, which takes thirty seconds, brush my teeth—two minutes—and do my hair—thirty seconds."

"There's a lot to unpack there," Brody said pensively.

Owen disappeared into the bathroom, promising to be

ready in a few minutes. I didn't have the heart to tell him that his efforts to rush didn't matter since I'd certainly take longer than six minutes to get ready, even though I'd already taken a shower after work.

I was just about to head to my own room to change, when Carter said, "Speaking of unpacking, is this all your stuff?" He pointed into one of the spare rooms.

"It's Minnie's. Some of it was already in there, but Owen brought down some other stuff from the attic so it didn't get ruined when the roof started leaking."

"Anything good?" Brody stood on his toes to look over Carter's shoulder since he was blocking the doorway. "Aamee wants to get a different place soon and make it more *hers*," he said with an eye roll as he turned toward me. "I'm thinking *hers* means bigger and nicer and less full of frat boy shit, but maybe I can spruce my place up a little and convince her to stay."

"By replacing *your* junk with someone else's?" Carter asked with a laugh. "Have you *met* Aamee?"

"It's not *all* junk," Brody told him. He'd given up trying to get into the room Carter was blocking with his solid body and had headed into the other guest bedroom that no doubt had an equal amount of not all junk. "There's a small dresser that Aamee could use for some of her clothes."

Poor, clueless Brody.

"I don't think adding more furniture to a small apartment is going to make Aamee want to stay," I told him.

Brody let out a long sigh. He had no choice but to accept that he'd probably have to give up his apartment, which for some reason meant a hell of a lot to him, and move into something else. His apartment wasn't bad, necessarily. I'd lived there myself and had no issues. It just didn't scream *newly married couple,* which he and Aamee would be soon. And which I also found ironic since Brody and I had pretended to be a newly married couple as well while I was living there.

"It's all right, buddy," I heard Carter say. "The apartment might be gone soon, but the memories will last a lifetime."

"I guess," Brody said, his voice holding an obvious sadness.

Owen had turned off the shower a moment ago, which meant he'd be ready to go soon. So I headed into my own room to change out of my T-shirt and cotton shorts. Maybe Owen would have better luck consoling Brody.

"You know what memories last a lifetime?" I heard Owen say. His voice was clear enough to make me wonder if he'd opened the bathroom door and was standing there in only a towel. Certainly the sight of him like that would last a lifetime. "The ones of your mom from last night."

I smiled to myself at Owen's comment. At least he seemed to be in a better mood.

I expected Brody to come back with an immediate rebuttal, or at least tell him that Mrs. Mason would never stoop so low as to allow Owen into his bed, so I was surprised when the next words out of Brody's mouth were, "Hey, can I have a couple of these?"

I quickly buttoned my jeans and searched for a nude strapless bra so I could wear the cream tank top I'd gotten out. Whatever Brody was referring to had distracted him enough that he'd ignored Owen's comment completely.

"Why would you want any of those?" Owen asked.

"Aamee'll love them! My mom has two by the same dude hanging in our house, and Aamee once told my mom how beautiful they were. I looked up the guy once to see if he had a website or something so I could get Aamee something of his for Christmas, but either all his stuff is already sold or he's not making anything new. My mom said I should try to email him since he's local, but I couldn't even find an email from him since he retired from teaching. He's gotta be like a million years old by now, so he probably only responds to telegrams and shit anyway."

"And you're sure it's the same guy?" Owen asked.

"Yeah. David Douglass. He does those weird curly things with his *D*'s. I'd recognize them anywhere. I used to stare at them during dinner while I pushed the vegetables around on my plate when I was a kid. I tried signing the B in Brody like that for at least a year before I finally gave up."

"Okay," Carter said. "Am I the only one confused here?"

Brody continued. "You could probably get some good money for these, O, because Dr. Douglass is like a Lazarus legend. But it'd be a solid declaration of our friendship if you gifted them to me instead."

A Lazarus legend?

I needed to get out there because if Brody was talking about what I thought he was talking about, Owen and I would have some detective work to do.

"Did he go to Lazarus with your mom?" Owen asked.

Nice. Already starting the investigation.

"No, that's where he taught," Brody clarified. "He was an art professor there. My mom told me his classes used to fill up before any other elective. Sooo, can I have them? Or at least one. I'll pay you."

Once I got myself together enough to open the door so I could see what was happening, I moved to stand next to Owen, and as I'd expected, sitting next to Brody were two of the paintings we'd found of Minnie in the attic.

"Holy shit," I whispered to no one in particular. Or maybe to everyone.

"I know," Brody said. "I think the naked preggo one is kinda weird too."

Chapter Sixteen

OWEN

As we approached the brick Cape Cod that turned out to be only three miles from Minnie's—or my—home, I wondered if we were making a mistake going to talk to Dr. Douglass. Only a few days prior, we hadn't even known his name, and now we were walking up to his front door to ask him about the painting he'd done that, when it came right down to it, was none of our damn business.

I'd been fine with letting the mystery lie when we had no way of discovering the truth, but once Brody had told us the painter's name and that he'd taught at Lazarus, the answers to all my questions felt too close to ignore. Especially when all of us had gone to the bar afterward and discussed all the possibilities.

But now I wasn't so sure. This whole thing felt like an invasion of privacy—of both Minnie's and Dr. Douglass's. Even though Dr. Douglass had agreed to meet with us, Minnie wasn't here to give her consent. And I couldn't shake the feeling that if she'd wanted me—or anyone else—to know about her past, she would've shared it.

I felt like I was staring at a scratch-off lottery ticket with a coin in my hand, trying not to let myself rub off the coating to see what existed underneath.

"Do you think he'll have other naked pictures of Minnie in his house?" Brody asked. "Like, what if there are tons of them hanging all over his walls and it feels like she's watching us?"

Or maybe this just felt like a mistake because I'd agreed to let Brody and Aamee come along. I panned my head over to Brody, who looked like his comment had been completely innocent.

"Ew," Aamee said as we stood on the porch, waiting for Dr. Douglass to answer the door. "Can you not talk about that poor woman like that? She's not even here to defend herself."

"You act like my comment was an insult. She was hot. I bet Owen will agree with me." He held out his hand toward me like he was looking for me to save him.

Aamee glared at both of us.

And as much as I didn't want to get involved in this conversation, Brody was...well, my bro, and what kind of friend would I be if I left him in the hole he'd dug for himself? Maybe I didn't have any tools to pull him out, but I'd be a dick if I didn't jump in with him so he had someone to keep him company.

"Um, yeah. Sure," I said. "I mean, it feels a little strange to say a woman I only knew as someone older than my own grandmother is...or *was* hot. Plus she's dead now, so that makes things extra weird."

Brody's eyes widened at me, and I realized I needed to do better.

"But yeah, I see what you're saying," I told him. "Minnie was hot."

It surprised me when no one responded to my comment. I'd been looking at Brody and Aamee, who were standing behind me, and Vee, but neither of them seemed to be paying any attention to me.

I heard a throat clear from behind me. "Good afternoon. One of you must be Owen?"

Without a word, everyone pointed at me.

"Hi, sir. We were just, um, I was saying how hot Minnie probably was all those years without air conditioning. It broke recently, and we could barely deal with it for a day or two."

Dr. Douglass stared through his screen door at me without a word.

"We were both so hot. Me and Vee"—I pointed to her—"Veronica. This is Veronica. She lives there with me after Minnie left me the house. She can tell you how hot both of us were when the AC broke, right?"

I looked at Vee, but we may as well have been Jack and Rose. I was clinging on desperately to the small piece of wood in the middle of a vast ocean, fighting for my life, and I didn't know if Vee would make room for me so I could climb on too.

"We were so hot," I said slowly again. "Right?"

Dr. Douglass remained quiet for another moment before he opened the door and waved us in. "Minnie *was* pretty hot," he said with a chuckle that reminded me of Santa Claus and helped me relax a little. "But I suppose that's not what you came to discuss."

VERONICA

Dr. Douglass had quite a few of his own paintings hanging

in his home, but none I could see from my spot on a chair in the living room were of Minnie. Though most were, in fact, portraits. He'd offered us some tea or coffee, and his wife, Diane, had brought out some croissants she'd gotten from a local bakery and placed them on the coffee table.

I'd wondered at first if Mrs. Douglass's presence might result in her husband not being as forthcoming about his relationship with Minnie as he might have been otherwise, but she'd joked early on that we weren't the first people to come asking about one of her husband's early muses.

"David was quite the ladies' man in his day," she said, patting her husband's shoulder lovingly.

Brody nodded his approval. "Nice, Dr. Douglass."

"Please," he said. "Call me David. I always hated how formal Dr. Douglass sounded. I tried to leave that title behind when I retired from teaching. So what is it you'd like to know exactly?"

David picked up the small mug of coffee and saucer carefully, his hands trembling in a way that I hadn't noticed until now.

"We were just curious . . . Owen and I," I said, "about the paintings of Minnie."

When he'd spoken to David on the phone initially, Owen had been open about his reason for wanting to meet, but David hadn't asked for details, and Owen hadn't provided them. We'd both kind of decided that we'd see where the conversation took us instead of trying to lead it. All he knew was that we'd found some paintings he'd done of Minnie.

"Ah, yes. I was an undergrad when I did those." He laughed to himself softly as nostalgia seemed to fill him. "Minnie was quite a bit older. Mid- to late-twenties or so maybe."

I prepared myself for Brody to make a cougar joke, but thanks to the croissants, his mouth was already occupied.

"Could you tell us a little about her," I said. "Anything at all would be helpful. How you met, anything about your... relationship maybe."

"Sure," he said. "I can try. Don't know how interesting any of it will be to you, but I'm happy to do my part to fill in some of the gaps for you where I can."

When he'd first spoken with Dr. Douglass, Owen had shared who he was and how he knew Minnie. He'd told him that he'd lived with her for a few years before she passed and that she'd left him the house, which Owen had noted afterward didn't seem to surprise Dr. Douglass much.

I wondered then if he and Minnie had remained friends throughout the years, but now it seemed that this man knew less about Minnie than we'd hoped. Or at least he presented it that way.

"I met Minerva, as she liked to be called back then, through my oldest brother, John. I think she was friends with John's girlfriend if I'm remembering correctly. I'm not sure of the exact connection, but I was looking for someone to be the focus of a painting for a show my art professor was putting together. My brother suggested I ask Minerva. She was kind of a free spirit, I guess you could say, so he thought she'd be willing to pose."

"In what ways would you consider her a free spirit?" Owen asked.

It wasn't like the comment was any sort of a revelation, considering we'd found out that Minnie had been selling pot brownies as a side hustle, but so many things about her seemed mysterious now.

David seemed to consider his words carefully before he spoke. "Like…she wasn't concerned with conforming to societal norms, like getting married, for one. While most women her age were already burdened by running a household and chasing after small children, Minerva didn't seem interested in any of that. I don't even think she had a boyfriend during the time I knew her."

"Do you know anything about her family?" I asked.

Like, did she have an estranged child?

David thought for a moment before answering. "Not really. She had a few siblings, I think, but I never met them. I'm not even sure if they were brothers or sisters." The wrinkles in his forehead became more pronounced as he thought back. Then he smiled in a way that made me think he was amused. "She told me once her parents would kill me if they knew I was painting her nude. She said they'd probably kill her too."

The casualness with which he said it, like he remembered the comment fondly, led me to believe Minnie had probably been exaggerating about their possible deaths, though I didn't doubt that her parents wouldn't have approved. I couldn't imagine what my dad's reaction would be if he discovered I'd been the nude subject of a college kid's paintings, and this was a good sixty or so years after Minnie had done it.

David continued. "I think that's part of the reason she let me paint her like that, to be honest."

"I can totally relate to that," Aamee said.

I hadn't even realized she'd been paying attention since she'd been touring the small downstairs as she would a gallery. Guess she really was a fan of David's work.

"It's such a thrill to do something when you know your parents wouldn't approve if they found out about it," she said.

"It's why I used to sneak out my window every night during the summer going into tenth grade to make out with Adam Levine."

"From Maroon 5?" all of us, except the Douglasses, asked in unison.

"Ew, gross. No. He was probably like thirty then or something. I would never," she said as if not making out with the lead singer had been a conscious decision on her part. "The Adam Levine that lived four houses down from us. Our dads despised each other. They would've freaked if they'd known. Adam was cute and a year older. He had a piercing—"

"Okay, that's enough," I said quickly.

Mrs. Douglass winked at her. "You'll have to tell me the rest later," she said.

"A piercing in his tongue," Aamee said to all of us firmly. "You really think I'd talk about a seventeen-year-old's penis ring in front of two senior citizens?"

"Do you really want us to answer that?" Owen asked when the room grew quiet.

If I didn't know better, I would've thought Aamee had been slightly offended by the implication. But if she had been, it was certainly short-lived. She returned her attention to the painting she'd been studying earlier, putting her face so close to it, I thought she might stick her tongue out to lick it.

"Is there anything else you can tell us about Minnie?" Owen prompted. "During that time in her life or later? I'm not sure how much the two of you kept in touch over the years."

"We didn't." David sounded almost regretful at the admission. "We were relatively close for a few years during that time in our lives ... when I was painting her and shortly after," he clarified. "But then ..." David cleared his throat and shook his head. "She kind of just disappeared."

"Disappeared?" I leaned farther forward.

"Not in the physical sense. To my knowledge, she was still in the area. But back then, there were no cell phones or"—he gestured wildly—"any of that other nonsense everyone uses to track each other nowadays." His voice sounded rougher than it had moments ago, like the idea of modern technology almost angered him. "She just stopped calling and hanging around with my brother's group. No one thought much of it at the time, I guess. People come and people go. It's the way life has always been and always will be. Most people are in our lives for a short time, not a lifetime."

His words hit me more than they should have, and I was surprised at my reaction to them. I thought about all the people I'd come to know here—all of them I'd consider close friends—and wondered how long I'd think of them like that. How long would they think of *me* like that?

"So you just..." Owen hesitated. "Never saw each other again?"

David set his coffee down, the dishes shaking against each other as he placed them on the table.

Diane put her hand on his thigh.

"We ran into each other once or twice over the years, but I didn't see her," he said. "Not the way I used to."

"Naked," Brody said, as if he was clarifying the meaning for the rest of us.

David laughed a little. "I didn't mean naked, though I never saw her like that again either. I meant... sometimes people are there but they don't want you to see them. You know?" Even Brody seemed to understand that was a rhetorical question, so he let David continue uninterrupted. "Whatever happened to

Minerva after I did that last painting of her... I wasn't privy to it."

"The *last* painting?" I said, needing him to clarify.

I studied David closely—the way the wrinkles around his eyes seemed to become more pronounced when his eyes narrowed, how his thin lips tightened.

"The one where she was expecting," he said. "I'm assuming that one was most intriguing to you." He sighed heavily, dropping his gaze from us for a moment like it made him uncomfortable to discuss her like that. "It was intriguing to me too, but it was also none of my business. So when it was clear she wanted to be left alone, that's what the rest of us did." He brought his eyes back to ours, and I thought they looked a little teary. "I don't know if that was the right decision," he said, "but it was the one we all made."

I think all of us could sense the conversation coming to a close. David didn't have much insight into who Minnie was or what her life was like after she'd withdrawn. It wouldn't do anyone any good to dig into a past that was so deeply buried.

"Thank you both so much for your time," Owen said. "And for the coffee." He took one last sip before standing. "Minnie was like a grandmother to me for the short time I knew her. I'm glad you were willing to speak with us."

"Likewise," David said. "And please tell your mother I said hello," he told Brody.

When we'd arrived, Brody had explained his and Aamee's presence there, sharing with the Douglasses that his mom had taken a few of David's classes during her time at Lazarus and had loved his work ever since.

I didn't know whether David truly remembered Brody and Sophia's mom or if he was just being polite. It had to be at least twenty-five years and thousands of students ago.

"Hang on just a moment," David said. Then he disappeared around the corner and into the kitchen. When he returned, he was holding two colorful serving dishes. He handed them to Aamee. "I haven't done any portraits in a long time because I can't keep my hands steady, so I've taken to painting designs on the pottery my wife makes."

"They're beautiful," Aamee said of the bright, abstract designs.

"They're yours," David replied. "Well, one for you and one for your future mother-in-law."

Brody raised his eyebrows like he found something amusing. "Penelope is gonna be so jealous when my mom shows her these."

"Who's Penelope?" I asked. I didn't remember there being a Penelope at the wedding we'd staged, so I didn't think she was a relative.

"My mom's best friend since high school," Brody explained. "They went to Lazarus together and both loved David."

The group continued talking, but I'd drifted out of the conversation with the mention of Mrs. Mason's best friend.

"Do you know who Minnie's best friend was?" I asked so suddenly even I wasn't prepared for the question. "Was it your brother's girlfriend who you mentioned?"

David was quiet for a moment before he answered. "No, they were friends, but I never felt like Minerva was exceptionally close to her. Why do you ask?"

"Was Minnie close to anyone in particular during that time? Anyone at all? Sorry to be so forward, but I thought maybe she had a close friend who might have known . . . what happened to the baby."

I said it as if the words felt shameful because, honestly, they kind of did. I was ashamed I'd pried into this woman's life, and the mention of a baby out of wedlock during that time period would've no doubt caused shame for Minnie as well as her family. Yet, none of us had directly mentioned it.

David sighed heavily but remained silent otherwise. I hoped I hadn't offended him with my question, but I couldn't leave here without exhausting every avenue I'd thought of.

"We should've been up-front with you," Owen added. "We're most curious about the painting where she's pregnant, because I didn't think Minnie had any family. But if she does have family somewhere—a child—I feel like that child has a right to know their mother passed away if they haven't heard already. Maybe they'd want some of the family photos or something."

All of us headed toward the front door, but we stopped when we got there. I could tell David had something to say by the way he glanced at his wife before turning his full attention to us.

"The only thing I know about Minerva's pregnancy is that when her parents found out, they wanted nothing to do with her or the child. Minerva was still living at home then because she was unmarried, as I told you, but once she couldn't hide the pregnancy any longer, her parents told her she needed to find somewhere else to live."

"Did she?" I asked.

"She did indeed. Minerva worked in a café owned by a husband and wife. I'm not sure how close they were to Minerva, but they felt bad for her and her situation, so they took her in. Nice people. They were around Minerva's age, I think. Maybe a few years older. Free spirts too, in a way. They didn't have any children then, so they had the room for her and the baby. They used to travel a lot during the holidays when the café was closed. Minerva went with them a few times I think."

Owen and I exchanged glances almost immediately.

The pictures we found.

"Do you by any chance remember the couple's name?" Owen asked.

"The husband, yes. His name's Milton. They owned the café by the same name that's still over on Kennett Street. Have you been there?"

I shook my head.

"I have. Fantastic cheese danishes," Owen said, looking almost catatonic.

"That's the place," Diane said with a smile.

But Owen continued like he hadn't heard her. "Until a couple of years ago, Milt's wife used to make 'em fresh herself each morning. I remember her name," he said. "It's June."

Chapter Seventeen

VERONICA

I'd spent the morning my family was supposed to arrive cleaning like some kind of fifties housewife. Owen had cast a number of concerned looks in my direction, but he hadn't voiced his thoughts.

Smart man.

He'd also been a bit lost in his own world. I think finding out that he knew June had been jarring for him, but he hadn't seemed to want to talk much about it. We'd tentatively decided to go down to the café they'd owned to see if anyone could put us in touch with June, but we needed to get through the day with my family first.

Ugh. My family would probably be here any second.

I wasn't even sure what my problem was. My dad knew it was a fixer-upper, not to mention the fact that it wasn't even my house. I obviously didn't want my dad thinking I lived in a hovel, but ultimately Owen's house reflected on him.

And that's what you're worried about, a very annoying voice at the back of my head told me. Did the voice the world heard sound as annoying as the one inside my head? Because if so, it was a wonder anyone liked me.

But even I couldn't force myself to be delusional enough not to accept the words were true. I *was* worried that my dad wouldn't like Owen. That he'd take one look at this house, find it and Owen lacking, and try to convince me to find somewhere new to live.

I could refuse, of course. My dad wasn't one to push his agenda too hard if it wasn't what we wanted. But still. The truth of the matter was, I wanted my dad to like Owen. And wasn't that a bitch?

My dad had tolerated a lot of my friends over the years, but he hadn't *liked* many of them. It wasn't that he was a difficult man, but he'd never considered being tight with my friends as part of his role as my father. He'd never tried to be the cool parent. If anything, he preferred my friends, and especially my boyfriends, to be a little intimidated by him. Which wasn't hard since the man was large in every sense of the word.

If he didn't like someone, I sure as hell heard about it, but on the whole, he kept a steady, protective, and silent eye on me and the people I surrounded myself with.

But I didn't want that this time. I wanted my dad to know Owen. I wanted him to like my quirky roommate who was quickly becoming the best friend I'd ever had. And if I sometimes wondered if my feelings for Owen went a little bit deeper than friendship, well, no one had to know about that. Romantic feelings were messy, and I didn't want to ruin a good thing by acting on my growing attraction. If it went bad, I'd be out a place to live and out a good friend.

The cost was simply too high. At least for now.

"Have you finally run out of battery?"

I jolted when Owen's voice sounded behind me in the kitchen. My hand flew to my heart as I tried to steady my breathing.

"Don't do that!" I scolded.

Owen smirked. "Sorry. I was just worried for your well-being. You've been using so many cleaning supplies, I thought the fumes had finally gotten to you."

"I was just . . . thinking."

He came closer and looked out the window I'd been staring through.

"Is it that you need to Windex it again? Because I can assure you, you don't."

I gave him a droll look, which prompted him to hold up his hands.

"I'm just saying. The windows in this place are so clean, I'm pretty sure we could see through them to alternate dimensions at this point."

I snorted a laugh and resumed looking out the window as we stood beside each other.

After a few seconds, he spoke. "You seem nervous."

"Nah," I lied. "It's only my dad and brothers."

"Yeah," he said, pushing his hands into his pockets. "Do you, I mean, should I . . . Is there, like, a certain way I should act or anything?"

I turned toward him, my brow furrowed. "What do you mean?"

"It's just that I wondered if maybe you were nervous for me to meet your dad? So if there's a way I should act or anything to make you less nervous, then you can tell me. I know I can seem a little out there sometimes, and I'll try to be on my best behavior, but if there's something specific I should or shouldn't do, it's totally fine to tell me. It won't hurt my feelings or anything."

My chest ached at his words. "Owen."

"Yeah?" he said, his gaze intent, as if he was prepared to take to heart whatever critique I was about to give him.

I couldn't help myself. I stepped into him and wound my arms around his stomach.

He jolted as if he'd been shocked, his body tense for a second, before he relaxed and returned my hug.

I tightened my arms as I spoke. "Don't ever be anyone else. If anyone ever tells you you're not perfect how you are, then you tell them to fuck all the way off."

I felt him chuckle—a rumble in his chest and slight shake of his body.

"I'm serious," I said, my tone fierce. "You're ... you're one of the best people I've ever met. Don't ever change to fit what other people think you should be. You're already exactly who you're supposed to be."

I didn't doubt the veracity of my words in the slightest. So many of us spent at least our early twenties trying to figure out what the future held for us, what kind of people we were going to be. But Owen was already ... Owen.

His cheek settled atop my head, and we stood there together for a bit. It felt as if we were being knitted together, and I didn't want to disrupt the process.

"Ooh, Frankie, it looks like we're interrupting something."

I groaned at the sound of my brother Manny's voice and buried my face in Owen's chest.

"Hmm, maybe we should've knocked," Franco said.

"Since this isn't your house, you definitely should've knocked, assholes," I grumbled as I pulled away from Owen.

Manny's face filled with contrived sympathy. "Yeah, but see, I didn't want to. And I'm so happy I didn't because then I would've missed all this," he said, gesturing at Owen and me.

"This is true," Franco agreed. "We want to be part of your special moment too."

"Group hug!" Manny yelled as he spread his arms wide and advanced on us.

I ducked quickly out of the way, but Owen stayed rooted to the spot, opening his arms and embracing Manny. They stood there for a few seconds as Franco and I watched them.

"Wow," Manny said. "This is weirder than I expected."

"It's only weird because society tells you it's weird," Owen said.

Manny was quiet for a moment before he said, "Nah, I'm pretty sure it's weird for many reasons."

They broke apart, and Manny took a couple of steps back. "So how you guys been? Looks like you're getting along," he said as he waggled his eyebrows.

Owen sighed. "I really wish we could move past this patriarchal notion that a man and woman can't be friends without it evolving into something more."

"Patri-what now?" Franco asked.

"Your brother is clearly implying something... romantic is happening between Vee and me simply because you saw us hugging. Friends can hug, you know." Owen looked almost indignant. It was cuter than it should have been.

Franco and Manny shared a bewildered look before Manny smiled widely and ruffled Owen's hair.

"He's adorable," he said to me.

"Yeah, I approve," Franco added because he was annoying.

I groaned. "Where's Dad?"

"Outside walking the perimeter," Franco explained. "He's going to be so upset when we tell him what he missed."

I glared at him. "You tell him, and I'll let it slip who broke his football trophy from high school."

Franco gasped. "You took a blood oath."

I moved closer to him. "It was ketchup."

Franco pointed to me. "Judas!"

"Dude," Manny said in a hushed tone. "Dad loved that trophy."

Franco threw his hands up. "It was an accident." He turned and pointed at me. "You are the spawn of Satan."

I smiled. "You bet your ass. Now behave or I'll unleash twenty-four years of misdeeds and bad behaviors." I turned and made my way out of the kitchen so I could go outside and greet my dad.

"How do you live with her?" I heard Franco ask.

My breath caught as I waited for Owen's reply.

"Happily," he said, his voice sounding fond.

His words had me smiling all the way out the door.

OWEN

I tried not to feel emasculated as I held the ladder steady for Vee's brothers as they trekked up and down it to fix the leak in my roof. After multiple Women's Studies classes, I knew better than to get hung up on the implied gender bias between who got to fix the problem versus who had to watch.

But knowing a thing and feeling it are two different things.

The fact that Vee's dad didn't trust me to help stung. It wasn't that it was an insult to my manhood, because I didn't subscribe to that line of thinking. It was more that he'd looked at me and decided that I couldn't be useful to him.

Normally, I didn't care much what parents thought of me. My mom had always said I marched to the beat of my own drummer, and I'd certainly met my fair share of people who were not into my brand of music. Ordinarily, I couldn't even blame them. I knew I wasn't for everybody. And that was fine because not everybody was for me either.

But damn, I'd really wanted Vee's dad to like me.

Not that he'd said anything that made me think he *didn't* like me, per se. He'd at least told me to call him Tomas instead of Mr. Diaz. But he still seemed sorta . . . ambivalent about me.

I'd done a lot of growing up since inheriting Minnie's house. I'd had to. I couldn't be scatterbrained and directionless anymore. It wasn't that I thought I owed it to Minnie to fix up her house. Hell, she'd been the one to let it fall apart to begin with. This wasn't about making anything up to anyone. It was about proving to myself—and my family—that I could stick with something. That I could commit to something and follow through on it.

My family was great, and I loved them to pieces. But there was a reason I hadn't asked them to help me fix up the house. They'd had to bail me out of various dreams I'd had when said dreams had gone south. They'd had to deal with me constantly contemplating a major change or showing up with a rogue animal or taking off for the summer to cruise around the country with a couple of guys I'd just met who made me ride in the trunk.

I could do this. And when they saw all I'd accomplished, they'd finally have something to be truly proud of.

"Watch out below!" someone yelled before a chunk of my

roof came flying down from above.

I'd breathed a deep sigh of relief when Vee's dad had told me it wasn't actually the roof that was leaking. Some of the caulking had deteriorated around the exhaust chimney, and water was seeping in. They'd also found a few loose shingles they'd hammer back in place, but overall, the roof was in good shape. Minnie must've replaced it within the past decade.

"Damn it, Frannie! You need to tell people to watch out *before* you throw it." Vee shielded her eyes from the sun as she looked up at the roof to yell at her brother.

"Did I hit anyone?" he asked, not much sounding like he cared if he had.

"That's beside the point," Vee argued.

"Is it, Bob the Builder?" Franco's voice was patronizing.

"Really? Bob the Builder? Are you five?"

"Can you two stop arguing so we can get this done?" Vee's dad grumbled.

"I was coming out to see what everyone wanted for dinner," Vee said.

"Yeah, whatever you want. My treat," I added. "It's the least I can do."

"I won't say no to free food," Manny called.

"There's a good sandwich place down the street," Vee said.

"How good?" Franco asked as he started down the ladder.

Vee looked thoughtful for a moment. "Better than Julio's but not quite DiSimone's."

He seemed to contemplate that for a moment before he shrugged. "Sounds good to me."

Vee took down everyone's orders, and I handed her my credit card so she could pay when she called.

When all the Diazes were back on solid ground, I began

picking up the debris that littered the yard. I'd just dumped a handful into the trash can when Manny sidled up beside me.

"So . . . you and Vee seem to be getting along swimmingly."

"Swimmingly?"

"Yeah. It means well."

"I know what it means," I replied. "I just didn't know anyone actually used that word."

"I'm full of surprises," he said. "Much like you."

I narrowed my eyes in confusion. "What surprises am I full of?"

His answering smile was full of mischief. "Vee was so adamant that you two were just friends when she first moved in."

"We are just friends."

Franco scoffed. "That didn't look like a friend hug in the kitchen."

I cast a glance at Vee's dad to see if I could get a read on his reaction to his sons' questioning. Secretly, I was hoping he'd tell his sons to leave me be, but the way he was organizing his tools let me know I wouldn't be getting any help from him.

"I wasn't aware there were different types of hugs."

Franco slid an arm around me. "Oh, Owen. That's the saddest thing I've ever heard."

"Haven't you ever had a girlfriend before?" Manny asked before his eyes widened as if something had dawned on him. "Or boyfriend? No shaming here, man. I'm very open-minded."

"That's . . . good," I answered, the words sounding like a question because I wasn't sure how the hell to respond. Being grilled by the Diaz brothers was a brand of psychological torture I had never experienced. "And yes, I've had girlfriends. And a boyfriend once because I didn't want to make assumptions about my preferences."

Franco looked at me curiously. "And what did you find out about your ... preferences?"

"That they definitely skew more toward females."

"But not exclusively?"

I shrugged. "I like to keep myself open to all possibilities."

"You two do realize none of this is your business, right?" Tomas interrupted.

"He knows he doesn't have to answer," Manny said. "Right, Owen?"

I knew no such thing. "Uh, yeah ... sure."

The older Diaz grunted and resumed his organizing. Looked like that was all the aid he was willing to send my way.

"So, back to the hug," Franco said.

I sighed. "I honestly don't know what you two want me to say. It was just a hug. A *friend* hug," I amended when Manny opened his mouth to interrupt. "Listen, I get it, okay? I even appreciate it. You care about your sister and want to make sure she's not staying with some dickhead who's going to try to take advantage of her. But seriously, do you know your sister at all? If I made one wrong move, she'd have my balls in a vise before I even knew what was happening. Not that it would ever come to that, because I respect your sister."

I took a deep breath, realizing I was babbling but unable to stop now that I'd started. "I'd have to be blind to not notice how beautiful your sister is. And I'd have to be stupid to not realize how great of a person she is. But she's never shown an interest in anything except friendship with me, and that's fine. More than fine. Because just knowing her is enough f or me. I'll never ask for anything she isn't willing to freely give." I paused and looked at them intently, hoping they could see the honesty in my words. "She's safe with me. I promise."

All three Diaz men were looking at me by the end of my speech, and my ears warmed in embarrassment. I'd completely shown my hand, but screw it. I didn't want them to worry about Vee, and a little discomfort on my part was worth it if it set their minds at ease. And if it meant I never had to be part of a conversation like this again.

It was Manny who broke the silence. "I changed my mind. I actually think it's Vee who's not good enough for *you.*"

Tomas headed my way and slapped Manny on the back of the head as he walked by. He stopped in front of me and gave me a long look before giving me a pat on the shoulder.

"I'm going to clean up before dinner," he said.

I watched him walk away, smiling inside. I would've bet money that was as close to a blessing as Tomas Diaz was ever going to give.

Chapter Eighteen

VERONICA

I watched my brothers rib Owen about an assortment of things as they devoured their sandwiches while my dad sat speculatively in a chair off to the side.

We'd gathered in the living room to eat since that was the place with the most space. My dad had seemed... weird. He'd always been on the quieter side, but he'd seemed almost reflective since coming inside.

"So an old lady just left you this place?" I heard Franco ask.

"Minnie. Yeah. It was definitely surprising," Owen answered.

"Was she like your sugar mama or something?" Manny asked.

"Gross," I muttered.

Manny shrugged. "What? Some people are into that."

Owen smiled. "I'm not kink shaming, but octogenarians are very much *not* my thing."

Franco's eyes sparkled with mischief. "What is your

thing? I suppose it wouldn't be dark-haired future lawyers who annoy the shit out of their older brothers, would it?"

Owen's eyes met mine, and he seemed uneasy for a moment. Deep down, I hoped that it wasn't because he didn't want to have to say no in front of me. Though I'd never admit it out loud, I wanted Owen to have a thing for me. Even if we never acted on it, I still *wanted* to be wanted by Owen.

When Owen looked back at my brother, he smiled, though it didn't reach his eyes. "I plead the fifth." He pointed a finger at my brother In mock-chastisement. "Stop trying to make things awkward between my roommate and me."

Franco laughed. "I'm sure, given enough time, you two will manage to do that all on your own."

"Does anyone want a cookie?" I asked, picking up the container of assorted treats I'd ordered from the deli. Tilting it toward Franco, I said, "Maybe you could choke on one."

Franco smiled as if I amused him. "Such a sweetheart. I totally get what Owen sees in you."

"Okay, that's enough," my dad warned in a low voice that wasn't threatening but still invited no argument.

"You're still in school, right, Owen?" Manny asked. "What are you studying?"

"Accounting."

"Really?" Manny looked surprised.

"Wait for it..." I murmured, knowing Owen would keep talking and his answers would be more in line with what Manny had most likely been expecting Owen to say.

"Yeah, I've always been pretty good with numbers. But it's boring, so I picked up a minor in Women's Studies. Now *that* is a fascinating subject. It's really informed my behavior in a variety of ways."

Manny and Franco were staring at Owen as if he'd just said he collected doll heads in his spare time.

Franco cleared his throat. "What do you, uh, do with a major like that?"

Owen hummed. "All sorts of things. I could be a professor, advocate, writer, therapist. But what I'd most likely go into is midwifery."

That one even got my dad's attention. His head snapped up, and he tilted it as if he thought he'd misheard.

"A midwife?"

Owen nodded enthusiastically. "I met a doula once in a haunted house. It's a long story, but we ended up in a closet together, and she told me all about her job. It was fascinating, and I immediately started looking into it." A look of disappointment washed over his face. "But when I told my parents, they thought it might be tough for a man to find a job in that line of work. So I agreed to stick with accounting and then decide what I was going to pursue after graduation. And it makes sense. If I start my own business, at least I'll know how to do the books."

Everyone was silent for a long moment. Finally, Manny and Franco looked at each other, and I held my breath in anticipation for them to shit all over Owen's dreams. My fists clenched as I prepared myself to shank a bitch, when they both broke out laughing. Which wasn't much better, but at least they hadn't immediately started putting Owen down.

"Dude," Manny said after a bit, wiping tears of laughter from his eyes. "You have to meet our Uncle Ricky. He'd get such a kick out of you."

Franco lightly slapped Manny. "You're so right. Ricky would adore this guy."

"Maybe I'll get the chance to meet him sometime," Owen said.

I involuntarily tensed. Owen obviously knew who my family was, and especially who Ricky was. While most of the rest of the gang had met him and owed him a lot of gratitude, I had no interest in Owen making his acquaintance.

It wasn't that I was ashamed of my uncle. He did what he felt he had to do, and while I didn't agree with his methods, I'd grown up knowing that I was on a need-to-know basis and to not ask any questions. I'd been able to separate my uncle from the mob boss.

But that didn't mean I didn't know what he was capable of.

Something about sweet, kind, caring Owen sharing space with my uncle made my chest tighten.

Franco clearly had no such reservations because he brightened like a little kid on Christmas morning. "You should come to my pop's birthday party in a few weeks."

"Oh, it's your birthday soon?" Owen asked my dad.

Frannie waved a hand at him. "No, pops is what we call my grandfather. How about it? You can drive up with Vee."

Manny smirked at me before turning excited eyes on Owen. "You have to come. The family will love you."

I didn't miss his added emphasis on *love*. It wasn't that Manny was lying—my family would love Owen—but not for a normal reason. They'd love how quirky and open he was. They weren't cruel people by any means, but they did like a good time. They'd spend the entire time peppering Owen with questions they thought would get a funny response.

Owen looked at me, and his brow furrowed at what he saw there. "Um, I don't know."

I opened my mouth to shut the conversation down, but my dad's voice stopped me.

"You'd be more than welcome," he said. "I'm sure everyone would love to meet Vee's roommate."

Maybe I imagined it, but it seemed like my dad had stumbled a bit when he'd called Owen my roommate. That, combined with the intense way he was looking at me, like he knew more than even *I* knew, made me shift uncomfortably.

"Oh, well, uh, I guess if Vee doesn't mind me tagging along?" Owen said, clearly looking to me for permission.

My brain scrambled for a way out of this, but I came up empty. In order to quickly fill the silence, I added, "Sure. It'll be fun."

I was aware my tone made it obvious I thought it'd be as fun as taking a blow to the head, but there wasn't much I could do about that once the words were out. I smiled to try to hide my uncertainty.

Judging by the way Owen's smile was dimmer than usual, I hadn't been successful at that either.

"Sounds like a plan," Owen said. "What could I bring as a gift?"

Franco leaned forward so he could slap Owen on the back. "Trust me, you're gift enough."

It was official. I was going to kill my brother.

OWEN

After Vee's family left, things between us felt awkward. We straightened up from dinner in silence that seemed deafening. Vee's body was stiff as she scooted around me, careful not to get too close.

I always felt so good around Vee, and I felt the loss of it like I would a missing limb.

She'd been that way ever since her brothers had invited me to their grandfather's party, so I could only assume she didn't want me to go—a realization that hurt more than I'd ever admit out loud.

I'd thought we'd become good friends, but maybe I'd misunderstood her feelings about me. Not that I could really blame her. My feelings for her went far beyond friendship. But the knowledge that she was on the complete opposite side of the spectrum gave me a deep sense of melancholy that would be tough to shake.

But I would. At least on the outside. It wasn't Vee's fault that I'd imagined there was more between us than there was. I'd save my sulking for when I was alone in my bedroom. Outside of there, I'd pretend everything was back to normal.

But to do that, *she'd* have to do the same.

When I lifted the trash bag from the can, I moved back a step and bumped into her as she passed. She jolted and performed some kind of advanced maneuver that looked like a pirouette combined with a stint in the electric chair.

"Sorry," she exclaimed, as if she'd stabbed me instead of lightly brushing against me.

Enough was enough. "It's okay if you don't want me to go to the birthday party."

"What?" she asked, though she didn't seem very surprised by my statement, letting me know I hadn't misinterpreted the cause of her unease.

"I get that I'm, like, kind of out there. I heard it all the time growing up. So if you don't want me to meet your family, that's cool." The words hurt to say. I'd always thought Vee got me like other people didn't. Being faced with the inaccuracy of that assessment was brutal.

I'd been told I was too weird, too immature, too irresponsible, too hyper, too...much, basically since birth. And while I'd chilled out considerably in the past year, I knew I could still seem like an airhead, even though my GPA was respectable and I'd taken on a lot more responsibility in my life. At this point, I was who I was. And ultimately, I really liked the guy I'd become.

I just wished other people did too.

"You're not *out there*. Has someone said that recently?" Vee spat the words as if she were genuinely angry, which made me feel slightly better.

"No, but I know how I come off. So if you don't want me going to the party, then that's fine. I understand."

"That makes one of us," she muttered.

And even though I heard her, I didn't understand. "What?"

She sighed and rubbed her eyes before focusing back on me. "Can I try something?" she said quietly.

"Sure," I agreed immediately.

She looked at me a second longer before closing the distance between us. As her chest pushed against mine, it felt as if my core temperature rose to dangerous levels.

I wanted to shift as pinpricks of awareness swept across my body. Willing myself to calm down—and my dick to behave—I focused on my breathing. I didn't want to do anything that would ruin this moment, whatever this moment was.

Vee stared up at me with an intensity I could only identify as lust, and I got lost in the deep chocolate orbs that often shone with so much warmth when she looked at me. She tentatively touched my stomach and slowly drifted her hand up to my chest and onto my neck, where she slipped it behind and nestled her fingers in my hair.

A slight tug was all it took for me to drop my head enough so that her lips could meet mine.

The kiss was tame, almost chaste, but it ignited a fire under my skin I'd never experienced before.

Her lips parted on a gasp, as if she felt the same overwhelming heat I did, and I allowed my tongue to trace the shell of her lips. I didn't push further. While my body longed for more, this was her show. I'd leave her to direct it as she saw fit.

The kiss seemed to simultaneously last forever and be over far too soon. She pulled away slightly, her hand still buried in my hair.

"Did you feel it?" she whispered.

"Yes," I replied, because despite her not clarifying what *it* was, I knew she was referring to the chemistry, the connection, that I'd always felt between us.

She pressed one more quick kiss to my lips before she stepped back. "That's why I'm nervous for you to meet my family."

Her words were so surprising they nearly gave me whiplash. "I don't understand."

She smiled, but it looked almost sad. "I don't really either. All I do know is that you're the best friend I've had in a long time. And I . . . I need that right now. More than I need anything else."

Okay, I had to admit that while the sentiment was nice, the reality was incredibly disappointing. Still . . . "I don't get why that means I can't meet your family."

"I guess it felt... complicated. Because my feelings for you are already complicated, and adding my family to any situation is a surefire way to ensure disaster. I don't want to ruin what we have because my family is crazy."

I smiled because what else could I do? "I'm pretty sure my family could give yours a run for their money in the craziness category."

Vee laughed. God, it was pathetic how much I loved that sound.

"You'll see. Once you meet mine, yours'll seem like the Cleavers."

My brow dipped. "But I thought you didn't want me to meet them."

She shrugged. "It's all out in the open now. And my brothers will probably drive down here and get you themselves if you don't show." When I didn't respond right away, she added, "As long as you still want to come. I get that I kind of dumped a lot on you. That was probably really rude, now that I think about it. Kissing you, saying I had feelings for you, but I wasn't sure whether to act on them." She was rambling and seemed to be speaking more to herself than me. It was adorable. "God, I'm really an asshole. Who does that? I'm so sorry. I didn't mean—"

I gently placed a finger over her lips to stop her downward verbal spiral.

"It's okay. I get it."

"You do?" she asked, hope lacing her tone.

Honestly, I didn't. Not fully. But I wanted her around more than I wanted to understand. "Yes. I promise."

She smiled. "My family really is going to love you."

I replied with a smile of my own, hoping I effectively hid the fact that her love was the only love I wanted.

Chapter Nineteen

VERONICA

Owen and I had almost been trying too hard to behave normally around each other. I worried I'd napalmed our friendship after I'd kissed him, but he'd taken it in stride. Owen could teach a master class in adaptability.

Thankfully Monday came and I was able to escape to Safe Haven. A place had never been so aptly named.

"Have you ever eaten mold?" Roddie, one of the other counselors, asked me.

"No. At least not knowingly." When he continued to look perplexed, I asked a question I really should've known better than to ask. "Why?"

He shrugged. "I was just wondering how bad it could actually be, ya know? Like, we're told not to eat raw cookie dough, but there's really no reason *not* to."

"Other than salmonella," I said.

"Exactly." He seemed to think we'd arrived at some sort of agreement. I was suddenly questioning Harry's discretion if he allowed this guy to watch over kids.

"I think it's a *better safe than sorry* kind of thing."

"Yeah, you're probably right." He looked almost dejected. "Guess I'll have to skip lunch today."

For fuck's sake. Had he really been about to eat something with mold on it for lunch?

"If you need to run out to buy something, I'm sure we can cover you," I offered.

"Nah, I'm trying to save money for an iguana." He then walked away as if he'd just been part of the most normal conversation ever.

Inez approached me as soon as Roddie walked away. "Was he asking you about drinking creek water?"

Oh my God!

"No, about whether it was safe to eat mold."

She shook her head. "I swear, I don't know how that guy has survived this long." She watched Roddie as he jumped into a game of basketball with a few of the kids. Her gaze was almost affectionate. "He's great with kids, though."

"Yeah," I agreed. "We probably shouldn't let him be in charge of feeding them, though."

She laughed. "True that."

The rest of the day passed as it normally did—some drama, a few tears, lots of crafts, and a ton of sweaty, tired kids. I had to admit, I liked it more than I'd thought I would. There was never a dull moment, and every day brought something different.

Just as they were finishing up afternoon snack, my phone buzzed. It was policy to only look at phones on breaks, but since everyone was occupied, I chanced a quick look. It was a push notification from the Temp Me app—a pharmacy needed a cashier from six to ten.

Even though I knew I should have faced my problems head-on and gone directly home to see how things were with Owen, I found myself jumping at the chance to stay out a bit longer. It wasn't like he could fault me for it. He'd been the one to suggest the app in the first place.

I quickly accepted the job and tucked my phone away. Four hours wouldn't bring in much money, but it was mostly about the experience anyway.

My day at Safe Haven ended, and I had enough time to grab a quick bite to eat as I made my way to the Rosato's Pharmacy. I shoved the last bite of my sandwich into my mouth as I walked in the door and promptly ran into a round-faced, balding man who scowled so hard it gave him a unibrow.

"Sorry," I muttered as I looked up at him.

He didn't return the apology.

"Do you work here?" I asked, noticing his white coat with the pharmacy's name printed on the breast.

"What gave it away?" he asked dryly.

I narrowed my eyes in confusion. "I don't . . . what?"

His scoff said he found me feeble-minded, and I balked at the assumption. But before I could say something snarky in response, he continued.

"I'm assuming you're Veronica? I saw your picture in the app."

If he saw my picture, why would he need to assume who I was?

"Yes, that's me."

"I'm Hugh. This way. You're later than I expected, so we'll have to go through everything in a hurry so I can get back to filling scripts."

I looked down at my watch. "It's ten of six."

He rolled his eyes before he began walking. "Since you've never been here before, I would've thought you'd want to get here early to settle in. I guess that was my mistake."

"I'm coming from my other job."

"I'm sorry. Did I give you the impression that I cared about your life story?"

That was it. "I'm sorry. Did I give *you* the impression that you could speak to me any way you wanted?"

Hugh jerked to a stop but turned slowly around to face me like he was auditioning for a slow-motion contest.

"What did you just say to me?"

"I'm pretty sure you heard me."

Goddamn me and my mouth. This was exactly the kind of encounter Owen had warned me about. But I was pretty sure that I was supposed to maintain my professionalism and try to make it work. Learning to deal with a difficult boss was all part of the process.

But seriously, fuck that noise and fuck this guy.

"Do you really think it's appropriate to speak to your boss in that manner?" he asked.

"You're going to be my boss for four hours." If that, since he'd probably fire me after this. "And you obviously need me more than I need you, or you wouldn't have used the app."

The way his mouth snapped shut let me know I had him there. He stood there glowering at me for a minute.

I sighed and said, "Do you want me to work or leave?"

"What I want and what I need are two very different things at the present moment," he muttered. "This way," he said again as he led the way to the checkout desk at the middle of the store.

He walked me through the basics and told me if I

encountered anything complicated to send the customers back to the pharmacy. He could ring them out from there. He mostly needed me to watch the store and make sure no one shoplifted while he was busy filling prescriptions.

He also looked like he wondered if *I* would shoplift while he was distracted, but he didn't voice it. I considered that progress.

A hotspot the place was not. A couple of people came in to pick up prescriptions, and I'd rung up some random things for three others, and that was it for the first two hours I was there.

Before he'd taken off for his pharmacological kingdom, Hugh had told me there was coffee in the back if I wanted any. And as the long day I'd had caught up with me, I took advantage of the near-constant lull to escape to the back and seek out some caffeine.

I pushed open the swinging door that led to the back and immediately heard voices. Was someone else working in the back? I crept closer because . . . well, I didn't really know why I did. Maybe it was because the voices were hushed and it made my Spidey-senses tingle. Or maybe I just had an overactive imagination.

I scooted along a wall and looked around the corner. Hugh was there with the back door ajar. Someone was outside, but I couldn't see them.

"Same amount as last time?" the voice asked.

"That's what we agreed on, isn't it?" Hugh answered.

I had to admit, it was nice to know he was an equal-opportunity dickhead. Hugh handed over a white prescription bag, and the guy on the other side of the door shook it.

Were those *pills*? Was uptight misanthrope Hugh running pills out of the back of his store? I wouldn't have thought the guy had it in him.

"See ya next week?" the guy asked.

Hugh grunted in what I assumed was assent. He began to let the door close, but the man outside flung his arm out, pushing it wider open.

They said a few more words to each other, but I didn't process them. I was too distracted by realizing I knew the guy outside.

I made my way to the front of the pharmacy, grabbed my things from under the counter, and exited the store, beginning to dial the police as soon as I hit the curb.

And as I explained what I'd just seen to the cops, I cursed my horrible luck. When they asked if I knew the man who Hugh had handed the drugs to, I took a deep breath and debated how to answer. If they asked for an explanation for how I knew him, I wasn't sure what I should say.

But screw it. Selling pot brownies was one thing, but peddling drugs from a pharmacy was another. *I think.* After all, who were the police more likely to believe—the whistleblower or the drug dealer? I told them the name I knew him by.

Fucking Mickey.

OWEN

When Vee had texted that she'd taken a temp job and would be late, I was almost ashamed to admit I was relieved. Since I was naturally a tad awkward, trying *not* to be awkward wasn't a strength. And there was a tension between us that definitely made things feel strained.

So when she walked in before ten p.m., I was surprised.

She plodded into the kitchen and plopped down onto a chair, letting her head fall forward onto the table.

"I'm guessing the job didn't go so well?"

She sighed heavily and lifted her head. "It depends on your definition of well. If you mean *well* like I had a boss with a winning personality who let me go early out of the kindness of his law-abiding heart, then no, tonight didn't go well. But if you define it as getting a crooked pharmacist and a drug dealer off the street, then it went perfectly."

My mouth gaped open, and as I tried to form words, I guessed I looked a lot like a fish out of water.

"I think I need some details," I finally forced out.

She went through what she'd seen and how she'd called the police. "I expected to be in for a long night of questioning," she said. "But it turns out, they were already on to the whole thing and had a guy stationed in the alley watching. So they just took my statement and let me leave."

My body had grown more and more rigid with every passing second of her story.

"You could've been hurt," I said.

She shrugged. "It all worked out."

She was being far too cavalier about the fact that she'd witnessed a crime being committed. I took a deep breath to quell the anxiety I felt at how close she'd been to two potentially dangerous men. I didn't want to be that guy who lectured a woman about being safe, but the thought of something happening to Vee made me feel like I was going to throw up.

"Maybe you shouldn't take any more temp jobs," I said. "This experience alone is enough to make up for any lack of employment history you may have had."

She offered me a small smile. "I agree. Mostly because it's

a pain in the ass and I'm over it."

"Okay then."

She smiled again as she stood. "I think I'm going to head to bed. I'm exhausted." She took the few steps that stood between us and lifted onto her toes to press a chaste kiss to my cheek. "Thanks for being worried about me."

I turned my head slightly, bringing our faces inches from each other. There were a million things I wanted to say, but my throat felt thick with them. She'd made it clear where she stood, and dumping my feelings between us would only cause the distance there to grow. Instead, I said the simplest truth I could.

"Always."

It felt like both too much and not enough all at once.

Chapter Twenty

OWEN

Vee and I had been looking forward to spending some time with our friends, so when we received a text from Taylor inviting us to a game night with the Scooby Gang, we were quick to say yes. But when the door to Brody's apartment swung open to reveal him wild-eyed, I worried we'd made a miscalculation.

He stared at us for a moment before grabbing Vee's wrist and gently tugging her inside. "I need a smart person."

I wanted to be miffed that he'd left me—an evidently *un*smart person—standing in the hall as he dragged Vee inside, but it was Brody, so being offended seemed fruitless.

When I entered the living room, everyone was gathered around the coffee table yelling at each other.

"You can't call dibs on teammates," Sophia yelled at her brother.

"I can because I *did*."

"You haven't done anything because we haven't made teams yet."

"I've made my team." Brody gestured to Vee, Xander, Toby, and Ransom, who all sat on his side of the coffee table that appeared to be the metaphorical line in the sand. "You're just mad you're not on it."

Sophia scoffed. "Like I'd want to be on your team."

"You clearly do since you're arguing with me about it."

"That's because you took all the smart people!"

Sophia looked like she hadn't meant to say that out loud as a chorus of affronted "heys" erupted.

"That was mean, Sophia," Brody chastised in the most patronizing way possible. "Besides, it's not even true." The offended people looked like they'd been avenged until Brody added, "I left you Taylor."

Drew threw his hands up. "This game night was a blast," he said dryly. "We should do it again sometime. Not." He started to stand, but Sophia grabbed his arm and pulled him back down.

"I'll even give you guys the extra player," Brody offered.

Everyone's eyes swung to me, and it was clear no one felt I was a valuable offering.

"I'd just like to address," Aamee said as she sat forward on the couch, "how my own boyfriend didn't pick me for his team."

"I picked you for life," Brody countered. "Isn't that enough?"

"Not really."

Brody sat down beside Aamee and took her hand. "It's not that I don't want you—"

"That's actually exactly what it is. You literally grabbed the people you wanted as soon as they walked in. And yet, here I am, totally ungrabbed."

"I just assumed that since you *live* here, you being on my team would go without saying," Brody hedged.

"Cut the bullshit, Mason." The glare Aamee aimed at Brody would've made the testicles fall right off a weaker man.

"Okay, fine, I don't want you on my team. You're a little . . . intense, and I don't think that's cohesive to the game night domination I'm going for."

Aamee stared at Brody for a pregnant second before turning to Sophia. "Let's show them what happens when you piss off a Zeta."

Sophia smirked. "Let's."

"What's a Zeta?" I asked, causing everyone to look over at me again.

Aamee looked disgusted by the question. She turned to Brody. "You can have Owen."

"It was their lame-ass sorority," Carter answered. "You remember, Owen. We filled all their bathtubs with bubbles the year you pledged."

"That was you assholes?" Aamee seethed.

"Of course. Who else would it have been?"

"You swore to me it wasn't you."

Carter scoffed. "There ended up being like a thousand dollars in damages after some of the pledges got too carried away filling up the tubs. No way was I copping to that."

"So you lied right to my face?"

"Yes." Carter responded as if Aamee was the one who'd made the error by expecting more from him.

She sat back and crossed her arms over her chest. "They can have Carter too."

"Sweet. He was next on my list," Brody said. To his team, he added, "He'll know all the sports questions."

"If they're taking Carter, then we need to keep Owen," Taylor said.

No one looked thrilled at this prospect, which would've bothered me more if I hadn't been used to being underestimated.

Vee, however, looked as angry as I've ever seen her. "Why are we only having two teams? Six and five are too big. We should split into three."

Brody's eyes widened in panic. "No, that does not work with my plan."

Vee stood up and walked over to stand beside me. "Well, your plan doesn't work for me. I want to be on Owen's team."

Xander raised his hand. "I wanna be on Team Owen too."

At that, Brody looked downright alarmed. "You can't both go!"

"Sure we can," Xander said as he joined Vee and me. "We'll even be the team of three."

It looked like everyone wanted to argue but couldn't think of a good enough reason to object, so they set about divvying up the remaining players. Toby stayed with Brody, and Carter joined them. Aamee and Sophia were still going on about their sorority, so they stayed together and absorbed Taylor into their team.

Everyone eyed Ransom and Drew. Drew sighed and withdrew a coin from his pocket. "Loser goes to the girls team."

A sound of outrage flared around us, but the two men ignored it.

Drew flicked the coin into the air and said, "Call it."

"Tails."

Drew caught the coin and smiled. "Heads."

Ransom looked less than thrilled.

"You know what?" Aamee said. "We'll be the team of three. Go on Team Owen. We don't need you."

Sophia and Taylor looked like they wanted to object, but Ransom had already perked up and hurried over to us.

"What are we playing first?" Toby asked as we all settled in with our teams.

"Trivia Wars," Sophia said as she opened the box and began to unpack the materials. She handed the directions to Taylor, who read through them. It was fairly straightforward and was a cross between Trivial Pursuit and Jeopardy. It even came with buzzers that showed who had rung in first.

"Okay, I'll read the first card," Sophia said. "What is the anatomical name for the external portion of the female genitalia?"

"Whoa!" Drew yelled.

"What the hell kind of game is this?" Brody asked.

Everyone else looked shocked except for Toby, who frankly looked a bit terrified.

I pressed the buzzer, and everyone slowly panned their heads toward me. Hesitating a second to make sure I was being recognized for pressing the button first, I said, "The vulva."

"That's . . . yeah, that's right," Sophia said.

"Dude, how'd you know that?" Carter asked, awe in his voice.

I wanted to argue that everyone in that room should know that because it was basic human anatomy but realized that would likely cause more arguing and there'd been enough of that already.

"I told you I was thinking of becoming a midwife," I explained instead. "Knowing female anatomy is kind of a must for that."

Brody reached over and gave me a hearty slap on the shoulder. "Bet that makes you real popular with the ladies, huh?"

I furrowed my brow. "It doesn't usually come up." What kind of weird conversations did he have with women?

"Can we read the next question?" Aamee snapped.

"Okay, okay," Sophia said. "This Latin phrase meaning *of unsound mind* is often—"

Vee's hand moved so fast it was almost a blur. "Non compos mentis."

Sophia sighed. "Yeah."

Aamee glared at Taylor. "What are you even on this team for if you're not going to get the legal questions?"

"She's going to law school too," Taylor defended.

"Are you going to complain about every question, or can we keep this moving?" Drew asked.

The slaughter that ensued would've been sad if it hadn't felt so wholly just. Between Vee, Xander, and I, we knew a wide cross section of information that was perfect for trivia. We didn't get every question, but our victory was decisive.

What felt even better was the fact that I hadn't been carried by my team. I'd buzzed in just as often as they had. Maybe even more since I had a larger well of useless trivia knowledge taking up space in my brain.

And when someone suggested Pictionary next, my confidence was further bolstered. I'd spent years dodging academic electives in favor of escaping to the art room in high school. Looked like tonight was going to be my night.

VERONICA

Watching Owen dominate game night was one of the hottest experiences in my recent memory. There was no one thing that turned me on. It was the way he was almost unassuming about his intelligence. He didn't gloat or excessively celebrate but rather quietly voiced his answers with the steady confidence of a man who knew he was right but didn't really seem to feel a need to prove it. He was also a profoundly supportive teammate, appearing to be impressed by the things we knew while not dwelling on the things we got wrong.

But the sexiest thing about all of it was the way he shoved victory after victory down the throats of everyone else in the room. Whether he was answering questions about ancient philosophers or drawing pictures of time machines that could've appeared in graphic novels, Owen *owned* game night.

And when we all lost our competitive steam and lazed around playing Truth or Dare, Owen also solidified himself as perhaps the most honest person who'd ever lived.

"My most embarrassing moment was probably when my grandmom Jimi walked in on me masturbating. Not so much because I was doing it—because it's healthy to explore our bodies—but because she slammed the door closed and then proceeded to talk to me through it from the hallway. She told me to continue what I was doing because it was my room and I was entitled to my privacy, but she just needed to know if I'd seen where she'd left the little wooden box where she kept her weed." Owen hesitated a moment before continuing. "It was also my most shameful moment because I told her no, even though it was sitting on my bedside table because I'd just smoked some of it."

Everyone was slack jawed for a second.

Xander recovered first. "Did you come clean about the weed?"

Owen sighed. "Yeah. I was able to lie to her through the door, but once I came out, she cornered me and shined a flashlight in my eyes as she interrogated me like some type of seventies crime drama. I couldn't withstand that type of scrutiny."

"How old were you?" Ransom asked through laughter.

"Oh, it just happened last time I was home."

I watched Ransom's face morph from pure enjoyment to something that resembled complete horror. He and Taylor exchanged glances, her expression mirroring Ransom's.

"Was that . . . when we were with you?"

Owen didn't need to answer verbally. His smirk said it all.

We all locked eyes with each other and burst into uncontrollable laughter.

"Dude," Brody said. "Who hasn't learned to lock their door by the time they're in their midtwenties?"

Owen huffed. "My door at home doesn't have a lock."

"Why not?" Toby asked.

Owen hesitated, which made us all immediately take notice. The guy had admitted his grandma had walked in on him jerking off. What could possibly give him pause after admitting that?

"It just doesn't have one," he said, his eyes darting toward the wall. "That's a really cool picture."

My poor Owen, the worst liar who ever lied.

Xander's eyes lit up. "Now you gotta tell us."

"Tell you what?" Owen said, his voice infused with so much innocence it made us all immediately suspicious.

"Come on, Owen," Aamee wheedled. "Why don't you have a lock on your door?"

He rolled his eyes. "There's no good story here."

"We'd like to be the judge of that," Sophia said.

Owen rolled his eyes again as his whole body slumped. "My dad took the lock off after I locked myself in my room and couldn't get out."

That was ... disappointing.

"Oh," Carter said. "That's ... not as good of a story as I was expecting."

"There's more," Ransom said. His shrewd eyes narrowed on Owen. "There's something else he's not saying."

We all looked expectantly back at Owen, hoping Ransom was right.

Owen sighed heavily, and I almost felt bad for participating in this mob that was determined to wrench a secret from him that he clearly didn't want to share. But at this point, I *had* to know.

"Fine, it didn't only happen once," Owen said.

"How many times did it happen?"

"I dunno, maybe like ... six."

"You locked yourself in your room and couldn't get out six times?" Drew asked, his voice loud and full of incredulity. "How is that even possible?"

"Why would you keep locking it if it was broken?" Taylor asked.

"I didn't lock it."

"Then how did you get locked in?" Toby said.

"Did your parents turn the knob around so it locked from the outside?" Xander asked.

We all looked at him, and he became defensive under our collective gaze.

"What?"

"We're going to have another chat about your childhood," Drew said to him.

Xander turned his eyes skyward before focusing back on Owen. "How did you get stuck in the room if you weren't the one locking the door?"

He shrugged. "It was just broken. It would lock on its own for no reason."

"How would that happen?" Taylor asked. "Don't most bedroom door locks either twist or push in? How could that happen on its own?"

"It just did. My family thinks my room was haunted, but—"

"Your family thinks their house is haunted?" Toby asked, excitement clear in his voice.

Owen nodded. "Only my room, but yeah."

Carter looked confused. "But didn't you say once that you don't believe in ghosts?"

"I don't. But I said I *do* believe in poltergeists. And since whatever entity lives in my room threw me out of my bedroom window, I'm fairly certain he, or she, qualifies as a poltergeist."

"What's the difference?" Aamee asked as I squawked, "You were thrown out of your window?"

Guess we had very different priorities in the conversation.

He looked over at me but answered Aamee first. "There are actually a lot of differences, but basically a ghost is the spirit of a deceased human being while a poltergeist is a malevolent energy. We can, theoretically, if you were to believe in such things, see a ghost, but they can't touch you. Poltergeists are globs of negative energy that create physical disturbances. They can't be seen, but they can move things and hurt people."

"So a poltergeist isn't a type of ghost?" Toby asked.

Owen looked almost offended. "Definitely not."

It looked like Toby wanted to inquire further, but I cut in first. "Get back to being thrown out your window."

"Poltergeist activity usually ebbs and flows, so I stupidly let my guard down. I had gotten rid of some things that I thought might have attracted the poltergeist, and when nothing happened, I relaxed. Then one day, my door locked again. My family was out for the day, so I decided to climb out my bedroom window so I could use the trellis to get to the ground. But as I leaned out the window, I felt something push me and went flying. I was lucky I only broke my arm."

"Jesus," I muttered.

"I'm pretty sure *He* wasn't there that day," Owen said dryly.

"That's exactly what happened to Bran on *Game of Thrones*," Brody said.

"Yes!" Xander said, sounding almost excited at the connection. "Do you have any incestuous kin who may benefit from your premature demise?"

After giving Xander and Brody a scathing look, Taylor turned to Owen. "Don't you think it's possible you just . . . lost your footing and fell?"

"Anything is possible." Owen glanced at Xander. "Well, *almost* anything. And I don't want to discount the possibility that I manifested the feeling of being pushed, but considering I wasn't even halfway out the window when it happened, I doubt I would've fallen if something hadn't pushed me."

Everyone began to clamor about Owen's story as I sat there and processed what he'd said. For a reason that wasn't logical, I felt like I'd experienced a loss. Even though Owen was sitting right beside me, I thought about how different my life would be if he weren't. The feeling was dark and oppressive and sad—probably the exact kinds of things that would fuel a poltergeist.

"You could've died." The words filtered through my ears and lodged in my brain in a way that seemed to make them stick there.

All the decisions I'd made, the rules I'd put in place about what Owen's and my relationship could be and what it couldn't, had been predicated on the fact that I didn't want to lose Owen.

But I could lose him at any time. I could've lost him before I even knew him. I'd been depriving us both, listing all the things that *couldn't* happen because I was afraid to confront what could. And what could happen was that I could fall head over heels in love with Owen, only for him not to feel the same. For him to move on. For him to leave.

But what if we tried...and he stayed.

"Vee?" I felt a tentative hand on my back, rubbing light, soothing circles.

I looked over to see Owen's concerned face.

"Are you okay?" he asked.

As my gaze focused on him, I was filled with so much want, I thought I'd burst with it if I didn't get it out. Figuring there was no time like the present, I said the thing I wanted most at that moment.

"Can we go home?"

Chapter Twenty-One

VERONICA

I hadn't thought much beyond asking to leave, which was an oversight on my part because Owen peppered me with questions the entire drive back to the house.

"Is your stomach upset? Tell me if you need to pull over."

I was sitting there thinking about macking on Owen, and he was asking if I needed to vomit. What a pair we were.

"I'm fine. I promise."

A better person would've put him out of his misery, but I was trying to get my thoughts in order while also worrying that Owen would crash if I told him I wanted to amend our arrangement. It was best to wait until neither of us was operating heavy machinery.

We finally pulled up to the house, and Owen immediately turned off the ignition and jumped out of the truck, hurrying around to my door and pulling it open. He extended a hand toward me as if I was some Victorian maiden dismounting from my trusty steed.

I looked at him curiously as I took his hand.

But instead of him holding mine as I climbed out of the truck, he slid it to his shoulder and then basically lifted me out. He placed me gingerly on the ground before he reached around me to close the door. When that was done, he slid a hand around my waist as if he was going to assist me inside. Owen began to move toward the front door, but I remained rooted in place.

"I'm not dying," I said as I looked up at him.

His eyes widened comically. "Why would you say that?"

I shrugged. "You're kind of acting like I'm dying."

"I'm being a gentleman."

"By carrying me inside?"

"I'm not carrying. I'm . . . supporting."

I smiled. Part of me wanted to balk that I could walk on my own accord, but the truth was, I liked having Owen close. I liked knowing I could depend on him. I liked . . . everything about him, really.

"Thank you."

He returned my smile, seemingly thrilled by my easy acceptance of his help. He wrapped his arm around me tighter, and I let myself lean on him.

When we made it inside, Gimli trotted over for some scratches as we took off our shoes. Then, Owen turned to me, looking a little uncomfortable.

"Are you sure you're okay?"

"Yeah. But I would like to talk to you. If you have time."

"Absolutely, yeah, I have time. Should we go to the living room? Or do you want a snack? We can talk in the kitchen." He seemed so nervous, and while I had no idea why, I still found it cute as hell.

"The living room is great."

We went in and settled on the couch, Owen still looking a bit anxious. I wanted to set him at ease, but I wasn't sure how to begin. I'd racked my brain the entire ride home and still had no idea how to ask for what I wanted.

"You're not moving out, are you?" Owen finally asked.

"Huh?" Where the hell had he gotten that from?

"You went quiet after the poltergeist thing. Was it too weird? I get that it's not a very . . . logical belief. I won't mention it again if it bothered you."

I wondered how often Owen had compromised who he was to make other people more comfortable. The thought made me angry. Owen had a right to believe whatever the hell he believed without needing to make himself more palatable to the people around him.

"I didn't get quiet because of that. Well, it maybe kind of was because of that, but not for the reason—"

"This can be a rage-fueled-entity-free zone. I won't mention it again."

"No, that's not—"

"Or if you're worried it followed me here, I can assure you, I haven't felt its energy at all."

"It's really—"

"But we could cleanse the house if it would make you feel better. I think it'd be hard to get a priest in to bless the place, but I bet I could find a paranormal expert to come in and do an energetic detox."

"I . . . I don't know what to say."

He put a hand on my shoulder. "You don't have to say anything. I'm sorry I scared you with my story."

"I'm not scared."

For some reason, that made him appear even more

crestfallen. "Oh. So you're just creeped out. Can we just forget I ever said anything? Because I don't want—"

"Owen, I wanted to leave so I could kiss you."

His words cut off abruptly at my admission. It wasn't how I'd wanted to broach the topic, but his self-deprecating rambling had to end. He hadn't done anything wrong, and I couldn't let him suffer any longer, no matter how unprepared I was for the conversation.

"Could you..." he started before he stopped to clear his throat. "I think I heard you incorrectly."

"Sorry, that was... abrupt. But it's true. I wanted to come home because I wanted to kiss you. And hug you. And maybe do some other things."

"Other things?"

"Yeah, you know, like, sexy things."

His lips parted in an O before he spoke again. "So, like, ghosts turn you on?"

I couldn't help it. I had to laugh. "No, *you* turn me on. And when you told the story about falling out your window, I thought about how you could've gotten hurt so much worse. And it made me not want to waste any more time ignoring how I feel about you."

"And how do you feel about me?"

I mock-glared at him. "Are you fishing for compliments?"

He smiled. "Honestly, I'm kind of worried I'm dreaming, so I just want to be very clear about what you're saying."

I slid closer to him on the couch, bringing my face almost close enough to kiss him. "I want you, Owen. I have for a while. And I'm tired of fighting it."

"Well, I am a pacifist, so..."

"So what are you waiting for? Kiss me."

The air between us grew thick with unvoiced wants and potent possibilities. Neither of us moved for what felt like an eternity but was likely only a few seconds. And then, just as I thought he didn't want the same things I did, he leaned in and brushed our lips together.

The kiss was soft and tentative and benign.

And then it grew into something much, much more.

OWEN

Kissing Vee had been beyond anything I'd ever experienced. There was a synchronicity that I hadn't even known was possible. It was in the way our mouths moved together, the way our bodies pressed close, the way neither of us rushed to take it beyond kissing and grinding together.

I tried not to undersell myself. I knew what some people's opinions of me were, and I'd worked hard not to let those things define me or impact who I knew myself to be. But there was no denying that Vee was out of my league. A law student who'd graduate with high honors did not seem to belong with a somewhat directionless kid who couldn't even get out of undergrad because he couldn't decide what he wanted his future to be.

But here, as we made out on the couch, we worked. We fit together like two puzzle pieces whose edges miraculously and unexpectedly snapped together.

I wasn't sure who pulled back first, but eventually our kisses slowed, and we cuddled up on the couch, my arm under her head as she traced patterns on the patch of stomach that had been exposed when my shirt had been rucked up.

"I want to go talk to June," she said quietly.

My body tensed from the abrupt words.

Likely feeling my reaction, she continued. "I know we already talked about going, but we haven't, and I don't want it to become one of those things we say we'll do but never actually follow through with."

"Okay," I replied because I'd likely give her anything. Not that I had any issues going to talk to June. I'd thought that had always been the plan, but Vee was right. It would've been easy to push off until it was forgotten.

Vee turned so she could look up at me and smiled. "This probably makes me a bad person, but I really like how you always agree with me."

I chuckled. "Is that why you like me?" I'd meant the words teasingly, but the way her face immediately grew serious, it was obvious my insecurity had bled through my words.

"No," she said sternly. "I like a lot of things about you. You're funny and sweet and kind and giving. Maybe too giving at times. But you'd never give something if it compromised your morals. You have such strong beliefs in things, and it's admirable how hard you'll fight for and stand by those things."

I pressed a kiss to her head because I wasn't sure what to say. I didn't think anyone outside my family had ever seen me that way.

"Is it trite if I list all the things I like about you now?" I asked, my voice teasing as I tried to lighten the mood.

She giggled and settled back against me. "Maybe, but you can do it anyway."

So I did. I waxed poetic about all the ways she was maybe not perfect in life but perfect to me. I didn't express that exact sentiment aloud, but I hoped she heard it anyway. Whatever had started between us, I wanted it to continue to grow. To build in ways that wove us together in a future that could belong to us both.

And a good beginning for that journey was to find out more about June.

Chapter Twenty-Two

OWEN

"Are you sure this is the best idea?" Vee leaned over to me as we waited in line at Milton's.

I probably hadn't been in the café in over a year —for no particular reason, really. But now I had a reason to go.

"Yeah. Well, maybe not, but it's *an* idea, and it's the only one I currently have. Why? Can you think of another way to contact her?"

"We could go knock on her door without warning. Like Stabler and Benson."

"Who?" I asked.

"The detectives from *Law & Order: SVU.*"

"Oh. I've never seen it, but I know who you mean. Can't we pick people a little younger than those two?"

"Ooh," Vee said, swaying a little as she moved up in line. "Do I detect a little ageism happening here?"

"I'm not . . . ageist," I said with a laugh. "But if we're gonna compare ourselves to TV detectives, I think we should choose ones that more closely resemble us."

"Who'd you have in mind?"

I thought for a moment. "Actually no one. Deciding I didn't want to be Stabler was as far as I got with my casting." Leaning a little closer to Vee, I asked, "Do you know what you want to get?"

"Well, I feel like I *have* to try the cheese danishes since you said how good they were. And I'll probably get an oat milk latte."

"Is it weird to you that they call liquid from plants milk? It's not like they have nipples. I don't even know how they get this so-called milk. Like there's almond milk and oat milk, cashew milk, sesame milk..." I thought for a moment. "Even hemp milk and banana milk, which I actually want to try because it sounds delicious and—"

"Okay, Bubba. Calm down."

"Nice," I said with a nod of approval. "A Forrest Gump reference. That one I like."

We approached the counter to order a few seconds later and were greeted by a petite girl with a septum piercing, a name tag that said *Serafina*, and a warm smile.

"Welcome to Milton's. What can I get started for you today?" she asked, the smile never fading from her face. She seemed genuinely happy to be here.

"I think we'll have three, actually make that *four* cheese danishes."

I could feel Vee's eyes on me.

"I'm hungry," I said with a shrug.

"You eat like a stray puppy." Then she squeezed my side in a way that made me giggle like a toddler getting tickled.

"Do you know of a lot of stray animals that find discarded fresh baked goods?"

Vee stared at me but didn't counter verbally.

Serafina looked back and forth between the two of us. "Is that all for today?"

"Oh, no, sorry," I said. "I'll have a matcha latte and..." I gestured to Vee.

"And I'll have a medium iced latte with oat milk. No sugar, please."

"Perfect, we'll have that right out for you. Can I have a name for the order?"

I gave Serafina my name, handed her enough cash to cover our order, and then dropped a couple of bucks into the tip cup once she gave me my change. I typically wasn't a fan of carrying cash because it also meant possibly carrying millions of microorganisms that could cause a whole host of sicknesses. But since some of the people who'd purchased items from us on Facebook Marketplace had paid in cash, I'd been using it more frequently.

"I was thinking we might be able to find their address if we look," Vee said to me as we made our way to the end of the counter to wait for our order.

"What makes you think that?"

Chances were pretty good that June and Milt were either dead or in some sort of assisted-living facility. I of course hoped for the latter, but we wouldn't know for sure without asking around here.

"I don't know, but we'll need to find it if we want to include it in our true crime podcast."

Thankfully I could tell Vee was kidding. At least about it being true crime. But I was willing to bet that if I agreed to the podcast thing, she'd have mics for both of us by tonight.

"How about we use that as our Plan B," I suggested.

"Doesn't work," a voice said from behind the din of the espresso machine.

Standing up a little taller, I craned my neck to see who had spoken. A moment later, a square-jawed, shaggy-haired guy peeked out at us, though most of his body remained behind the machine so he could finish whatever drink he was making.

"I'm sorry?" I said.

"Plan B. It's bullshit. My ex got that three years ago, and now I have a toddler and an obligation to pay child support."

What the fuck?

"Oh," Vee said. "Oh, we weren't... Not that kind of Plan B," she clarified. "We were actually talking about a real Plan B. Like a backup plan for when the first plan doesn't work out."

Did this dumblefuck actually believe we were discussing birth-control options in a public café?

"Hey, listen, I'm the last person to judge. Just thought I'd warn you it might not work." Then he pulled the metal cup from the machine, poured it into a mug and headed over to a nearby table to drop off the drink to a man on a laptop.

Vee and I exchanged wide-eyed glances at each other but didn't comment any further. A moment later, Serafina came over holding the box of danishes. She handed them to me and then told us our drinks would be right up.

"Take your time," I told her, relieved that I wouldn't have to interact with Plan B Guy again.

Serafina didn't waste any time, and our drinks were up quickly. "Sorry about the wait. We're short-staffed today."

"Oh, no worries," Vee said. "We're not in a rush."

Serafina smiled again. "Can I get you some plates and napkins? Are you eating here or taking it to go? I should've asked you when you ordered. I've been a little scattered today," she said with a self-deprecating smile.

"Plates and napkins would be great," I said.

She reached below the counter and grabbed two plates then placed napkins and two forks on top and handed them to me.

"Thank you," I said, noticing there wasn't anyone in line at the counter. "Um, I know you're probably busy, but I wanted to ask you a question if you have a moment."

Her dark eyebrows pressed together curiously. "Sure. I have a sec."

"I'm Owen. And this is Vee." He nodded in my direction. "We live in the area and were wondering about the former owners. June specifically. Does she happen to come in anymore?" I didn't even know if she was still alive, and that would make for an awkward answer if Serafina had to tell us she doesn't come in . . . because she's dead.

"She doesn't anymore. Hasn't been coming in for at least a year."

"Oh, okay." She didn't mention her death, so that was a good sign. "I haven't been in here in a couple years, but I remember June used to make the danishes herself every day."

"She did," Serafina said with a smile. "I didn't work here then, but I used to come in after school a lot to see her. Now my dad makes them. He learned from her, but they don't live up to Nana's, if you ask me."

"Oh wow, so June is your grandmother, then?"

"Great-grandmother," she corrected me.

That made sense if I'd thought about the math. Serafina couldn't be more than twenty, and June had to be close to ninety, give or take, based on what David had told us.

"Would you mind giving her a message for us?" Vee said.

It hadn't been how we'd planned on making contact with June, but maybe *that* would be our Plan B. "We were hoping to talk to her about something if possible."

Serafina seemed to sense the importance of our request because she stopped restocking the bagels a man had brought out from the kitchen. I wondered if he was her father. She turned to face us and crossed her arms in front of her, though not in a way that felt angry.

"Is everything okay?"

"Yes, fine," I was quick to assure her. "I was just hoping to run into her here, and I don't have her contact information or anything, so we figured giving you a message to pass along might be the best option."

"Sure," Serafina said. "I can give it to her next time I see her. Should be sometime this weekend."

"Great. We appreciate it," Vee said. Then she went into her bag and pulled out a small notebook that had a pen clipped to it. She jotted down a note along with our numbers and her email address and then handed the small piece of paper to Serafina.

"Thanks so much," I said as Serafina looked quickly at the paper.

The fact that she didn't ask questions about anything led me to believe that Vee hadn't written anything odd or cryptic on it.

Serafina assured us she would relay the message to her great-grandmother. Then she told us to enjoy our danishes and drinks before returning to her place at the register to help the couple who'd just approached the counter.

VERONICA

"Where do you want these?" Owen asked as I moved around the front yard, slapping different color stickers on items.

I turned around to see him holding a large tray with piles of dishes from Minnie's china closet on it.

"You know, you'd make a better server than I did," I told him.

"Gimli would make a better server than you," he said, earning him a slap, though I made sure it was light enough that he didn't drop anything.

"Where should I put this? My hand's beginning to lose feeling."

"Oh, sorry." Glancing around at the setup so far, I tried to find a place that would make the most sense and also have room for everything Owen had brought out. "I guess you can put them over on the buffet table."

"What happens if we sell the table before we sell the stuff *on* it?" he asked after putting the tray down carefully. He began unloading the dishes and stacking them into neat piles.

"I have some blankets I can set down on the grass if we need other places to put things. They're right on the front porch. I'll get them at some point."

The yard sale wasn't set to officially begin until another half hour or so, so when I saw a car pull up and park across the street, I wasn't sure if it was someone visiting the neighbor or if it was an early shopper hoping to get the jump on some of the more desirable items.

"I'll grab 'em when I come back out. I'm gonna go up to get

the rest of the stuff from the extra bedroom."

I watched Owen jog up the front steps, his shorts fitting perfectly around his strong thighs and ass. When I turned back toward the car that had pulled up, I saw Inez and Roddie get out.

"Hey," I said, the word sounding more like a question than an enthusiastic greeting. "What are you guys doing here?"

"We're here for the flea market," Roddie said. He pulled his aviators up onto his head and jogged around to the passenger's side to cross the street with Inez. "Taylor told us you guys were selling a ton of shit."

I hoped what we had wasn't something people thought of as shit.

"It's more of a yard sale than a flea market."

"What's the difference?" Roddie asked.

Was he serious?

"A flea market has a bunch of different vendors, and people sell more than just used items. They have crafts and food and all sorts of stuff."

"Oh, yeah, I've been to those," Roddie said with more excitement than the realization called for. "I bought a tooth from one of those dinosaur sharks from one a few years ago."

"There was a dinosaur selling teeth?" Inez joked.

Despite his strange phrasing, I knew what Roddie meant, but like Inez, I couldn't help but picture an abnormally large prehistoric shark "standing" behind a table filled with teeth.

Roddie looked at Inez like he wasn't sure how to answer. "Dinosaurs haven't been around for a long time" was his only explanation for why Inez's interpretation wouldn't be possible. "This dude scuba dives for sharks' teeth for a living!" Roddie explained. "He said sometimes he finds small ones worth a few bucks and other times he finds some worth thousands."

I hadn't even realized that Owen had come out of the house until he was beside me again and said, "I know that dude!"

The chances of Owen having met the same dinosaur shark-tooth guy as Roddie seemed slim, but having *two* such men in the area seemed even less likely.

"I'm Owen," he said, holding out a hand to shake Roddie's.

Something told me these two would be fast friends before long.

"Roddie. I work with Vee at Safe Haven. Great to meet ya, man. Vee's told us a lot about you."

Had I? I'd maybe mentioned him a few times in conversation, maybe a little more, but all kinds of topics and people came up when we were trying to pass the time there.

"Well, she clearly hasn't mentioned my shark tooth collection," Owen said with a wink toward me that caused me to redden even further.

"And I'm Inez. Also from Safe Haven."

"Nice to meet you as well," Owen said. "I think some of our other friends are stopping by too, but I don't know that there's anything here you'd want to buy. Unless you're into doll collections or glass elephants."

"You had me at doll collections," Roddie said, his eyes lighting up as he seemed to spot the doll table. He was gone within a few seconds.

"That was . . . odd," Owen said. Which was pretty telling coming from Owen.

"Not for Roddie," Inez said. Then she headed over to where he was already examining a porcelain doll with a purple bow in her hair.

"Inez seems nice," Owen said. "I'm surprised Taylor and Ransom never mentioned her."

"Oh, yeah, I don't know if she's ever hung out with them. Taylor said Inez was pretty quiet when she first started in the winter, but I think she's opened up a little more because she's never seemed shy around me."

Owen put his arm around me and pulled me in close. "That's because everyone loves you." He planted a kiss to the top of my head as we walked toward the house again.

I tried not to focus on his choice of words, but how could I not? He'd said everyone loved me, which presumably meant him too, though he obviously hadn't meant it like that. But that didn't change the fact that I liked the way it sounded coming from him.

"Thanks," I said. "Everyone loves you too."

We both continued getting ready for the yard sale, and neither of us said anything else about which people loved the other or why. I wasn't sure if that made the moment more weird or less, but I guessed it didn't matter now.

Owen finished setting up the last table while I taped the QR codes I'd printed to some of the tables to make for easy payment. I'd decided at the last minute to take Owen's suggestion and allow people to pay in cash too. I'd originally figured it would be easier to not worry about change or keeping track of actual money, but he was right that many people probably wouldn't plan to pay electronically, especially a lot of the older crowd.

So I'd gone inside to hunt around for whatever cash I'd put away from some of the Marketplace sales. After searching through my things, I found a small clutch for myself and a thin travel makeup pouch that I could give to Owen to have as well.

I split up the money—some dollars and change for each of us—and placed it into the clutch and makeup bag.

I didn't think I'd been gone very long, but by the time I got back outside, I was greeted by some of our usual crew. Sophia, Drew, his younger brother, Cody, who I hadn't seen lately, and Xander and Aniyah, who'd come down for a visit.

"I can sell blood to a doctor," Cody announced proudly. "Where do you want me?"

All of us looked at him strangely.

"What does that mean?" Drew asked.

Cody let out a small laugh like he couldn't believe his brother didn't understand the reference. "Doctors are around blood all the time."

"So?"

"So why would they buy it?"

"I don't know," Drew said. "Why would *anyone* buy blood?"

"That's the point, dummy."

"But you specifically referenced doctors."

"Because they have easy access to blood," Cody said slowly, like his older brother was incapable of understanding the metaphor simply because of the speed of his explanation. "So if they wanted it, they could just steal it." With a shake of his head, he laughed again and pointed a thumb in Drew's direction. "Can someone please explain this to him?"

Drew sighed loudly, presumably because he'd decided to give up on his line of questioning, and asked, "How can we help?"

Owen looked around at the yard, which held everything from essential everyday items to unique collectibles that only a small portion of the population would even take a look at.

"I don't know," he said. "There isn't much to do. I guess we'll play it by ear and see what the turnout's like. Thanks for coming out."

"Of course," Xander said. "We're happy to help. And also, rumor has it you have a telescope here somewhere?" His eyes searched the yard behind us as he spoke.

I noticed Aniyah roll her eyes like it wasn't the first she'd heard about the telescope.

"It's over by the table of books." I nodded toward it, and Xander's eyes lit up.

He grabbed Aniyah's hand. "Come on," he said, already leading her toward the telescope.

The morning passed quickly, with people coming and going, and we'd sold a good amount of the little items and some of the larger ones. Our friends helped by carrying purchases to people's cars, wrapping some of the more fragile items, and directing people to the QR codes if they wanted to pay through an app.

By lunchtime, we were all famished.

"You want me to order some pizzas or something?" Xander asked.

"We always get pizza," Drew practically whined.

I didn't think I'd see the day when any of our crew, especially Drew, would get sick of pizza, but there was a first time for everything.

"Okay," Cody said. "What about sandwiches? Or Chinese? Or there's this little Greek place right on Seventh Street that lets you pick four spreads if you order the warm pitas." Cody's eyes closed as he seemed to daydream about the spreads. "I'll actually get whatever you guys want because I'll eat anything."

"That's shocking," Drew deadpanned.

The group began debating what to order, but Owen had remained noticeably quiet. Until he wasn't.

"I think I have a better idea," he said before looking toward the house. "Cody, Xander, and Aniyah, can I borrow you for a couple of minutes?"

They nodded hesitantly and uttered their "sures" and "okays" before following Owen inside. A few more customers purchased some things before the guys returned. Cody and Owen were carrying the grill from the backyard, and Aniyah and Xander had their arms full of condiments: mustard, ketchup, barbecue sauce, and spices, among other things.

Xander handed Drew a list he'd made. "Can you run to the store and grab these things as quickly as you can?"

Drew took a cursory glance at the list. "You got it." Then he headed to his car with Ransom beside him.

"What are you doing?" I asked Owen. "Where did you get all that?"

They'd just set down a cooler filled with frozen hot dogs and hamburgers.

"I always keep extra easy dinners in the basement freezer," he answered. He leaned down to turn on the propane.

"Enough for an impending apocalypse?" I asked.

"Maybe." He smiled as he fired up the burners. "Or a lunchtime yard sale."

An hour or so later, we had a full spread of burgers, dogs, grilled chicken, baked beans, and some other easy and inexpensive sides like chips that Drew had picked up when he'd gone out for the other things Xander had requested.

Inez and I had put out a salad and filled a cooler with sodas and waters. And Sophia had made several pitchers of sangria. Eventually, someone brought out some speakers so we could play music.

Not only did we get to meet some of the neighbors we hadn't spoken to until now, but we managed to make a ton of extra money selling plates of food and drinks once the word was out on social media.

When it was all said and done, Owen and I had brought in well over a thousand dollars and gotten to hang out with our friends on a beautiful summer day. We were fucking exhausted.

"You were pretty impressive out there today," I said to Owen as I lay beside him in his bed, watching some movie I was sure neither one of us was actually paying attention to. "The food was a great idea."

"I have my moments," he joked before pressing a chaste kiss to my head and pulling me closer to him. "You were pretty great yourself. I wouldn't have been able to even organize the thing to begin with without you."

"So you're the fun one, and I'm like the Type A boring planner."

"Yeah," Owen said with a laugh. "I think we complement each other well, though, don't you?"

"Mm-hmm," I said with a nod as my lips parted to meet Owen's. "We *are* pretty great together." And as our mouths grew hungrier and our bodies grew more alert with every movement against the other's, I thought about how well Owen and I fit together.

It didn't get much better than that.

Chapter Twenty-Three

OWEN

I'd been a little surprised when we'd heard from June and even more surprised when she agreed to meet us at her old shop. I knew she was an older woman, and I hadn't thought meeting with a couple of kids to discuss the past would be high on her list of priorities.

But evidently it was, because we sat across from her as she bit into a cheese danish.

"Not quite like mine, but still delicious," she said with a smirk that let us know she was teasing.

June was a well put together elderly woman who was likely older than she seemed. She was short, her shoulders slightly stooped in a way that showed she'd spent much of her life hunched over a kitchen counter baking. Her gray hair was straight and fell to just below her chin in a sleek bob that went well with her black slacks and cream blouse. June kept herself in good shape, and I hoped I'd be half as vivacious when I was her age.

I toyed with the wrapper of my muffin, anxious for

reasons I couldn't quite identify. There was no weight to this meeting, nothing I *needed* to get out of it. But it still felt important somehow.

June rubbed her hands together to rid them of crumbs before she regarded us with an almost bored expression. "So you're living in Minerva's old house?"

"Yeah," I started, but my voice sounded gravelly, so I cleared my throat and began again. "Yes, she left it to me."

She nodded and her face looked thoughtful, as if this was interesting news, but she didn't expound. Instead she said, "I'd heard she passed, but it was a few weeks after it had happened. We hadn't spoken in..." Her face drew tight, and she looked down at her lap for a split second before focusing back on us, her face blank again. "A very long time."

"We found pictures of the two of you together. I assume you were good friends?" Vee asked, her voice soft and gentle.

June shifted as if the question made her uncomfortable. "We were close for a time. Minerva had gotten herself in a bit of trouble, and my husband and I tried to help her through it."

"Do you mean the pregnancy?" Vee asked.

June looked a bit shocked at Vee's question for a moment before she schooled her expression again. "Yes. Her parents had kicked her out, and we took her in. She stayed with us for a little while, but after losing the baby, she didn't have much reason to spend her time with a boring married couple."

Vee's hand gripped mine under the table. "She lost the baby?"

June looked between the two of us. "Yes. I'm sorry. Since you knew about the pregnancy, I assumed you knew the full story. It was a stillbirth. Very traumatic. For all of us, honestly."

"And then Minnie just... moved out?" I asked.

The pictures had made it seem like June and Minnie had been close, and I figured Minnie would've wanted someone to lean on after going through something so heartbreaking. But maybe I was projecting my feelings onto Minnie. Everyone dealt with difficult things in their own way.

June looked pensive before continuing. "It was a mutual decision. Things became . . . strained. It was in the best interest of everyone for her to get her own place."

Vee and I both nodded to show we were following.

"Did she move away or stay in town?" I asked.

Again, June looked like we didn't know something she'd expected we would've. "She moved into the house you own now."

"Oh. Wow. I'm surprised she could afford to move there all on her own," I said.

June studied her hands, which were clasped together atop the table. "She couldn't. It was my family house. My husband and I wanted to live closer to the shop, but my mother had left me the house I'd grown up in. We'd meant to rent it out, but when Minerva needed a place to live"—she shrugged—"it just made sense to sign it over to her. She was in need, and even though things between us weren't good at the end, we cared for her very much. In our own way. We hadn't wanted to kick her out on the street like her parents had, but we also knew she wanted to be independent. Renting from us would've made her feel beholden to us. At least with the house in her name, she was responsible for its upkeep from then on."

Something about her words didn't feel right. I understood wanting to help someone out, but June was acting as if they'd been not much more than friendly roommates. Who left a house to someone they barely knew? And why were their pictures of the two of them together hidden all over Minnie's house?

"That was very kind of you," Vee said.

If I hadn't been watching June so closely as I tried to figure out what she wasn't saying, I would've missed her flinch. That was interesting.

"It was the least we could do."

It actually sounded like close to the *most* they could've done, but that didn't seem appropriate to say. Maybe people were radically different back then. Or maybe June and her husband were just exceptionally charitable people.

But something about the almost rote way June relayed all this information didn't sit right.

"You sound like you were almost surrogate parents to Minnie."

She blinked hard, as if the comment had hurt her, and damn, I wanted to know why. I was becoming too invested in a situation that had nothing to do with me. I had enough on my own plate just trying to keep the house standing. Why did its history and the history of its inhabitants matter so much to me? Why did who Minnie had been suddenly matter as much, if not more, than who I'd known her to be?

No matter how ridiculous it may have sounded, it felt like the house couldn't ever truly be mine until I knew its full story. I wasn't sure when that had even become important to me. When the house had gone from a property I'd keep for a while, fix up, and sell off when it was time to move on to the next phase of my life, but here we were. And I was desperate to not only know, but to understand.

June looked at her teacup as she spun it in her hands, not taking her eyes off it when she said, "If that's the case, then I guess we failed her like they did."

Vee and I were quiet after that, exchanging a look that said neither of us knew where to take the conversation from there.

June clearing her throat again prevented us from having to take it anywhere. "At the risk of being blunt, I'm not sure what you came here expecting to hear. We were part of Minerva's life for a very short and difficult time. There was a time when I thought we'd be friends forever, but that wasn't to be. She left, and none of us looked back."

She was lying. Her gaze was steady, her chin squared, her shoulders set—all the marks of the truth being told. But there was also a quiver in her voice and resignation in her tone. There was definitely more to the story of Minnie and June. But it seemed as if we might never get to hear it.

June stood and said, "Now if you'll excuse me, I promised Serafina I'd show her some more of my recipes before my grandson takes me home."

We stood and said our goodbyes and then watched her disappear into the back room.

"Well that was weird," Vee whispered.

"Yeah," I agreed, not able to shake the feeling that it was also indelibly and remarkably sad.

VERONICA

I hadn't been on many road trips with friends in my life, which made me feel like Owen had a point when he'd basically called me sheltered a few weeks ago. I hadn't worked a bunch of menial jobs, and I hadn't hit the road with other careless youths. What was with me?

Owen had volunteered to drive up to White Plains, where my grandfather had moved almost a decade ago when he'd turned the family business over to Ricky. The ride would only be a little over two hours, which likely didn't even qualify as a road trip, but no one was going to steal my shine.

I'd been singing along to a playlist on my phone, when I glanced over at Owen and saw a small smile playing on his lips.

I turned the radio down. "What are you smiling about?"

He looked over at me quickly. "You."

"Are you laughing at my impressive vocal talent?"

He glanced at me again. "Something like that."

I pretended to be offended for about point-two seconds and then relaxed back in my seat and studied him. God, I liked him. Everything about him. From the way his wavy blond hair pushed out of the bottom of the ball cap he was wearing to the soft slope of his nose to the plush fullness of his lips to the squareness of his jaw. I liked the way his body flexed with every movement without bulging with popcorn muscles. And I liked his kindness. His quirkiness. His intelligence, which not many people gave him enough credit for, even though it was vast and deep.

"What?" he asked, pulling me from my thoughts.

"What *what*?"

"You're staring."

"You're fun to look at."

His eyebrow quirked. "Am I now?"

I nodded even though he wasn't looking at me. "Not just now. All the time."

He smiled, clearly loving my compliment. "You're pretty sweet on me, huh?"

"I was until you started talking like a nineteen seventies cowboy."

"Know a lot about cowboys from the seventies, do you?"

I smiled, loving the back and forth between us and how

it always felt a little bit like foreplay. "Yup. I even read a cowboy romance not too long ago."

"Hmm, interesting." was all he said in reply.

It seemed neither of us knew where to take the conversation from there, but I wanted to keep talking to him and enjoying his company.

"What do you think is the real story with Minnie and June?"

It was clearly the wrong thing to ask, because the smile slipped from his face and he straightened in his seat, his hand gripping the steering wheel more tightly.

Damn it, I should've enjoyed his company silently.

We hadn't spoken too much about it. We'd debriefed when we'd left June's shop, but neither of us had gotten our thoughts straight yet, so the conversation had fizzled out quickly. Now I realized that it had maybe fizzled because Owen, for some reason, didn't want to talk about it.

"There was definitely more to it than June said," he replied after a few moments. "There's no way Minnie would've kept pictures of them for her entire life if June and Milton hadn't meant something to her. But she hid them behind other ones, so she clearly didn't want to have to see them every day. It's . . . odd."

"Maybe she put them back there when she moved in and the feelings were fresh and then just forgot about them."

"Maybe," he replied, sounding doubtful.

I reclined back farther so I could kick my feet up on the dash. "Okay, lay your theory on me."

He glanced over at me. "It's very dangerous to sit like that."

"I like to live on the wild side," I deadpanned, causing him to laugh.

"I'll tell you my theory if you put your feet down."

I sighed dramatically as I sat up again. "Spoilsport."

"Spoilsport's my middle name," he relied dryly.

I laughed but then grew contemplative. This was Owen after all.

"It's not really, is it?"

The laugh that burst out of him was boisterous. "No."

I was about to ask him what his middle name really was, but he began talking.

"I think there was more between them than friendship. I don't know that they were full-on lovers, but I think at least Minnie had romantic feelings for one of them, or maybe even both. And when June and Milton realized, they freaked and kicked her out."

"That's ... sad."

Owen nodded. "But it makes sense. There were times where June was clearly trying too hard to make it seem like she wasn't to blame for what happened. Like she was trying to assuage her own guilt for overreacting badly to Minnie's feelings."

"Maybe Minnie just couldn't handle being close to people after she lost the baby," I reasoned.

Owen shrugged. "Maybe. But I don't know. I feel like while that would explain why Minnie pulled away initially, would it *keep* her away?"

"It could. That's a pretty traumatic loss."

"True."

"Let's think on your theory a little more," I said. "Minnie loved June and/or Milton, and so they hid her away in the family house like a dirty little secret and never spoke to her again?"

The thought of that made me want to cry. I hadn't known Minnie, but hearing about her through Owen made it feel like I did, and I hated that she'd had to live with that kind of rejection and that she'd seemingly never moved on from it.

"I can't imagine having people you think you can count on and then having them just . . . abandon you when you need them most," I said.

"Sometimes people do shitty things" was Owen's frank response.

"The pictures made it seem like they'd had such great times together. The affection in those photos—you can't fake that kind of thing. It's crazy that it all fell apart so quickly."

Owen sat for a minute, his face pensive. "I don't know that I think it's that crazy. Sometimes people fall hard for others, whether it be romantically or platonically. You meet someone and think *this is a forever kind of person*. And then you get to know them and realize . . . they're not who you thought they were." He looked over at me and smiled. "It's like your true crime podcasts always say. How well do you ever really know a person?"

I'd turned toward Owen at some point during our conversation, but I flopped back into my seat as his words sank in. June and her husband had invited Minnie into their home when she'd needed a place to stay. They'd become fast friends and maybe even something more, at least on Minnie's end of things. Then when it had become uncomfortable or too much, June and Milton had sent Minnie away and never spoken to her again.

I didn't have to be Freud to see the similarities between Minnie's situation and mine. There were vast differences too, though. Namely that I believed Owen's word was his bond, so when he'd promised we'd always be friends, I believed him.

But Minnie had probably believed in June, and I'd seen where that had gotten her.

As every insecurity I'd ever had about getting involved with Owen reared its ugly head, only one thing was certain. I was really fucking mad I'd ruined my road trip by bringing this up.

Chapter Twenty-Four

VERONICA

We pulled into the parking lot of the hotel my family had taken over for my grandfather's party. Uncle Ricky had blocked off a bunch of rooms and wouldn't hear of any of us paying, which was incredibly generous and very much like him.

The hotel was part of a larger property that included a golf course and private restaurant. My dad had told me Ricky had rented out one of the rooms in the restaurant for the party. Last I'd heard, there'd be only twenty Diaz and Diaz-adjacent partygoers. My grandfather had wanted to limit the party to family only, which was a relief because parties could get rowdy when we started including friends and business associates. It was better to ease Owen in.

I couldn't wait to get out of the car. Owen and I had kept up idle chitchat for the rest of the drive, but my heart hadn't been in it after the Minnie talk. I needed some space to get my head back on straight. Not that hanging out with my family would ever make someone think *more* clearly. Which was why

I needed a few minutes to breathe and gather my strength.

I knew my family would be nice to Owen. But I also knew they'd want to know everything about him, including what was going on between the two of us. And while I knew there was *something* between us, we hadn't labeled it, which we probably should have done on the two-plus hours we'd just spent in a car together. But the last thing I wanted to do after discussing Minnie's dumpster fire of a potential love life was try to define my own. I felt… frayed. I hoped a weekend with my family would help stitch me back together rather than shred me apart more.

Owen found a parking spot, and we carried our bags to the lobby. Immediately upon entering, I heard a familiar voice screech, "Oh my God, is that little Veronica? It's been so long since I've seen her, I can't be sure."

No one did guilt quite like Aunt Ana. She was the younger sister of my dad and Ricky but acted as if she was older and wiser than everyone around her. Someone had given her a clipboard, and she held it tightly against her chest as if it held state secrets.

"Hi, Aunt Ana," I said as I walked over and gave her a hug, which she accepted but didn't return. "How have you been?"

She sniffed. "Pretty good. Just trying to keep everyone in this family alive. Your grandfather barely takes care of himself, and your dad and uncle aren't much better."

Drama, thy name is Ana.

"It's a good thing they have you," I said because agreeing would end the conversation faster than inquiring further.

"Isn't that the truth," she agreed. She looked past me. "Is this your plus one?"

I moved aside to invite Owen into our conversation. "Yes.

This is Owen. Owen, this is my aunt Ana, my dad's younger sister."

"Pleasure to meet you," Owen said as he dropped one of his bags so he could extend a hand to my aunt.

"Ooh, well isn't he a charmer?" she asked as she put her hand in his as if she expected him to kiss it.

Owen just awkwardly pumped it up and down and smiled.

"Franco and Manny have told me all about you. Which is a good thing since I never hear anything from my niece anymore."

I wanted to ask her if she'd misplaced her cross, since she was clearly going for martyrdom, but I managed to refrain.

"Sorry. I've been busy with working and getting ready for school."

She reached out and patted my head like I was a Shih Tzu. "I know. And we're so proud of you. Law school! Such an accomplishment. I could barely get my two to finish high school."

She wasn't kidding. My cousin Adrien was three years older than me and had been wearing an ankle monitor by eighth grade. Natalia was a year older than me and, while more kindhearted than her brother, was a total ditz. She'd never encountered a mistake she wouldn't make, but it wasn't duplicitous. It was as if her frontal lobe had never developed fully, causing her to never consider the consequences for her actions.

She'd once been put in charge of a school fundraiser when we were in high school, and she'd given away all the baked goods for free to anyone who asked because they'd said they were hungry. Needless to say, the fundraiser didn't earn any money, and Natalia was never put in charge of anything of substance for the remainder of her time in school.

"Are Adrien and Natalia here yet?" I asked.

"Natalia is. She and I drove up together. Who knows about Adrien. He said he was coming, but he hasn't answered any of my calls today. You know how he is," she said with an eye roll.

And I did, which meant Adrien was likely in jail and hadn't been allowed to make his phone call yet.

"Natalia is already up in your room getting ready for tonight," my aunt continued.

Our room? Why would she be in Owen's and my . . .

"Oh, Natalia and I are sharing?" I gave Owen a quick glance that I hoped conveyed that that was news to me.

"Yes. And your brothers said Owen could bunk with them. I said I'd put him in with Adrien, but Manny insisted on keeping Owen with them. They must really like you." Ana said the last bit to Owen.

I wanted to say that it was more likely they didn't want Adrien to drug Owen and put him in a bathtub of ice in order to harvest his organs, but again, my restraint came up clutch. I had to remember to thank my brothers when I saw them.

My aunt studied Owen as if he was a specimen in a lab, which let me know it was time to get the hell out of there.

"I guess we better go get ready for dinner."

She smiled. "Of course, my beautiful niece." My aunt leaned in and gave me a hug. "You're room 302 and the boys are 307." She handed us our keys, and we said our goodbyes before making our way to the elevator.

OWEN

Vee seemed nervous, and my old insecurities reared their heads again. I hoped it wasn't because she was worried about me saying or doing something that would embarrass her.

Once we were safely in the elevator, Vee leaned back against the wall and let out a sigh. "I can't believe we got out of there without her telling embarrassing stories about me as a kid."

Her words soothed me a little. There were limitless stories my family could tell about me doing dumb shit, so I could relate to Vee not wanting those kind of stories to come out.

Still, I couldn't resist teasing her a little. "I'm going to have to head back down there, then."

She shot me a glare that lacked any heat and then sighed again before rolling her neck around a few times.

"You okay?" I asked.

She'd gone quiet on me for a bit after we'd discussed Minnie and June. I hoped thinking about it hadn't bummed her out, especially when we were supposed to be here celebrating.

"Yeah, just tired. Long car rides always make me sleepy."

Her answer made sense, but there was something about her tone that made me think she wasn't being completely honest.

The elevator arrived at the third floor, and we followed the signs toward our rooms. I stopped with Vee outside her room as she slid the keycard into the lock. When she had it open, she turned to me with a small smile.

"I'll see you in a couple hours?"

"I'll meet you out here."

"Perf—"

"Is that him?" Suddenly, the door was wrenched open farther, sending Vee stumbling back. "He's all anyone's been able to talk about."

The girl giving me a very thorough once-over had to be Vee's cousin, since that's who her aunt had said Vee was sharing a room with.

Vee looked like she'd rather swallow a live wasp than introduce us, but she forged ahead anyway.

"Lovely to see you too, Nattie. And yes, this is Owen. Owen, this is my cousin Natalia."

"Nice to meet you," I said as I extended my hand, which Natalia just stared at.

She pointed at me and looked at Vee. "He serious?"

"Well, he doesn't know you yet, so he'll probably change his mind about it being nice to meet you soon," Vee replied dryly.

Natalia rolled her eyes. "I meant with the handshaking thing. But whatever." She took my hand in hers. "The fifties were probably cool."

"Fifties?" I asked. Was this girl speaking a different version of English than I'd been raised on?

"Yeah. That's the last time shaking hands was cool," she quipped.

I furrowed my brow. "I don't think that's true."

"Ignore her," Vee said. "She gets off on making people uncomfortable."

"That's not all I get off on," Natalia purred, arching her back and shooting me a wink.

Vee stared at her. "That was beneath you."

Natalia's posture drooped as she seemed to drop the sex-kitten act. "I know, but I still couldn't resist it." She gave me an appraising look again. "So this is *the* Owen, huh? Gotta say, I expected someone ... bigger."

"Why?" I couldn't help but ask.

Natalia shrugged. "That's Vee's usual type. Tall, muscular, dark features, barely able to read."

Vee made a sound of outrage while I tried to ignore that Natalia had basically just described Vee's almost-husband Brody, who was basically my antithesis.

"That's such bull," Vee yelled.

Natalia rolled her eyes. "Okay, fine, some of them could read a little."

Vee squawked again, but Natalia moved closer to me. "So, Owen, tell me about yourself. What's your major, ten-year plan, financial outlook, and astrological sign?"

I opened my mouth to say ... something, but Vee grabbed Natalia and pulled her back.

"Ignore her." Then she turned her attention to her cousin. "Would you stop grilling the poor guy?"

Natalia laughed. "If you think this is grilling, you're in for a rude awakening at dinner." She pointed at me. "They're gonna be all over Wonder Bread here."

"Don't call him that," Vee snapped. "Can you just ... give us a second?" she asked Natalia.

She shrugged. "Sure. See ya later, Owen."

"Bye," I replied, my voice timid even to my own ears.

Natalia was overwhelming, and I wasn't convinced it was in a good way.

When Natalia was back in the room, Vee looked at me. "I want to apologize in advance for my family tonight. They seriously don't know how to act around outsiders. If they make you uncomfortable and you want to leave, I won't blame you. They're . . . a lot."

This wasn't exactly the pep talk I needed before facing the Diazes, and seeing Vee so nervous made my own nerves intensify. As much as I wanted to get to know Vee's family, maybe this was premature.

But it was too late now, so I was going to have to roll with it.

"I'll be fine. My family is basically the one from *The Texas Chainsaw Massacre*—minus the killing. It'll be okay."

Vee's lips quirked. "That's an interesting description."

I shrugged. "It's also very fitting. Just ask Taylor."

Vee's eyes narrowed a bit when I said that, and I wondered if she didn't like that Taylor had met my family when she herself hadn't. But that was probably just wishful thinking.

"See you in a bit?" she asked.

"Absolutely."

"Okay. Tell my brothers to be nice," she added as an afterthought.

I would absolutely *not* tell them that, but to Vee, I said, "Will do."

She gazed at me for a second as if she had something else to say, so I stayed where I was. Just as I was about to step back, she surged forward, pressing a hard kiss to my lips. She pulled away before I could reciprocate and offered me another smile before stepping into her room and letting the door close firmly behind her.

I shifted my bag higher on my shoulder before going in search of my room, trying to ignore the way that kiss had felt almost desperate. Almost like an unwilling goodbye.

Chapter Twenty-Five

VERONICA

"Are you almost ready, Nattie?"

She'd been in the bathroom for over an hour doing God knew what while I waited for her so I could get in there and get ready myself. We'd told Manny, Franco, and Owen to come to our room at six so we could all go down to dinner together— which I thought might make it less awkward for Owen—but it was already a quarter of, and I still needed to get in there.

"I hate that nickname," she called. "It reminds me of the cheap beer."

"Well, that's part of the reason you have that nickname, so…"

"I know. But I don't like to be reminded. I didn't want to bring it up in front of Owen earlier, so I let it go."

"Can I at least grab my curling iron and makeup bag? And Owen already knows why you have that nickname."

The door swung open abruptly to reveal an almost completely naked Natalia. She wore a full face of makeup and a blue lace thong but nothing else.

"How dare you?" she screamed.

I reached into the bathroom for my curling iron as I tried not to brush up against her.

"Who cares? The story's funny."

"Yeah, to everyone else. You weren't the one who fell into a pond in the middle of winter because you were too drunk to realize it wasn't completely frozen."

I laughed out loud hearing her replay it. "It was only three feet deep."

Though I was happy I'd been there to witness it live. She'd gone out to try to ice skate in her boots, and before anyone could stop her, the thin sheet of ice had cracked beneath her, sending her plummeting into the water like someone had opened a trap door beneath her. I was sorry I hadn't thought to catch it on video. Damn me and my concern for someone and their potential hypothermia.

"You were fine. It wasn't anything a few blankets and a warm car couldn't fix. And you gotta admit, Nattie Ice is a pretty badass nickname."

Our whole school had known about it by Monday, and even some of the teachers took to using the nickname. Some just called her Ice, or even Vanilla Ice. Nattie was the best of the options, in my opinion.

Natalia came out of the bathroom and headed over to where her dress was laid out on the bed. "Yeah, I guess it is pretty cool."

She was so easy to placate.

"Totally. They should really interview you for that show about the people who shouldn't have survived."

After all these years, I knew how to placate Natalia. And making something she'd endured sound more dramatic than it had actually been always worked like a charm.

In the reflection of the mirror, I could see the wheels turning in Natalia's head she thought about being featured on a show. I also noticed how incredibly perfect her boobs were. She didn't even need a bra under her black strapless dress. Somehow her boobs held the dress up without anything holding *them* up. Damn her.

As I did my hair and makeup in the less-than-ideal lighting of the room, I considered moving to the bathroom, but since I was pressed for time and the guys would be here any minute, I finished quickly and then slipped on my heels.

The boys arrived a few minutes later, all of them looking dapper. Manny and Franco barely dressed in anything nicer than a T-shirt and jeans, and I realized I'd never seen casual Owen like this either.

"Well, don't you look fancy," I said before giving him a kiss on the cheek.

When I pulled back, he held on to my hands and let his entire head move down my body and then back up again.

"You look... Jesus, you look..." He couldn't seem to get the words out, which made me feel more gorgeous than I possibly ever had. Owen lifted my hand and guided me to spin around. As I did, he exhaled loudly like the sight literally took his breath away.

But our moment was interrupted by Franco smacking him on the back of the head. "That's my sister you're gawking at, so watch yourself."

Owen didn't take his eyes off me. "I can't watch myself when I'm watching her," he muttered.

That earned him a smack from Manny too.

"You look beautiful," Owen finally managed to get out.

"Absolutely perfect."

"Well, isn't he the chivalrous gentleman," Natalia said. She stepped into the hallway. "What about me?" She did a little spin of her own.

"You look nice as well," Owen said.

"Manny? Frankie? What do you think?" She did a few poses with her hand on her hip and then her head looking over her shoulder and back at them like she was walking a runway.

"I think you're our cousin, and I'm not judging how you look," Franco said as we headed toward the elevator.

"But if you weren't my cousin, what would you think?"

My brothers stared straight ahead at the elevator after Manny pushed the button.

"What do you think they'll have to eat at this thing?" he asked.

"You're still guys," Natalia pointed out. "You can tell if a female looks pretty."

Franco ignored her. "Hopefully prime rib or steak. It's Grandpop. No way he's having this thing without some high-end meat."

"Fine," Natalia said.

"Even chicken parm would be good," Manny said. "That real thick kind that takes up the whole plate so they have to give you another plate just for the pasta."

Natalia rolled her eyes and turned toward Owen and me. "This is just like when guys claim they can't tell when another guy is good-looking because they think it'll make them seem gay."

"That's not true," Manny said. "Owen's a good-looking guy." He looked to Franco as we all boarded the elevator.

"I agree. He gelled his hair so his blond waves are styled. A crisp black shirt and light-gray slacks that fit his ass perfectly, the dude looks fresh."

He gestured to Owen, who instead of looking embarrassed, appeared to light up at the compliment.

"Thanks, man. You guys clean up pretty nice yourselves," Owen said as the elevator doors opened to let us off on the ground floor, where the restaurant was located.

Manny came up behind Nattie as she stepped out and squeezed her shoulders. "You look good, Nattie," he told her.

"Yeah," Franco agreed. "You know if you looked stupid we'd tell you."

I laughed at that, and Natalia pretended to be more annoyed than I figured she actually was. She was used to her own brother's jibes as well as Manny's and Franco's. We'd all grown up together and had lived on the same block. We'd gone to the same school and spent every holiday and birthday at each other's houses, which was why we knew each other as well as we knew ourselves. It was also why it was so easy to annoy the shit out of each other. And Owen seemed to fit right in.

It didn't take long for the rest of my family who hadn't met him yet to warm to him as well. He'd introduced himself with the casual confidence I'd become used to, but I could tell my grandfather, Uncle Ricky, and some of the other older men in my family were impressed by it.

It wasn't that they were used to being disrespected by my brothers and cousins—they knew better than to cross anyone in the older generation—but it wasn't often that someone who'd just met them stood up tall, squared their shoulders, and looked them in the eye. Mostly because my dad and his uncles and cousins could be scary as hell.

But by the time the salads were served, Owen had

everyone engaged in a story about the time he'd encountered an alligator on a golf course in Florida.

According to Owen, the animal had crept out of the pond on the eleventh hole when Owen's dad had gone to look for the ball he'd shanked.

"Wait, wait, wait." My dad's cousin Gabriel leaned forward from a few seats away with his glass of bourbon in his hand. "You're telling me you *tried* to get an alligator to chase you?"

Owen looked almost as surprised at the question as Uncle Gabriel was at the image of Owen seeking out a wild animal who could probably swallow him whole.

"I didn't have much choice. It was me or my dad."

Franco pointed at our dad from across the table. "Don't expect me to make the same sacrifice."

My dad laughed. "Well, you two got no balls. That's not news to anyone here."

Manny looked offended. "Hey, why am I a part of this?"

"Cause you always gotta be part of everything," my uncle Ricky called out. He was always louder than he needed to be, and that certainly didn't change when he was more than a few seats away.

"Okay, okay," my dad said. "Let's not forget what we're all doing here."

Adrien, who'd shown up a half hour late wearing jeans and a black T-shirt, grabbed his beer. "Drinking on Uncle Ricky's dime," he said, lifting the bottle to his lips and taking a long swig.

The next few minutes consisted of my great-uncles complaining that they'd chipped in too and my aunt Ana saying it never would've come together without her meticulous planning. My uncle Ricky stayed pretty silent for once because he probably hadn't had much to do with any of this coming together.

At least they'd moved the conversation away from Owen. My family had done such a thorough interrogation upon meeting him, they could probably create an online dating profile for him. Not that I'd want him to have one.

I put a hand on Owen's thigh under the table and squeezed just enough to let him know I was thinking about him. His hand found the top of mine beneath the table.

"You know who would've loved this," my grandfather said.

I could tell when he seemed emotional, which was more often than people who didn't know him well would've guessed. And right now felt like he was a few words away from tears.

"Angela." He looked to my brothers and me and then to my dad. "She could never get enough of the big dinners and holidays, always tellin' us we were family and tryin' to keep our asses in line."

Somber nods and *mm-hmm*s made their way around the table, but I felt myself unable to do much more than stare at my pasta.

"She definitely kept my ass in line, that's for sure," my dad said, and I could tell in his voice that the words hurt a little to say.

It was true. As much as my mom hated that my dad was still involved in his father's and brother's shady activities, even if only peripherally, she still loved the people. And if she were anywhere right now, it would've been at this table with the people she loved more than anyone.

When she had been alive, my dad had kept more of a distance from my grandfather's and my uncle Ricky's dealings. But since then, though the change had been gradual, my dad found himself more wrapped up in the family business than my mom ever would've approved of.

I couldn't blame him, though. Not really. The life she'd asked him to leave was the one he'd grown up in. And it was easy to slip back into old habits when there wasn't pressure not to.

I heard my family's chatter like a low din, but they took a back seat to my own thoughts. Thoughts of how strong my mom must've been to marry into a family like my dad's—even though it was, in a way, what broke her in the end.

I looked at Owen chatting with my family, seemingly at ease with the people around him, even though he knew who they were—what they were capable of. Just like my mom.

Over time, she'd found it more and more difficult to separate the people she ate meals with from the people they were on the street. I remember my dad and her fighting about it. Hell, they'd fought about it right before—

God, I missed her. I missed her every second of every day. It was a feeling I'd become so used to, I wasn't even aware of it until I forced myself to be. Like the steady beating of my heart or the subtle rise and fall of my chest with each breath, the void her death had left in me had been lasting—something I'd carry with me for the rest of my life even when I wasn't aware of it.

"Veronica, you okay?" I heard my grandfather ask, and it pulled me away from the fuzziness of my memories and brought me back to this moment. "Vee?"

"Yeah. Yeah," I said with more conviction this time. "I'm fine."

But that was a lie that most people at the table probably saw right through because memories could only be bottled up for so long. I felt like a sieve with feelings pouring out of me in uncontrollable quantities.

My mother had been beautiful, honest, sincere.

I looked over at Owen, my gaze settling on him for a long time before I let it roam over the rest of my family. A family I loved. A family who'd always had my back. A family who sometimes, maybe even oftentimes, did bad things. Bad things that had driven a wedge between my parents, even though they'd tried like hell to bridge it. Until it had all been too late.

Because wasn't that always how it went? We thought we had all the time in the world, and then suddenly it was all over. No take backs. No do-overs. Just an empty place at the dinner table.

I suddenly felt broken. Like I'd shattered right here, all my pieces scattered around for everyone to see. Pieces I wasn't sure could ever be put back together even if I wanted them to.

I was used to the pain of my mother's loss. That pain I could withstand. It was more of a dull ache. But the pain I experienced now felt deeper, like someone had plunged the knife fully into my chest and then twisted it for good measure. It was intense and sharp and a pain I knew I'd never be able to ignore.

After my mother's death, my dad had told me how appropriately named she'd been. *Angela.* She'd been an angel in life, and now, he'd said, she'd be my angel in death—with me always, watching over me, guarding me, helping me make difficult decisions.

And there had been times I'd turned to her for advice, hoping she'd give me a sign that would help me know what to do, which choice to make. But right now, for the first time, I wished I didn't feel her so strongly, because she only reinforced what I already knew.

I couldn't let Owen join a life that was so different from his own.

OWEN

Vee had left the table so suddenly, I didn't know if she was sick, which was why I'd waited a few minutes before excusing myself also. I didn't tell anyone I was leaving to check on her, but I was sure they knew because it was clear to everyone she'd been upset.

I couldn't even begin to imagine how Vee felt hearing everyone talk about her mom, how it felt to be sitting with so many people who reminded her of what she lost.

I didn't know what I planned to say to her when she finally came out of the bathroom, but whatever words might make her feel better than she did right now, I'd have to find somehow.

"Excuse me," I said to a woman who'd exited the restroom. "Did you see a woman in there? Midtwenties, long dark hair, dark eyes."

"No, I don't think so. I think I was the only one in there."

I wasn't sure if she was saying that because it was the truth or if she thought I was some creep who hangs outside women's bathrooms hoping to find my next victim, but I decided to believe her.

If Vee wasn't in the bathroom, she must be around somewhere. I decided to text her, and though she didn't respond immediately, it didn't take her too long to reply.

I'm outside.

I found Vee sitting on a low brick wall outside the doors that led to the hotel restaurant, her hands folded on her thighs as she seemed to stare off at nothing in particular. Taking a seat next to her, I waited a moment before I said or did anything. She clearly needed space, but I wanted her to know I was here.

"You didn't have to come looking for me," she said without looking in my direction.

"I was worried about you. I think everyone's worried about you."

"They don't need to be."

"But that doesn't change the fact that they are. Look, I'm not going to pretend I know what you're going through right now, but I'm here for you however you need me to be."

"That's the problem," she said quietly.

"What?"

She finally looked at me, and I thought I saw a bit of anger in her teary eyes.

"Did I ever tell you how my mom died?"

That hadn't at all been what I'd expected Vee to say, and I was startled by it.

"No."

"She had a heart attack. It was the craziest thing. She hadn't even been sick. It came completely out of nowhere."

"Jesus, that's . . . Vee, that's horrible. I'm so sorry."

She sniffled, but she didn't look at me, so I couldn't tell if she was crying.

"My dad blamed himself for a long time. Maybe he still does. They'd been arguing. My uncle Ricky wanted my dad to do some jobs for him. It was the same old same old. My parents had been fighting about it a lot. I used to sit at the top of the steps and listen to them."

She sighed heavily and was quiet for a moment before continuing. "She left. Slammed the door behind her and just took off. We never saw her again."

Reaching over, I took one of her hands in mine, hoping I could show her I was there in silent support.

"That's the price, Owen."

"What price?" I asked quietly.

She looked over at me then, tears glistening in her eyes. "The price of loving someone in this family."

"Oh, Vee, no. What happened to your mom, that was a tragedy. But it wasn't because of your family."

She dashed harshly at her cheeks as the tears slid down them. "Maybe. Maybe not. But there's always a risk. A risk that the stress will wear on someone. That some asshole my uncle pissed off will come looking for revenge and hurt one of us." She hesitated for a moment. "A risk that being part of this family will turn you into someone you're not."

I laughed, but it was humorless. "Come on. They're nice people. They've been great to me tonight."

"That's because they adore you. Just like they adored my mom. And who wouldn't? You're kind and pure. Just like she was. But that didn't save her, Owen. And it won't save you either."

She stood, and I joined her.

"I don't need anyone to save me, Vee. I can take care of myself."

When she looked at me, the tears were no longer falling, and there was a steeliness to her posture. "I can't do this with you, Owen."

"Do what?" I asked, even though the last thing I wanted to

hear right now was her answer.

"Be with you." Tears appeared in her eyes again, but mine fell first. "Fall in love with you."

"You can't help who you love," I told her. Wasn't that the first rule of romance and relationships? "Well, *I* love *you*, and I can't just *will* myself not to. I don't *want* to will myself not to. Loving you is the best thing that's ever happened to me."

Her tears fell again at that, but she wiped them away quickly, almost harshly. Then she smiled, but it was sad.

"Sometimes the best things end up being the worst. No matter how much we wish they didn't."

I couldn't help but laugh roughly at that. "But you're the one making it the worst by throwing it all away."

"I'll never throw your love away, Owen. But I can't keep it either. You deserve—"

"If you say something better, I'm going to freak out."

She smiled again. "Something else. Something that suits you. Something *worthy* of you."

"You're selling yourself really short. You're the one who's too good for me," I argued because it was the damn truth. This brilliant, beautiful, compassionate woman couldn't have been serious when she said she wasn't worthy of me.

"I'm not having a self-esteem crisis. I just know who I am. I know what I can do and what I can't. And I can't do this. I'm sorry. I truly am." She took a few steps away and then stopped and spoke again without turning around. "I'll tell my family you weren't feeling well. And if you'd rather me get a ride back with my brothers, I understand."

And then she was gone.

I had no idea where we'd go from here or what would happen next, but I couldn't even bring myself to think about it. So I did what any guy who was too sad to be alone with himself and his thoughts would do. I headed to the hotel bar.

I was on my fifth vodka soda when I noticed a few of Vee's relatives walk through the restaurant toward the doors that led to the hotel lobby. Dinner must've just finished, but I wasn't in any kind of state to speak to any of them and thank them for inviting me. That would have to wait until tomorrow.

"Vee said you were sick," a female voice said beside me.

Unfortunately, it wasn't the one I wanted to hear.

Managing to lift my head enough from where I'd been staring at my glass, I turned to look to my left. Sitting next to me was Natalia. She was holding a martini glass with a clear green liquid in it.

"Nah," I said.

"What happened?"

I let out a sigh. "It's a long story."

"Good thing I got time." She pointed at the two empty glasses on the bar in front of me. "And it looks like I got some catching up to do."

"I had two more before these," I admitted.

"Guess I better get started," she joked, signaling to the bartender.

"You're probably better off without me near you. I'm not a very fun drunk right now."

She shrugged. "Maybe. But I don't know that you're better off with *me*. Whenever I've felt how it looks like you feel right now, it always helps to have someone to talk to."

I nodded but wasn't so sure.

"Wanna tell me what happened with you and Vee?"

"Not really, but I figure you're probably gonna make me, so I will anyway."

So I told her everything. Even in my drunken state, I remembered the conversation practically word for word because I'd replayed it in my head countless times since I'd sat down.

"Wow," Natalia said. "Vee can be a little unpredictable, but I can't understand why she'd do something like that. I can tell she's crazy about you. Though now I'm starting to think she's just plain crazy." She was quiet for a moment, and I did nothing to fill the silence. "What are you gonna do?"

I shrugged. "Nothing I *can* do. I can't make her think it's okay for me to associate with your family, let alone be part of it one day. We haven't even discussed marriage because all of this is so new. If she's this freaked out now, I can't imagine what she'll think if things got more serious."

"There's always something you can do," she said confidently. "You just have to figure out what that something is." Resting her elbows on the bar, she plopped her head down into her hands like she was deep in thought.

I downed the rest of my drink and lined it up next to the other empties. "Well, let me know if you figure out what that is, because I'm five drinks in and my brain is becoming more useless by the second."

Natalia stayed quiet, as did I until the bartender came over to clear my glasses and I asked him for another.

"I got it!" Natalia said, practically jumping off her bar stool. "I know how to make Vee see that you can be part of the family."

I was skeptical. "How?"

"Do you trust me?"

Chapter Twenty-Six

VERONICA

I was devastated. I'd never broken my own heart before, and I wouldn't recommend it. The feelings running through me could only be described as agonizing, and it took everything in me to not run back to Owen and try to fix it, if only to make the pain stop.

But that would be wrong. What I'd done had been the right thing, even if it made me feel like I was bleeding out internally. A relationship with Owen would never work for a whole host of reasons I didn't need to drag myself through again. I'd been thinking about all of them since the very beginning, and the time for action had finally come.

I could only hope that Owen's promise that we'd always be friends was a solid one. But if it wasn't, I'd deal with it. What choice would I have?

I sequestered myself in my hotel room, locked the door, put earbuds in, and lay down on the bed, deciding I needed to cry it all out of my system before I faced the world again. I just had to pray Natalia didn't come back anytime soon.

It didn't take long for the tears to make my eyes feel heavy and scratchy. I closed them in an effort to rest them and promptly fell asleep.

I awoke an hour or so later, my cheeks stiff with dried tears and my head feeling fuzzy. After rubbing my face a few times to wipe the sleep and sadness away, I grabbed my phone to see the exact time. On the screen, I saw a bunch of missed calls and texts from my family. And from Owen. There was also an alert about a voicemail from a number I didn't recognize.

I instantly worried it was Owen calling from an unknown number in the hopes that would get me to answer, but I instantly dismissed that idea. Owen wasn't that duplicitous.

Not wanting to deal with my family or Owen yet, I checked the voicemail from the unknown number.

"Hi, Veronica, this is ... um, this is June. I still had your number, and I ... I wanted to talk." She gave a stilted chuckle. "Or *confess* maybe a more accurate word."

There was a long pause, and I looked down to see if the message had ended, but it hadn't. Finally, June began speaking again.

"I lied to you. I've lied to a lot of people, actually, and I think maybe it's time to stop all of that. It's not good for the soul, and I don't have much longer to make things right in that regard. Though I can't lie, I'm a little relieved you didn't pick up so I can tell all this to a machine. It'll be easier without having to worry about what you might say once I tell you everything.

"I loved Minnie. *We* loved Minnie. God, it feels so weird to say her name like that. I'd conditioned myself to call her Minerva when she left. Or when we *made* her leave. I guess in some silly way it gave me more distance from her. But we'd always called her Minnie back then. It was almost jarring to hear you and Owen use the nickname so casually, because she never let anyone else call her that. Only us."

I heard the sense of pride at having had the gift of using a nickname no one else had been privy to. But there also seemed to be a sense of sadness at having lost that right. Or having realized that, with Owen and me using it too, that it had meant less than June had thought.

"Minnie came to us looking for work so she could support herself and her unborn baby, and we leaped at the chance to hire her. There was just something about her. She exuded life and joy, even with all she'd been through. We knew she'd be important to us. We just didn't realize all the ways she'd be important at the time.

"It didn't take us long to both fall in love with Minnie. And she fell right with us. It was almost . . . easy. We fantasized about what it would be like to live together, work together, raise a family together. But, in the end, that was all it could ever be. A fantasy."

June sniffled, and I suspected she was crying, but her voice was steady when it came again. "Rumors spun out of control so quickly. It was nearly impossible to stay ahead of them. You have to understand, society was very . . . conservative back then. People weren't accepting of a relationship like ours, even though we weren't open about it. They suspected, and even when we denied it, I think they could see the truth. We vowed to do better, be more discreet. But the damage was done. Our business started to suffer, and we had to make a choice.

"When Minnie lost the baby, we were all devastated. And Minnie needed us so much more, but we couldn't, or maybe wouldn't, be there for her how she needed us to be. She wanted to be able to hug us whenever she wanted, to lean in for a kiss of support, to hold our hands in public, but we couldn't give her that without losing everything we'd worked so hard for."

June made a soft sound that sounded like a repressed sob, and my tears began all over again. "When Minnie came to us one day and said she was leaving, it was clear she wanted us to fight for her. But we didn't. We made a choice, and Veronica, I swear at the time it felt like the right one. And for years, we convinced ourselves it was. Giving her the house made us feel as if we'd done right by her, but . . . we didn't. We didn't do right by ourselves either. We had a family, we poured ourselves into making our business a success, we joined PTAs and rotary clubs. We filled our lives with things and people, but none of it, not even for a second, filled the hole Minnie left. My husband and I never acknowledged it, but we both knew it was there."

She laughed, but it was humorless and depressing. "Milton's and my marriage was never the same. We were always missing something vital, and it's difficult to look back and know that that piece was only a few miles away, living in the house I'd grown up in, but we never went after it. It was like she was sitting there, waiting for us, and we never showed. We just . . . left her there. Alone."

June's sob did come out then, loud and clear, and I was both sad to hear it and thankful that this was painful for her. A dark part of me felt that she deserved to hurt for what she'd done to Minnie.

And wow, was it a smack to the face to realize that I *also* deserved to hurt like that. I'd abandoned Owen after ripping his heart out, and for what? Because I was scared? It was all just . . . noise. I shouldn't have let it factor into what my heart had known for months.

Owen was a once-in-a-lifetime kind of love. Just like Minnie had been. I wondered if Minnie had known that—had been able to see something kindred in Owen, and that was why she'd left the house to him. She could've just...done nothing. But instead, she'd taken herself to a lawyer and drawn up a will that made sure that the young man, who she'd barely known, would inherit her house upon her passing.

It had been the only thing she'd had to remind her of the great love she'd lost. And she'd given that token of love to Owen. Because he was worthy of it. Because he was strong enough to carry it. Because he was...everything.

God, I am such a dipshit.

June continued through as her voice shook. "She's my greatest regret. And God, she'd hate that. To be anyone's regret. She was above that. Better than it. Better than me. She deserves to be someone's truth. And I want to give her that, even if it's too late. I hope"—she paused, and I assumed she was trying to get herself under control enough to continue—"I hope she knew. That even if we didn't show it, she felt it all the same."

There was another long pause before she said, "I'm so sorry."

Then she hung up.

I wasn't sure if the final words were to me or to Minnie. Maybe they were meant for both of us. But I guessed that didn't really matter.

What mattered was what I did from here. And my only way forward was Owen.

Chapter Twenty-Seven

OWEN

I awoke slowly, groaning as my head throbbed.

Jesus, what happened last night?

I sat up carefully, the comforter pooling around my waist as I rubbed my eyes. After taking a few deep breaths, I looked around the room, realizing immediately that it was unfamiliar.

It was clearly a hotel room, but not the one I was sharing with Vee's brothers. I racked my brain, trying to recall last night's events.

I remembered the fight with Vee—though I wished I could forget it—then Natalia comforting me. We had a couple of drinks, and she asked me if I trusted her. Then we'd gotten in an Uber and ended up in ... Connecticut. That was right. I remembered seeing the *Welcome* sign.

The rest of the night was hazy and out of order. I'd need to shake this hangover to remember the rest.

I spotted the door to the bathroom and stood to make my way toward it. A shower would go a long way to helping me feel more normal. As I walked, I heard a shuffling sound from my left. I headed that way instead, and when I rounded the couch, I saw Natalia curled up on it, using my dinner jacket as a blanket.

I was relieved we hadn't shared a bed, though it seemed odd that I'd allowed her to take the couch. I leaned down and gently shook her leg to wake her.

Despite how softly I'd shaken her, she jolted awake like I'd electrocuted her.

"What? Why?" Her eyes focused on me. "What the fuck, Owen? I need my beauty sleep."

"I think we need to get back to the hotel more than you need to sleep."

God only knew what Vee would think when she realized I'd skipped town with her cousin. I didn't even want to think how much worse that could make everything between us.

Though I wasn't sure how much worse things could get. Vee had dumped me last night, and the memory of that moment ached so badly I had to keep myself from rubbing my chest. But maybe we could still find a way forward. She'd been upset, but maybe with time, she'd calm down and see things differently. But if Vee thought I'd had sex with her cousin, I was sure a reconciliation would be off the table.

"We're in a hotel," Natalia said, settling back down and closing her eyes.

"Come on. I'll even buy you breakfast."

She cracked one eye open. "Waffles?"

"Whatever you want."

"Okay," she said, much more perkily. She tossed my jacket aside and swung her legs around so she was sitting.

"I was going to grab a shower, unless you want to take one first," I offered.

"Nah, you can go."

I nodded and then made my way toward the bathroom. On my way, I passed a desk with a sheet of paper on it. Something about it prickled my senses, so I stopped to look it over.

"Natalia?"

"Yeah."

I turned and showed her the paper. "This is a marriage license."

"Yeah," she said slowly, as if I should know what it was.

And I did know. Fuck, did I know. Because the night was suddenly there in my mind with stunning clarity. But I continued to ask questions anyway, as if maybe it had been a nightmare instead of reality.

"Why do we have it?"

"Because we hassled some poor woman into opening her office after hours and giving it to us. Well, technically she just gave us a copy because she needed to file the original. But we begged her for a copy."

And fuck, we had. The office had been, rightfully, closed since we hadn't gotten there until late. But somehow Natalia had tracked down the woman who ran the office in the small town we'd ended up in, and she'd opened it. Natalia had spun some tale that had sounded suspiciously like the plot of *Romeo and Juliet*, and *goddamn* that play and fucking Shakespeare because that piece of trash story kept coming back to haunt me.

And after the woman had fallen for Natalia's tale, she'd also informed us she was an ordained minister. And that Connecticut didn't require witnesses. And wasn't that just great?

Natalia had said to trust her. That she'd show Vee that me

being part of the family wouldn't be a bad thing. And I'd been sad and drunk enough to believe that Natalia's plan would work.

I'd imploded my whole life—my present *and* my future, because surely that was what Vee was, right? My future? But not anymore, because I'd stupidly reverted to the old Owen who went about things in a totally ass-backward way.

So, yeah, Natalia and I would show Vee that I could be a member of the Diaz family. But I wouldn't show them that I could make Vee happy, because this was sure to devastate her.

Forget worrying about what Vee would think of my sharing a hotel room with Natalia. Just wait until Vee found out I'd married her.

ALSO BY ELIZABETH HAYLEY

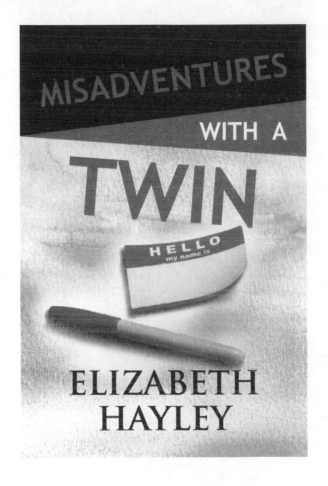

Keep reading for an excerpt...

CHAPTER ONE

COLTON

"I can't believe we're actually going to this thing," Corey said as he zipped up his jacket and exited my truck. "Why's it so cold this weekend?"

"Um...because it's Boston in November," I said. I closed my door and ran to catch up with him on the sidewalk. "We've lived here all our lives. You should be used to this."

"I'm used to being at home. Let's go there instead," he said, turning toward me.

Except for his pathetic expression that was silently pleading with me to let him off the hook, it was like looking in a mirror. Dark hair with cropped sides—long enough to style on top but short enough that we didn't have to—and dimples that were noticeable even when we weren't smiling, causing elderly women to call us cute like they would a baby in a grocery store line. Even after almost thirty years, it was tough for most people to tell us apart.

"I can't understand why you haven't had a date in a couple of months. You're a blast," I said dryly. "Aren't you supposed to be the friendlier one?"

"It's just that we haven't talked to most of these people in years. It's weird."

I rubbed my hands together to get them warm. Corey was

right. It was freezing tonight. "That's why we're here. We can talk about all the crazy shit we used to do."

He raised an eyebrow at me. "You *still* do crazy shit."

"Okay, so we'll tell everyone about all the new crazy shit." Corey rolled his eyes and laughed.

"Come on, you know it'll be fun." I wrapped an arm around his neck and pulled him toward me to mess up his hair so I would look better than him.

Corey laughed as he broke free of my hold and put an arm out in front of my chest to stop me. He raised his eyebrows at me, and then somehow—like we used to when we were kids—we telepathically counted to three and then took off at full speed to our destination, which in this case was the hotel hosting our ten-year high school reunion.

I'd promised Corey we'd have fun, and I'd meant it. We hadn't made it to our five-year, but it was just as well. Five years ago we were still living at home and working part-time. Corey had just graduated college with a business degree he wasn't using, and I was spending every cent I made buying and restoring old motorcycles. Sometimes I made a few bucks, and sometimes—most of the time, if I was being honest—my pastime had been more a labor of love than anything that might have turned into a career.

It wasn't until we put our minds together and decided to open a custom bike shop about forty minutes outside Boston with a buddy of ours that our lives really began.

Stepping through the door to the hotel ballroom where our reunion was being held, I scanned the room for familiar faces. Whether it was to find ones I wanted to avoid or ones I wanted to talk to, I wasn't actually sure. When we didn't recognize anyone right away, we headed to the bar. "What are we drinking tonight?" I asked Corey.

"We *are* at our high school reunion, so let's throw it back to 2006."

"You're going to tell Ava Blaine you've loved her since the second grade and then pass out on the hood of Dad's Sentra?"

Corey's eyes grew serious, like they were lost in the memory of that ridiculous moment. "That was a bad night. I didn't drink for a full year after that," he said with a shake of his head. He put his hands on the bar and called to the bartender, "Two Captain and Cokes, please."

"Ahh," I said, tossing some money onto the bar after we got our drinks. "I forgot about your Captain phase."

"Me too," Corey said. "I don't think I've even had one in almost a decade. They were my go-to for most of junior and senior year, though." He craned his neck and scanned the room. "You think Ava's here? I heard she's divorced now."

"Where'd you hear that?"

I looked at him, but he avoided eye contact. "Facebook."

"Seriously? You're such a stalker." I laughed. "If you plan to talk to her, you should probably make sure it happens before your seventh drink this time."

"You're a wise man, Colton," Corey said with a smile before taking a sip.

I shrugged. "Well, I *am* your older brother." I loved making this distinction, but the truth was, Corey and I shared everything. We always had. From our birthday to our group of friends to our clothes and cars. Growing up, nothing belonged to only one of us.

Well, everything except girls. That was a line we would never cross. If one of us was into someone—or especially if one of us had hooked up with someone—she was off-limits to the other brother. Forever. That rule limited Corey's selection of females greatly when we were in high school, but I couldn't be blamed for taking opportunities as they arose just because it made his potential dating pool smaller.

We talked at the bar for a few more minutes until we spotted a few of our old lacrosse teammates sitting at a table with their wives. We hadn't seen any of them in person in at least seven years, and time didn't appear to have been kind to them. Josh Graham and Scottie Gibson sat, their hands toying with beers they absentmindedly brought to their lips every so often, as their wives chatted. The guys didn't look thrilled, but they didn't exactly look annoyed either. Just . . . spacey.

"CJ!" they yelled as we approached the table, greeting us with the name everyone used in high school. It was easier for people to just use our first and last initials—which were the same—than to tell us apart. I'm not sure what they would've done if we'd had different first initials.

We spent a half hour or so catching up with Josh and Scottie who, it turned out, both had infants at home. Tonight was their first real night out since their kids had been born, and they were exhausted. It had been their wives, Marissa and Sophia, who had really wanted to come, since they were both graduates of our school as well. They didn't look familiar to me, and their names didn't ring a bell either. Which hopefully meant I hadn't messed around with them in high school.

"I'm already dreading getting up in the middle of the night," Scottie said. "Nicholas wakes up every three hours."

"You act like you're the one who has to get up to feed him," Sophia joked. "I know you gained a few sympathy pounds, but I'm pretty sure your breasts still can't feed a newborn."

They all laughed until Josh explained that Marissa

pumped as well as nursed, and in order for Josh to bond with their daughter, Marissa had gotten him some sort of bra that held bottles so the baby could "nurse" from him as well. The table got eerily quiet, and I realized what had most likely caused Josh's gray hairs.

"You're a good mom, Josh," I said.

"And you're an asshole, CJ," Josh countered with a laugh. "What's up with you guys?"

"Well, I'm not breastfeeding," I answered. "So nothing too exciting. We live in the suburbs now."

Corey added, "We opened a custom motorcycle shop with a buddy of ours a few years ago in Canton."

Scottie and Josh looked simultaneously heartbroken and envious. "Oh wow," Scottie said.

"They build bikes," Josh added sadly.

Marissa rolled her eyes at Scottie and her husband. "You two are pathetic."

"Thank you," Josh said. "That's what we're saying."

"That's awesome, though," Scottie said. "I'm happy for you guys. You seem happy, and you're both in great shape. Don't ever get married and have kids. It sucks the life out of you."

I didn't disagree. Why Corey longed for that life—one that would most likely ruin the one he had—made absolutely no sense to me. I would much rather live life as it comes instead of getting attached to something that most likely wouldn't last.

"Well, as much as I love talking about male breastfeeding, I'm gonna have to excuse myself for a few minutes. Anyone want another drink?" I stood, waiting to see if anyone wanted to take me up on my offer, but no one did.

"Captain and Coke, right?" the bartender asked, probably

remembering me because there had been two of us when we'd ordered.

I nodded.

Instead of heading straight back to the table of desperate housewives—and I wasn't talking about the women—I decided to hang out at the bar for a bit. It would be a good vantage point to see the rest of the room, and I could skim the event page on my phone to see who was even here.

All these people looked so different from what I remembered...and from their profile pictures, which all seemed to be taken from a height that indicated the photographer was a drone and not an actual person.

I couldn't help but feel a little out of place, and the realization surprised me. I looked back at Josh and Scottie's table and saw Corey talking to them and laughing with another woman who looked completely unfamiliar to me. Maybe I was getting early Alzheimer's. For some reason, it had seemed important to go to this thing, to show everyone I actually made something of myself. Though I wouldn't have admitted it at the time, I hadn't been anything to idolize in high school. I had been an okay athlete with an even less okay GPA.

I was busy scrolling through the reunion event page when a woman a few seats down the bar said, "You look like you're having about as much fun as I am."

I smiled at her and gave a wave as I mentally flipped through our graduating class in my head. But for the life of me, I couldn't think of anyone who looked like this woman—shiny blond hair that stopped at her chin in a trendy asymmetrical cut and eyes so blue it was like looking at the sky on a summer day.

"Yeah." I laughed to myself about how I must look, sitting

at the bar alone on my phone instead of catching up with people I hadn't seen in ages. "Guess I thought more of my old friends would be here. I'm blaming their absence on the fact that this thing was held on the night before Thanksgiving. Who the hell planned this?"

"I'm assuming our class president. But I can't quite remember who that is."

When she stopped talking, I realized I'd been nodding absently as she spoke. She was beautiful. *Who is this woman?*

"Gotcha," I said, ceasing the awkward movement of my head. "What about you?" I asked, hoping to buy myself some time before she realized I had no clue who she was. "Did you see many of your friends?"

She brought her hand up to tuck her hair behind one ear, even though it was already there. "A few." Her gaze dropped to the stem of her wineglass, and she spun it back and forth between her fingers like she was deciding whether she should say what she was thinking. She opened her mouth but then closed it quickly.

"What? What is it?"

"It's going to sound stupid," she said, closing the small gap at the bar between us. "But seeing you actually made a dull night a little better. I was hoping you'd be here, but I didn't see you post in the group, and you were only a 'maybe' to attend. Are you here with anyone?"

"Just my better half," I joked, though the statement held more truth than she probably realized.

Her smile, which had been beaming only seconds ago, faded. "Oh." I didn't miss her glance at my hand. "So are you engaged, or..."

"Engaged?" I asked, confused. "No, I'm not engaged."

"So she's your girlfriend, then?"

Suddenly realizing where her confusion must have come from, I quickly corrected her. "I'm not here with a fiancée or a girlfriend. When I said my better half, I meant my brother."

"Of course," she said, her voice sounding relieved. "I shouldn't be surprised. The only time I remember you being apart is when you had separate classes." She laughed, looking embarrassed, but she wasn't the one who should have been feeling that way, when I still had no clue who she was. "That's nice of you to say he's the better half." She took a sip of wine and scanned the room for a moment. "Though I'd have to disagree. I always liked you much better."

Continue reading in
Misadventures with a Twin

Also by
ELIZABETH HAYLEY

The Love Game:
Never Have You Ever
Truth or Dare You
Two Truths & a Lime
Ready or Not
Let's Not and Say We Did
Tag, We're It
Trivial Pursuits
Duck, Duck, Truce
Forget Me Not

Love Lessons:
Pieces of Perfect
Picking Up the Pieces
Perfectly Ever After

Sex Snob
(A Love Lessons Novel)

Misadventures:
Misadventures with My Roommate
Misadventures with a Country Boy
Misadventures in a Threesome

Acknowledgments

We have to start by thanking Meredith Wild for her continuous support. It's an honor to be part of the incredible Waterhouse team.

To our swolemate, Scott, we're not sure what we'd do without you. Thanks for reeling us in when we need it while still allowing us the freedom to express ourselves.

To the rest of the Waterhouse Press team, thank you for all you do for us and for not making us feel like the disasters we are.

To our Padded Roomers, what can we say? You do so much for us, and there's no way we can ever repay you. From the bottom of our hearts, thank you for sacrificing your time to help us spread the word about our books. We love you all dearly.

To our readers, there's no way to accurately thank you for taking a chance on us and for your support. Thank you for letting us share our stories with you.

To our children, who are starting to realize what we do for a living. Guess we couldn't prevent you from learning to read forever. We hope we make you proud.

To our husbands, we know it's not easy. Thanks for hanging in there. We honestly don't deserve you.

To each other, for pushing one another forward when we stall. The ride hasn't been easy, but it's sure as hell been a lot of fun. On to the next.

About

ELIZABETH HAYLEY

Elizabeth Hayley is actually "Elizabeth" and "Hayley," two friends who love reading romance novels to obsessive levels. This mutual love prompted them to put their English degrees to good use by penning their own. The product is *Pieces of Perfect*, their debut novel. They learned a ton about one another through the process, like how they clearly share a brain and have a persistent need to text each other constantly (much to their husbands' chagrin).

They live with their husbands and kids in a Philadelphia suburb. Thankfully, their children are still too young to read their books.

Visit them at AuthorElizabethHayley.com